SLAM!™

VOLUME ONE

BOOM!
BOX™

BOOM! BOX

SLAM! Volume One, August 2017. Published by BOOM! Box, a division of Boom Entertainment, Inc. SLAM! is ™ & © 2017 Pamela Ribon & Veronica Fish. Originally published in single magazine form as SLAM! No. 1-4. ™ & © 2016, 2017 Pamela Ribon & Veronica Fish. All rights reserved. BOOM! Box™ and the BOOM! Box logo are trademarks of Boom Entertainment, Inc., registered in various countries and categories. All characters, events, and institutions depicted herein are fictional. Any similarity between any of the names, characters, persons, events, and/or institutions in this publication to actual names, characters, and persons, whether living or dead, events, and/or institutions is unintended and purely coincidental. BOOM! Box does not read or accept unsolicited submissions of ideas, stories, or artwork.

BOOM! Studios, 5670 Wilshire Boulevard, Suite 450, Los Angeles, CA 90036-5679. Printed in China. First Printing.

ISBN: 978-1-68415-004-5, eISBN: 978-1-61398-675-2

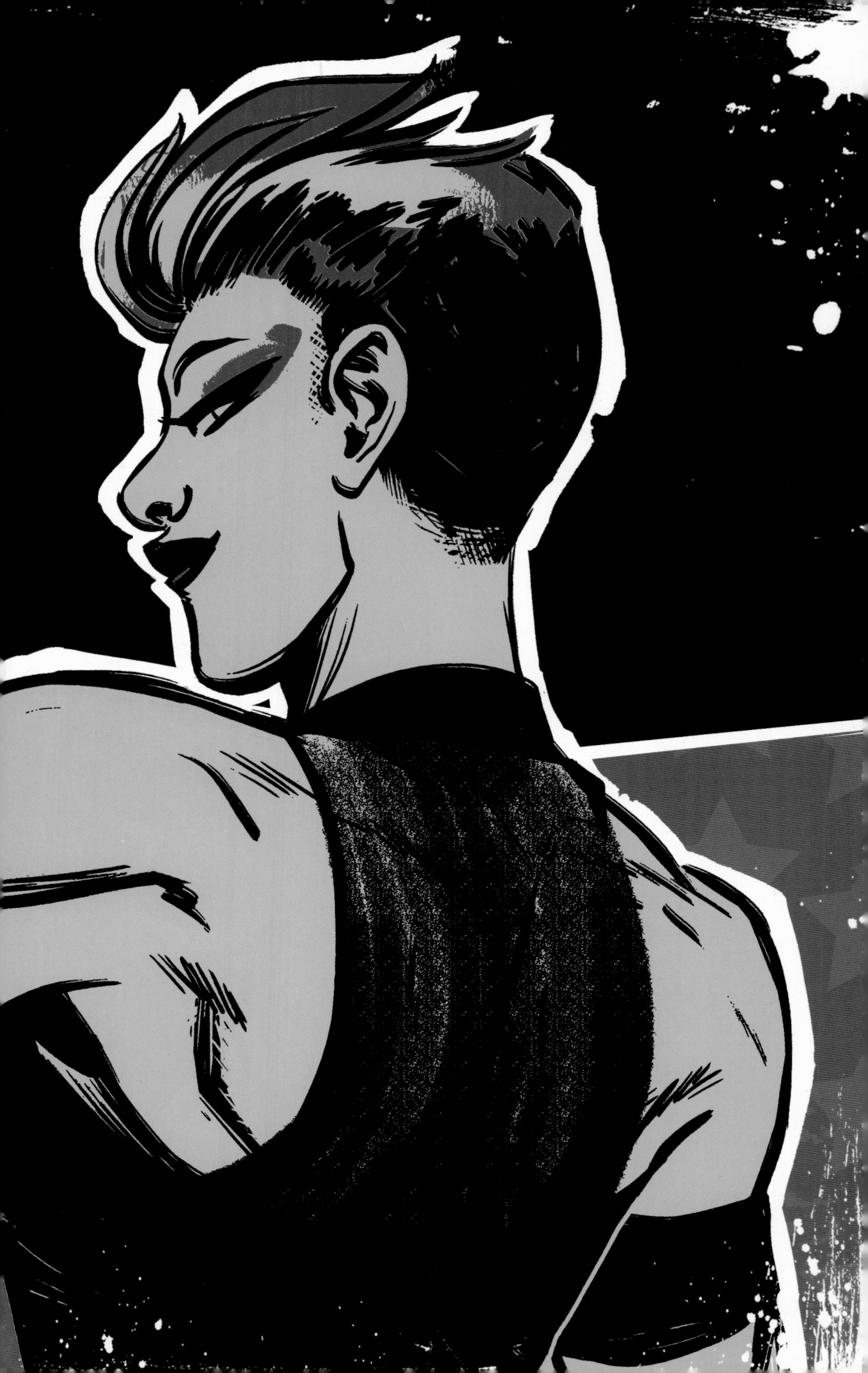

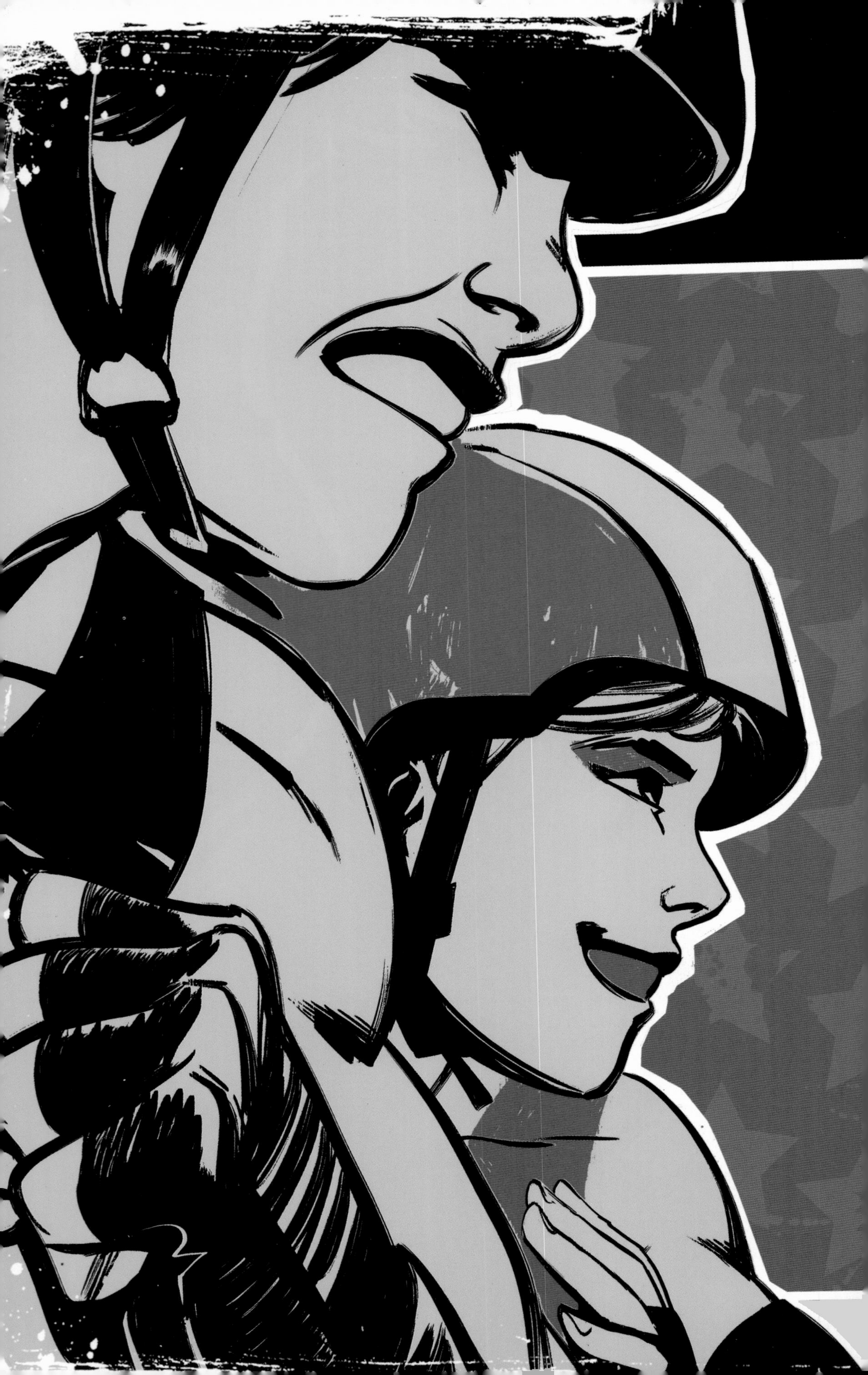

SLAM! ™

CREATED BY **PAMELA RIBON** & **VERONICA FISH**

WRITTEN BY
PAMELA RIBON

ILLUSTRATED BY
VERONICA FISH

COLORS BY
BRITTANY PEER
WITH **LAURA LANGSTON** (CHAPTER #3)

LETTERS BY
JIM CAMPBELL

COVER BY
VERONICA FISH

DESIGNER **KELSEY DIETERICH**
ASSISTANT EDITOR **SOPHIE PHILIPS-ROBERTS**
EDITORS **WHITNEY LEOPARD** & **SHANNON WATTERS**

CHAPTER
ONE

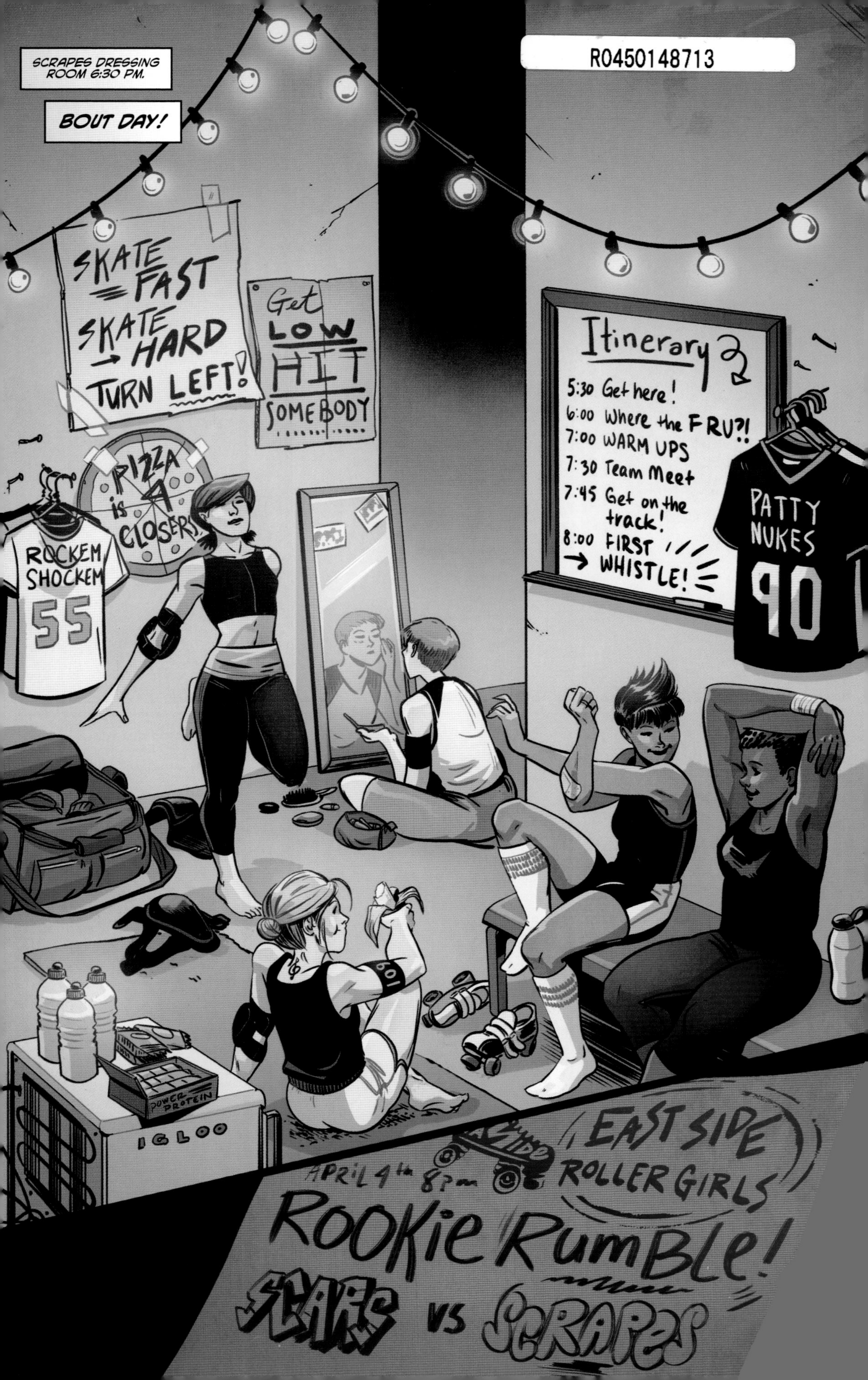
SCRAPES DRESSING ROOM 6:30 PM.
BOUT DAY!
SKATE FAST SKATE HARD TURN LEFT!
Get LOW HIT SOMEBODY
PIZZA is 4 CLOSERS
ROCKEM SHOCKEM 55
Itinerary
5:30 Get here!
6:00 Where the FRU?!
7:00 WARM UPS
7:30 Team Meet
7:45 Get on the track!
8:00 FIRST WHISTLE!
PATTY NUKES 90
POWER PROTEIN
IGLOO
EAST SIDE ROLLER GIRLS
APRIL 4th 8pm
ROOKIE RUMBLE!
SCARS VS SCRAPES

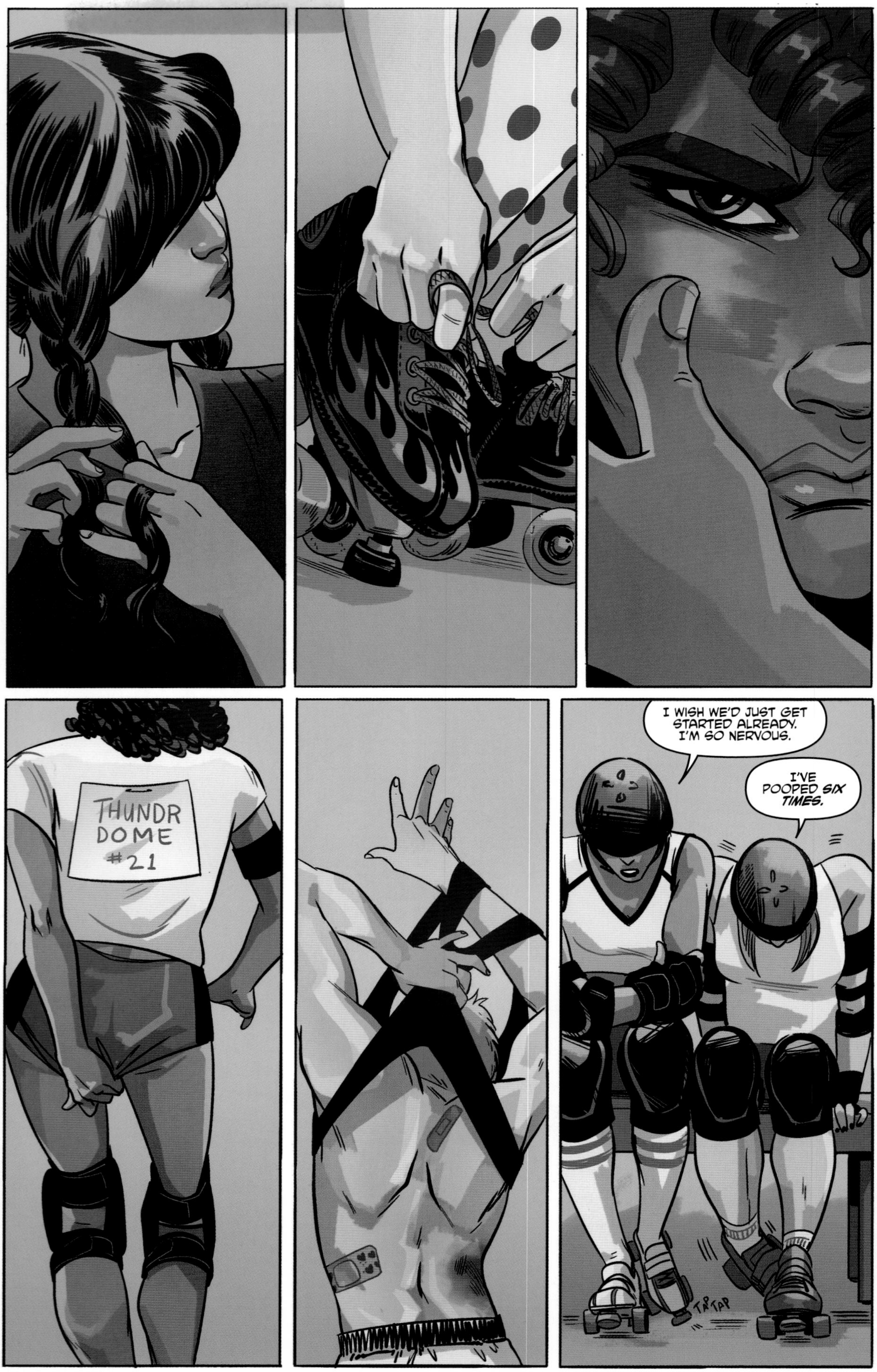
THUNDR
DOME
#21
I WISH WE'D JUST GET STARTED ALREADY. I'M SO NERVOUS.
I'VE POOPED *SIX TIMES.*
TAP TAP

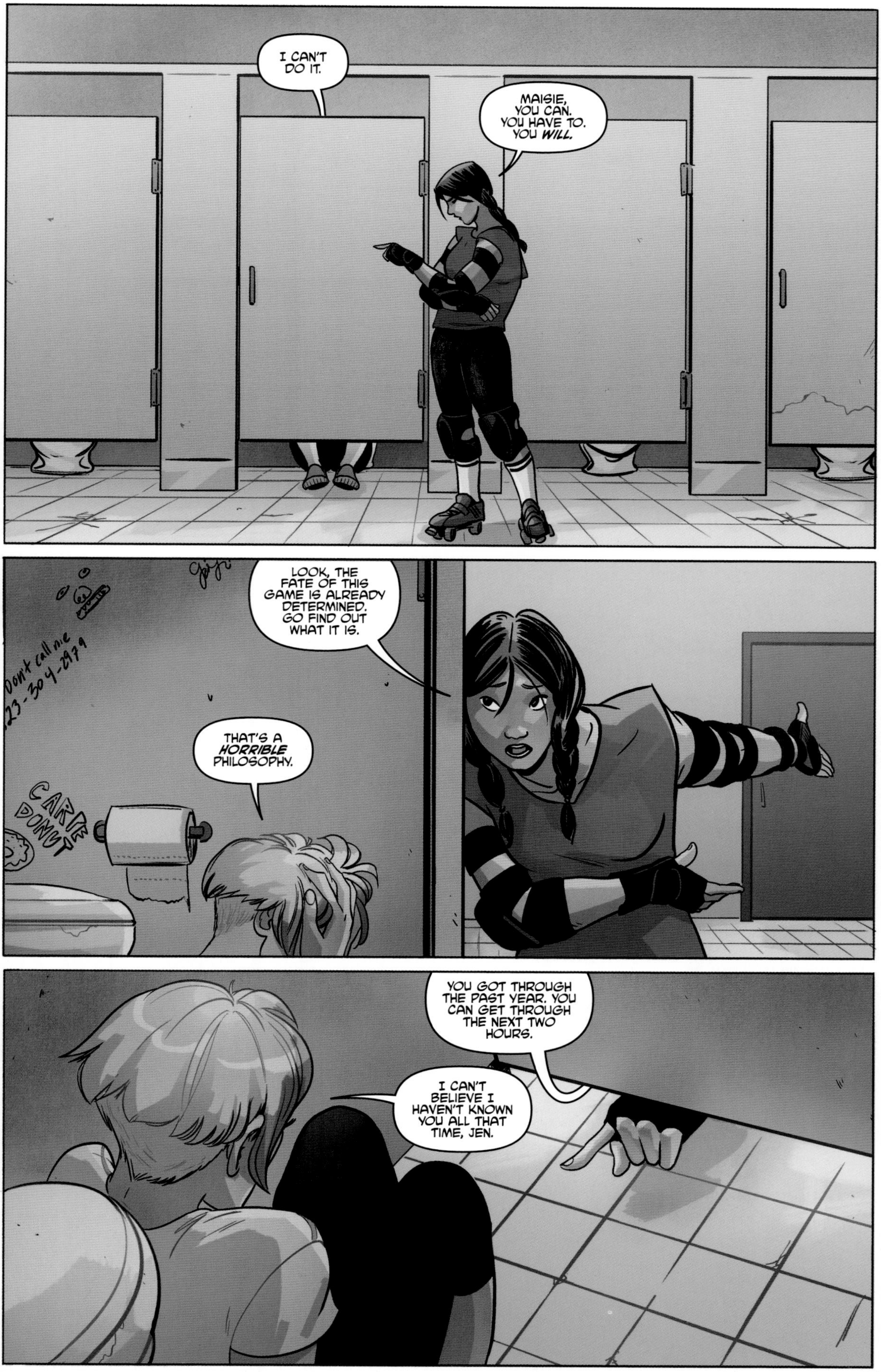
I CAN'T DO IT.
MAISIE, YOU CAN. YOU HAVE TO. YOU ***WILL.***
LOOK, THE FATE OF THIS GAME IS ALREADY DETERMINED. GO FIND OUT WHAT IT IS.
THAT'S A ***HORRIBLE*** PHILOSOPHY.
YOU GOT THROUGH THE PAST YEAR. YOU CAN GET THROUGH THE NEXT TWO HOURS.
I CAN'T BELIEVE I HAVEN'T KNOWN YOU ALL THAT TIME, JEN.

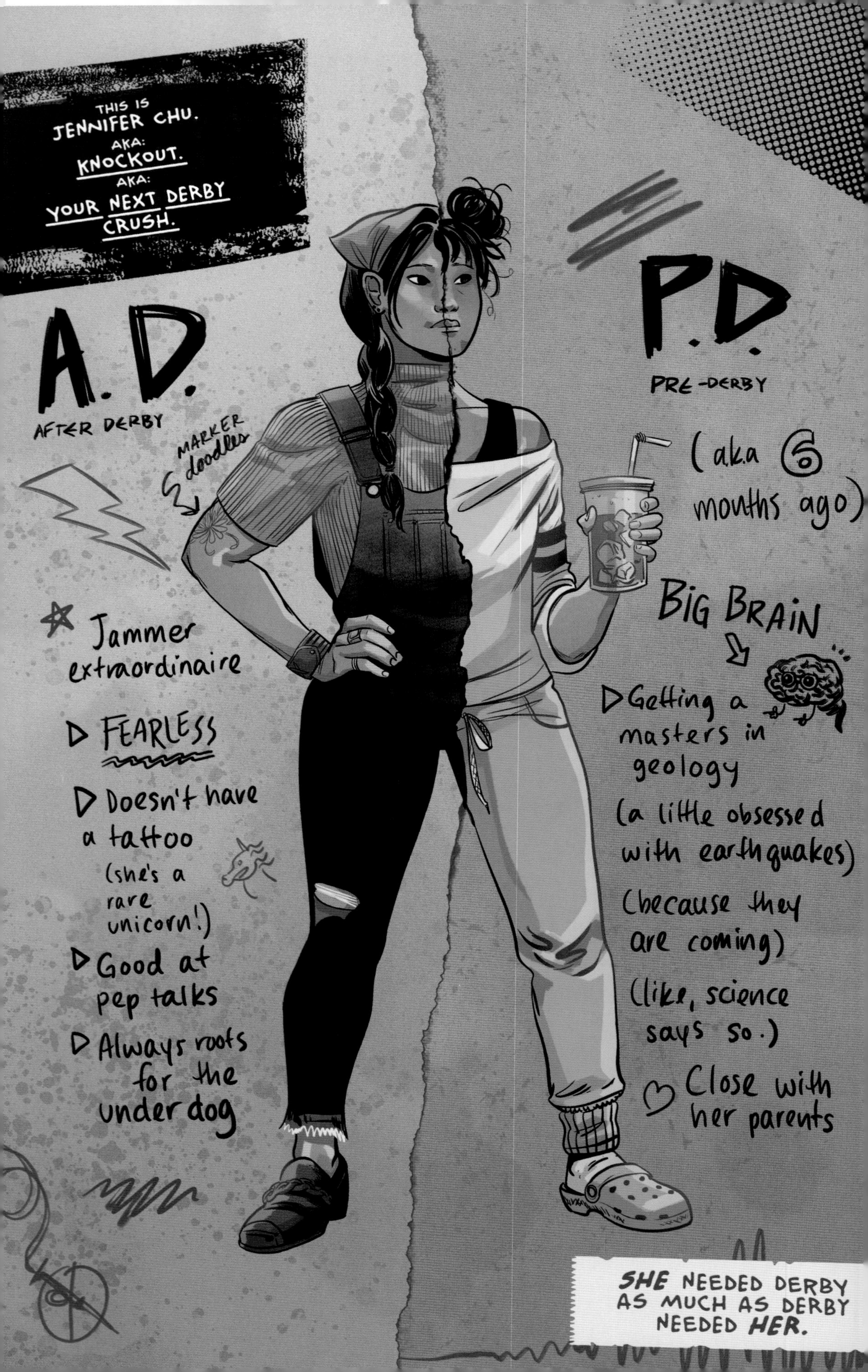
THIS IS JENNIFER CHU. AKA: KNOCKOUT. AKA: YOUR NEXT DERBY CRUSH.
A.D.
AFTER DERBY
MARKER doodles
Jammer extraordinaire
FEARLESS
Doesn't have a tattoo
(she's a rare unicorn!)
Good at pep talks
Always roots for the underdog
P.D.
PRE-DERBY
(aka 6 months ago)
BIG BRAIN
Getting a masters in geology
(a little obsessed with earthquakes)
(because they are coming)
(like, science says so.)
Close with her parents
SHE NEEDED DERBY AS MUCH AS DERBY NEEDED HER.

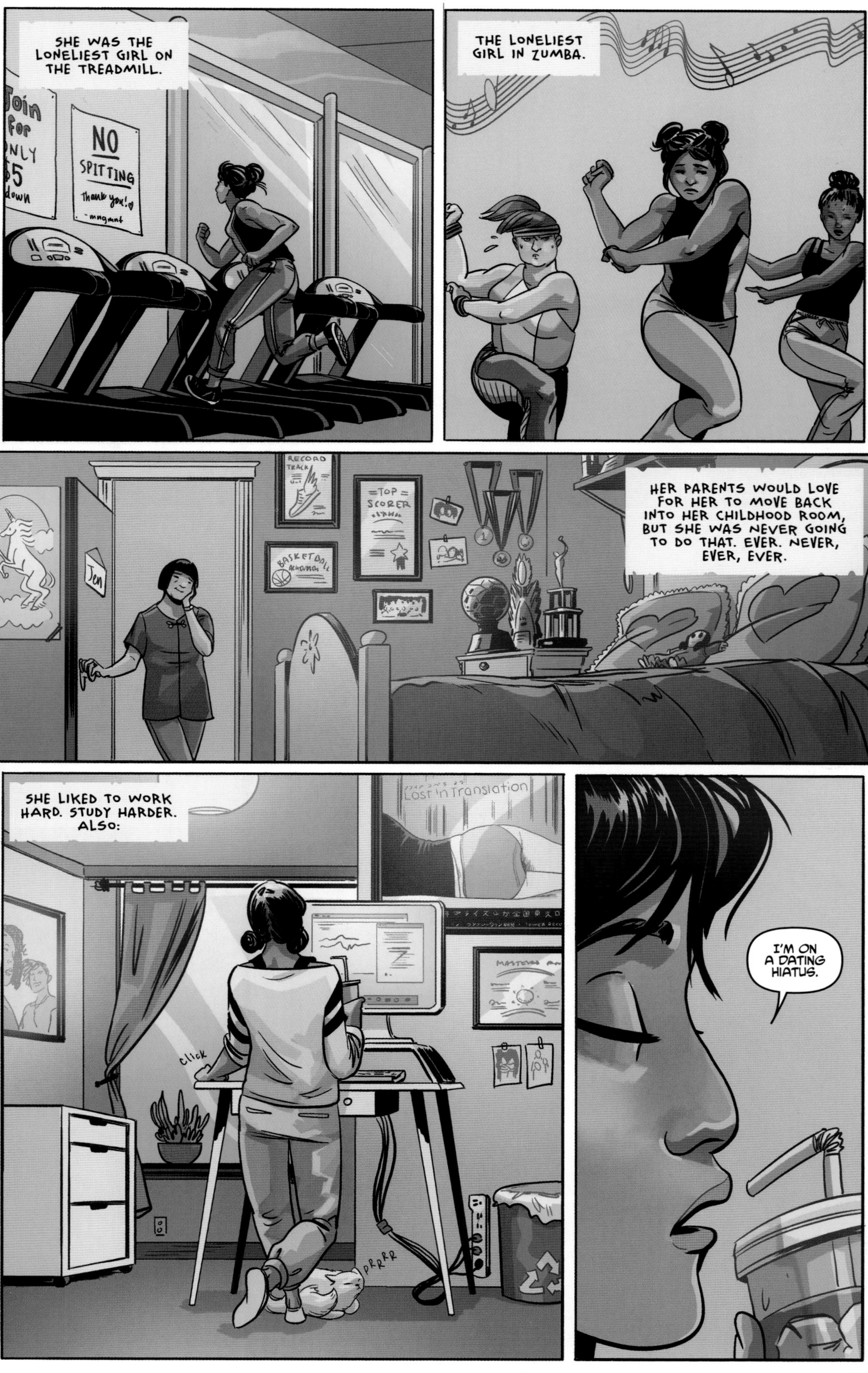
SHE WAS THE LONELIEST GIRL ON THE TREADMILL.
Join for ONLY $5 down
NO SPITTING thank you! -mngmnt
THE LONELIEST GIRL IN ZUMBA.
HER PARENTS WOULD LOVE FOR HER TO MOVE BACK INTO HER CHILDHOOD ROOM, BUT SHE WAS NEVER GOING TO DO THAT. EVER. NEVER, EVER, EVER.
RECORD TRACK
TOP SCORER
BASKETBALL
Jen
SHE LIKED TO WORK HARD. STUDY HARDER. ALSO:
Lost in Translation
click
PRRRR
I'M ON A DATING HIATUS.

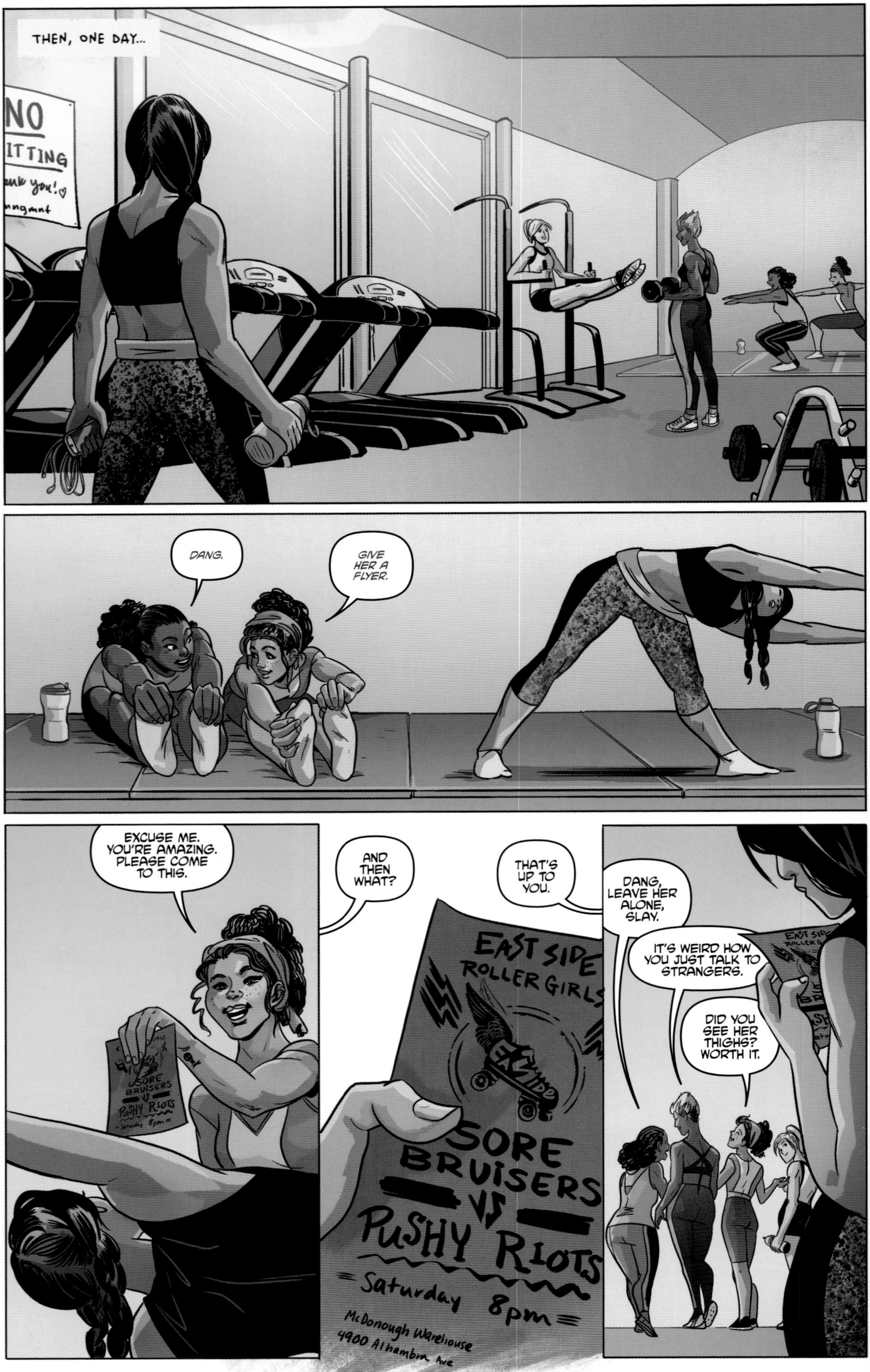
THEN, ONE DAY...
NO
ITTING
ank you!
nngmnt
DANG.
GIVE HER A FLYER.
EXCUSE ME. YOU'RE AMAZING. PLEASE COME TO THIS.
SORE BRUISERS VS PUSHY RIOTS
AND THEN WHAT?
THAT'S UP TO YOU.
EAST SIDE ROLLER GIRLS
SORE BRUISERS VS PUSHY RIOTS
Saturday 8pm
McDonough Warehouse
4900 Alhambra Ave
DANG, LEAVE HER ALONE, SLAY.
IT'S WEIRD HOW YOU JUST TALK TO STRANGERS.
DID YOU SEE HER THIGHS? WORTH IT.

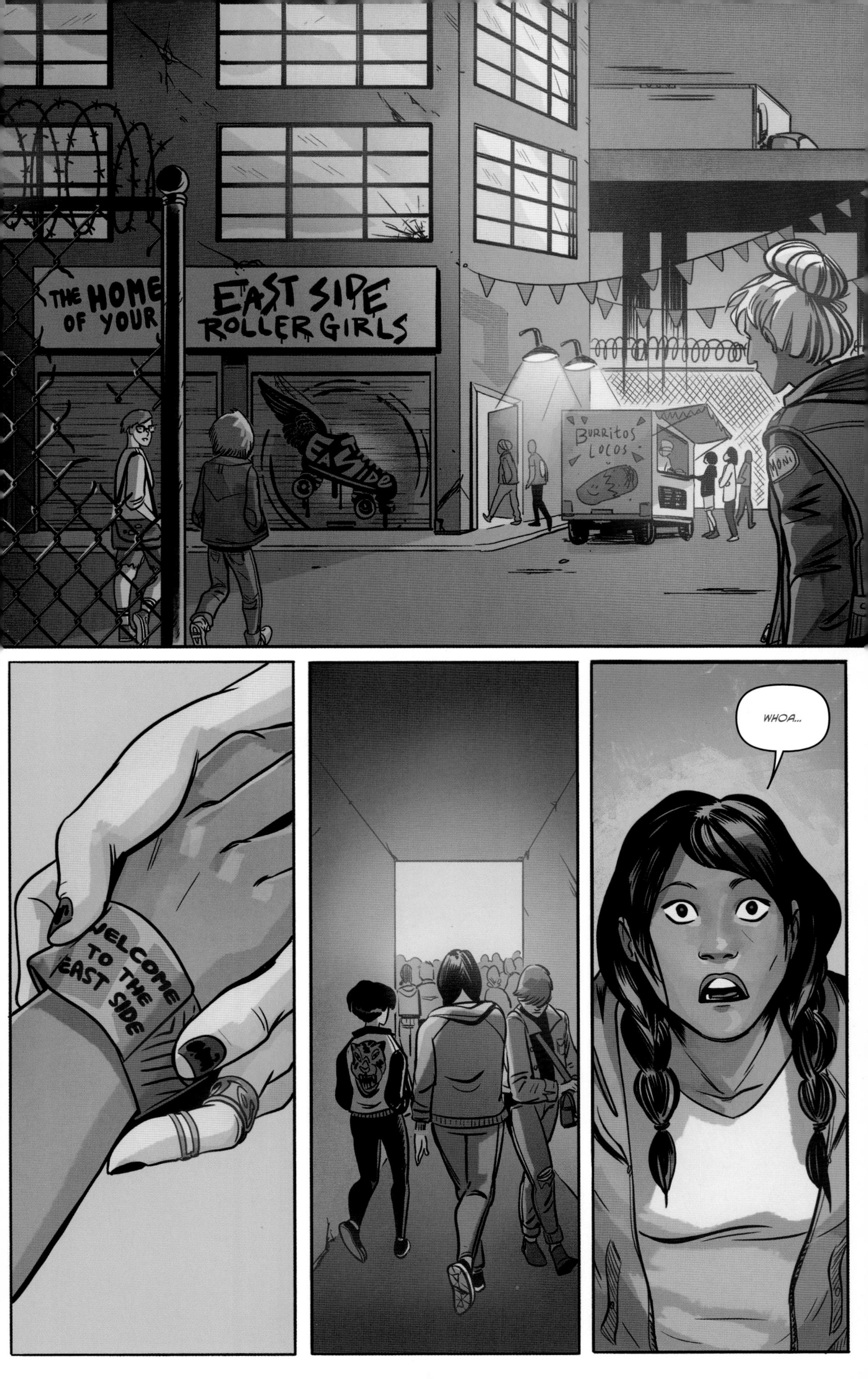
THE HOME OF YOUR
EAST SIDE ROLLER GIRLS
EASIDE
BURRITOS LOCOS
MONI
WELCOME TO THE EAST SIDE
WHOA...

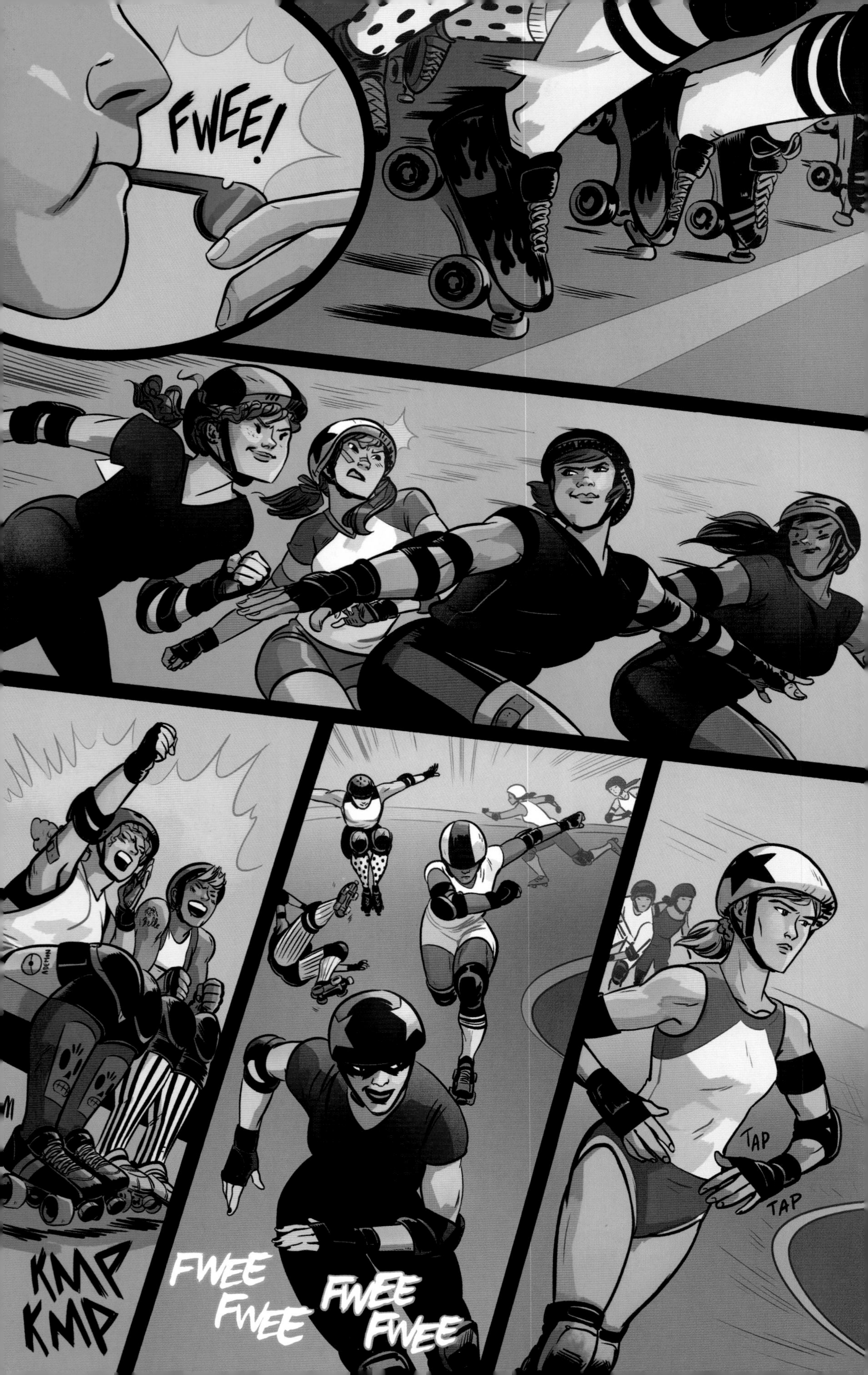
FWEE!
KMP
KMP
FWEE
FWEE
FWEE
FWEE
TAP
TAP

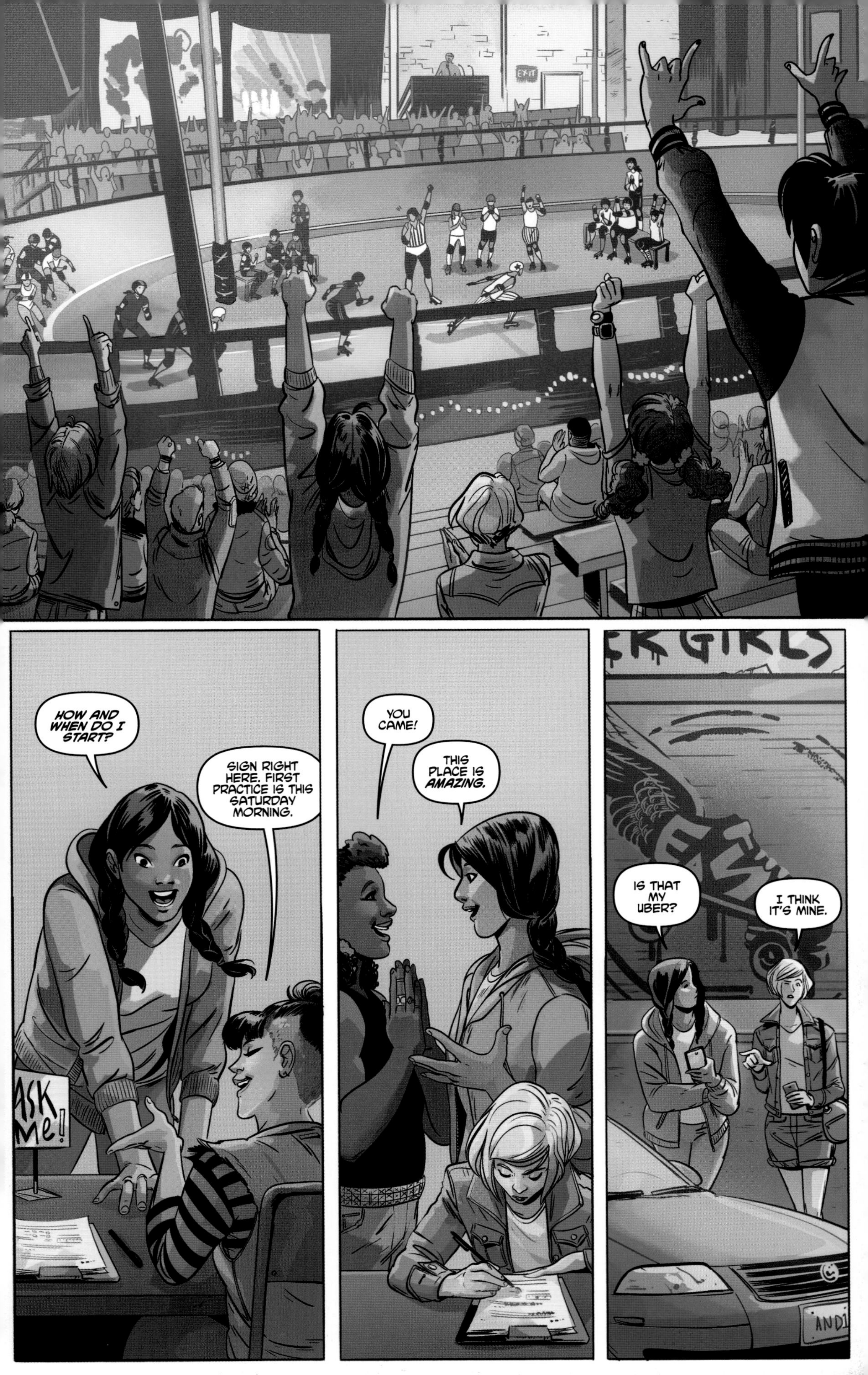
HOW AND WHEN DO I START?
SIGN RIGHT HERE. FIRST PRACTICE IS THIS SATURDAY MORNING.
ASK ME!
YOU CAME!
THIS PLACE IS *AMAZING.*
IS THAT MY UBER?
I THINK IT'S MINE.

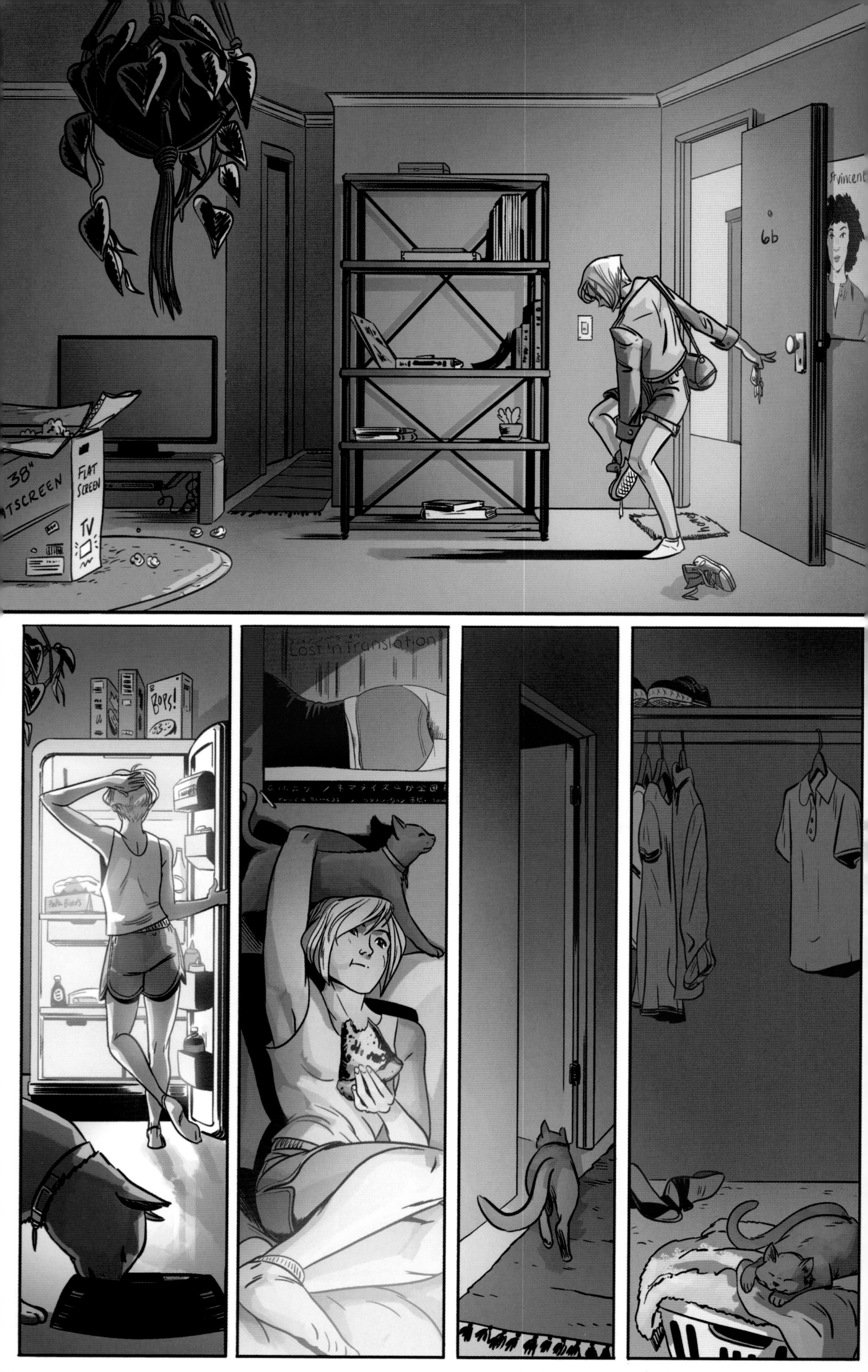

38"
TSCREEN
FLAT SCREEN
TV
6b
St. Vincent
BOPS!
Lost in Translation

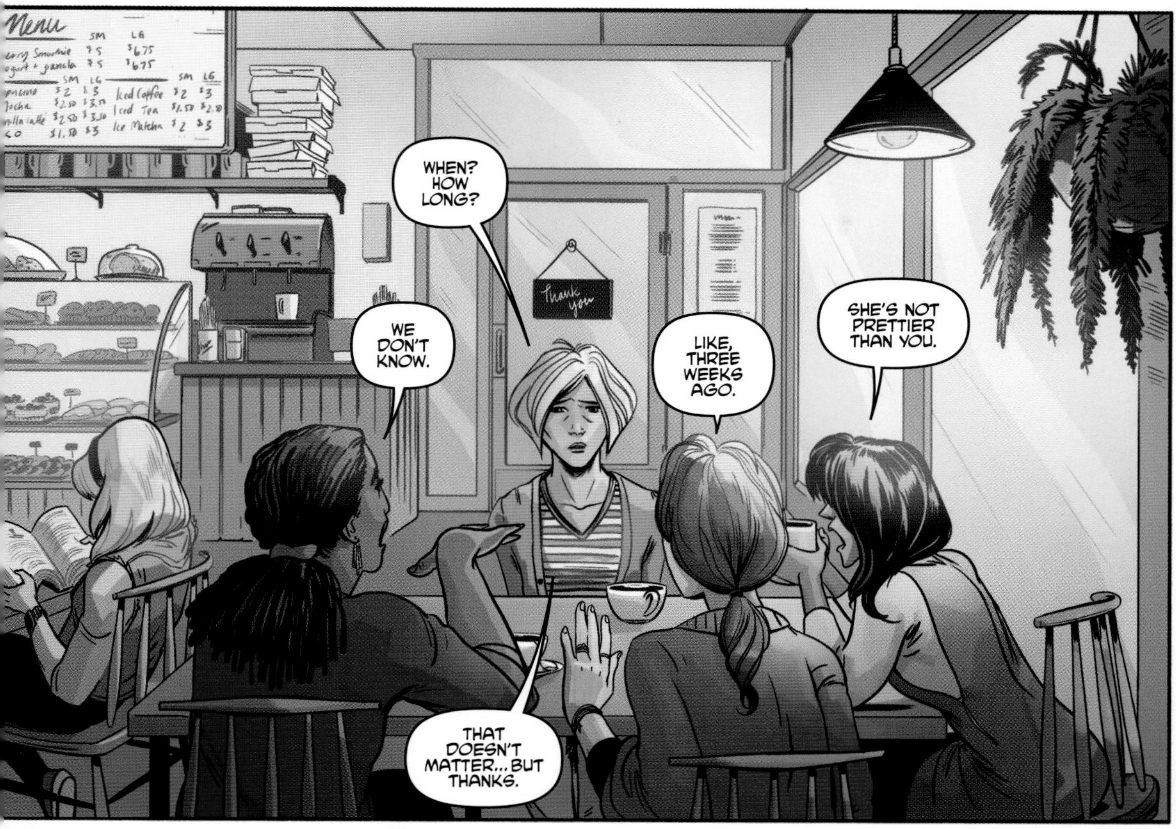
Thank you
WHEN? HOW LONG?
WE DON'T KNOW.
LIKE, THREE WEEKS AGO.
SHE'S NOT PRETTIER THAN YOU.
THAT DOESN'T MATTER... BUT THANKS.

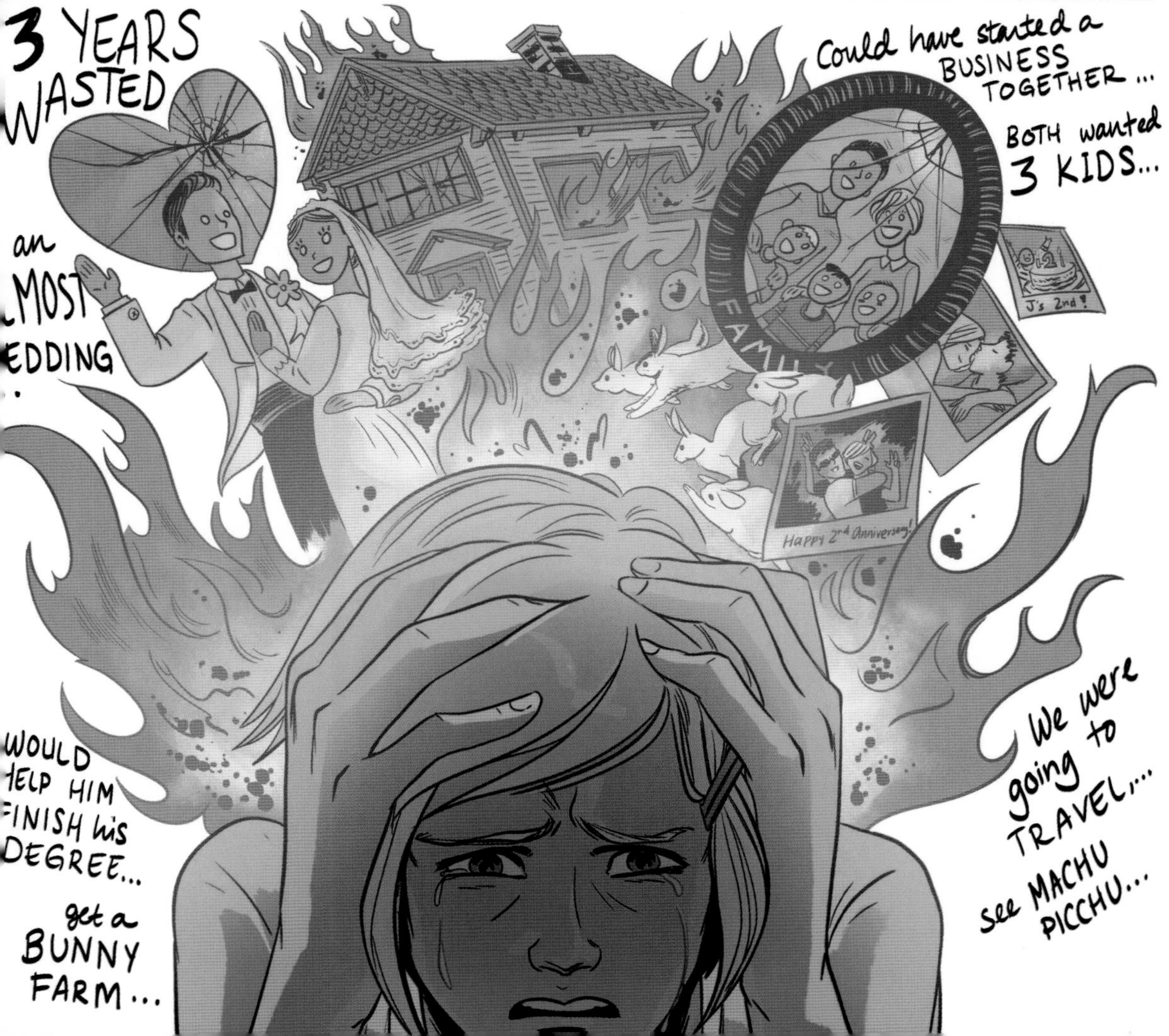
3 YEARS WASTED
an MOST EDDING
Could have started a BUSINESS TOGETHER...
BOTH wanted 3 KIDS...
J's 2nd!
Happy 2nd Anniversary!
WOULD ELP HIM INISH his DEGREE...
get a BUNNY FARM...
We were going to TRAVEL... see MACHU PICCHU...

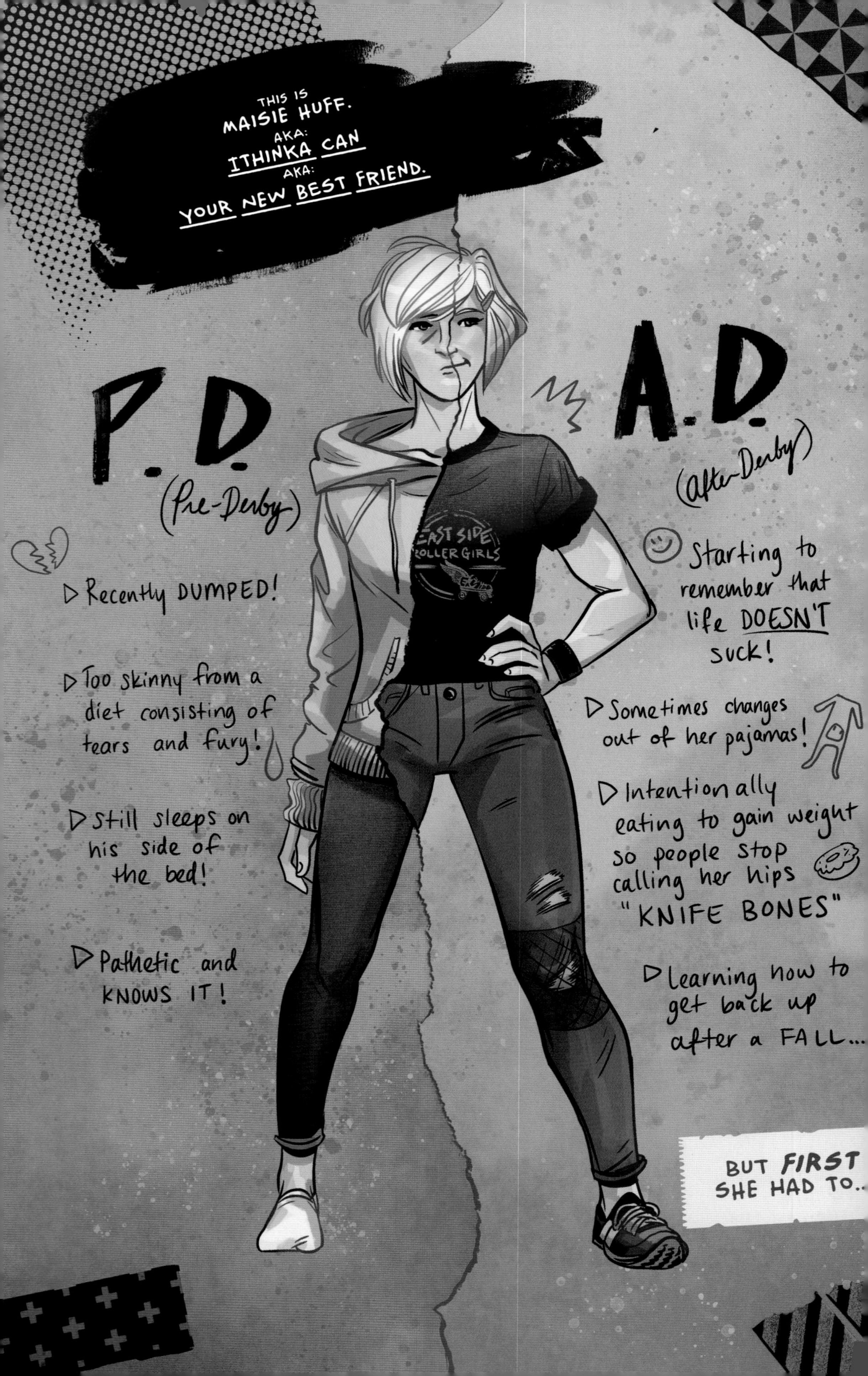
THIS IS MAISIE HUFF. AKA: ITHINKA CAN AKA: YOUR NEW BEST FRIEND.
P.D. (Pre-Derby)
Recently DUMPED!
Too skinny from a diet consisting of tears and fury!
Still sleeps on his side of the bed!
Pathetic and KNOWS IT!
A.D. (After-Derby)
Starting to remember that life DOESN'T suck!
Sometimes changes out of her pajamas!
Intentionally eating to gain weight so people stop calling her hips "KNIFE BONES"
Learning how to get back up after a FALL...
EAST SIDE ROLLER GIRLS
BUT FIRST SHE HAD TO...

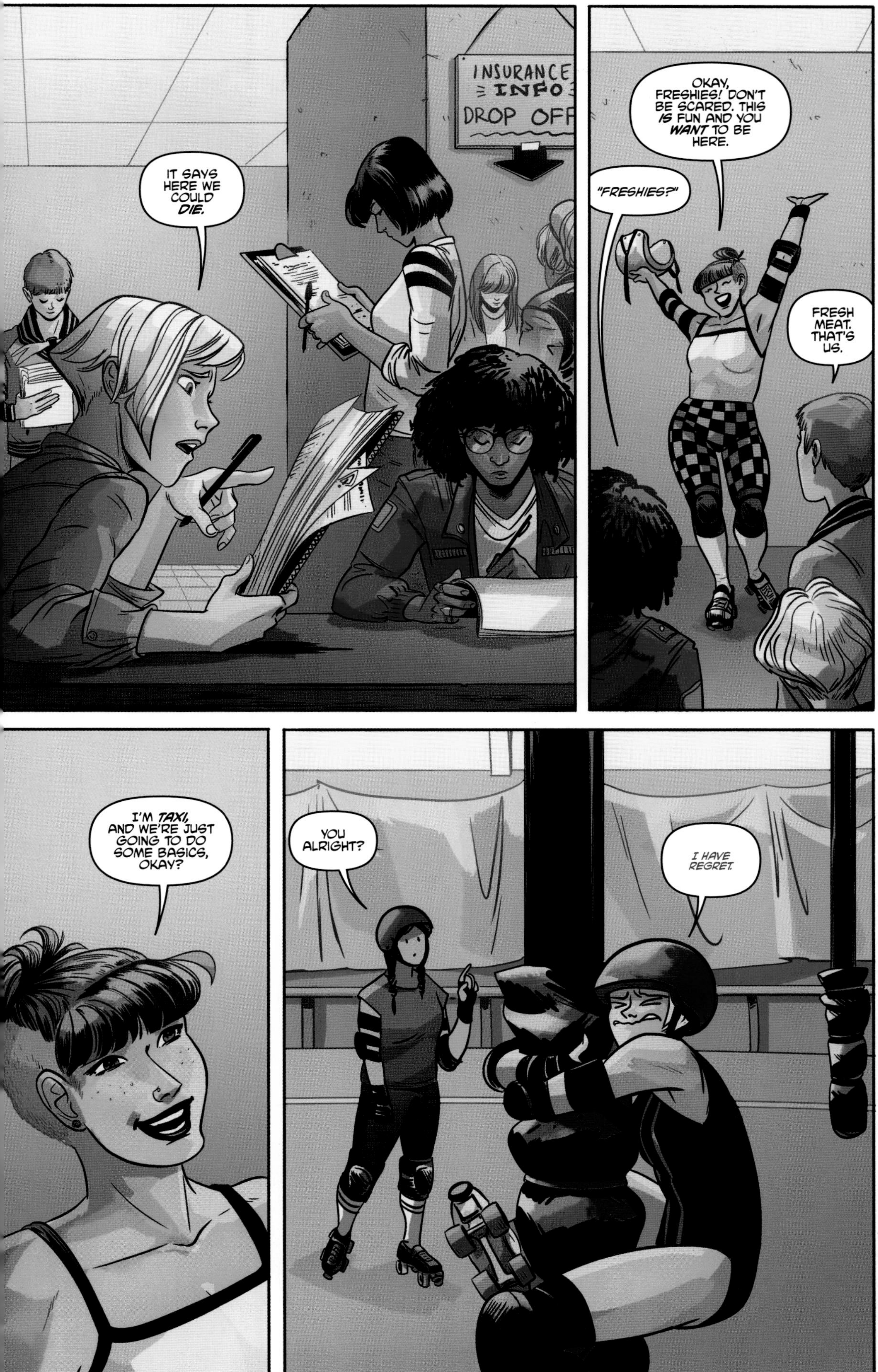
INSURANCE INFO DROP OFF
IT SAYS HERE WE COULD DIE.
OKAY, FRESHIES! DON'T BE SCARED. THIS IS FUN AND YOU WANT TO BE HERE.
"FRESHIES?"
FRESH MEAT. THAT'S US.
I'M TAXI, AND WE'RE JUST GOING TO DO SOME BASICS, OKAY?
YOU ALRIGHT?
I HAVE REGRET.

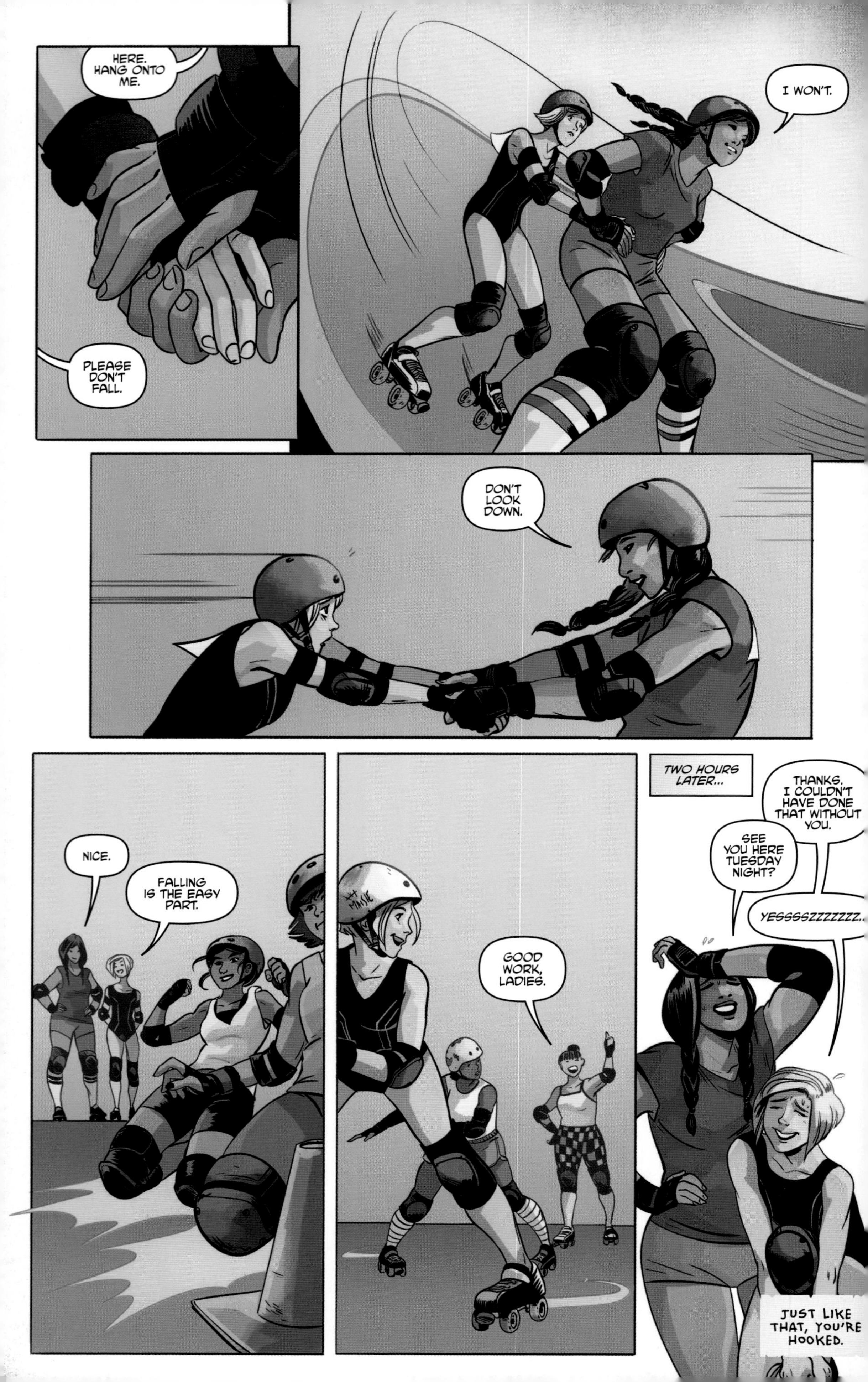
HERE. HANG ONTO ME.
PLEASE DON'T FALL.
I WON'T.
DON'T LOOK DOWN.
NICE.
FALLING IS THE EASY PART.
#MASIE
GOOD WORK, LADIES.
TWO HOURS LATER...
THANKS. I COULDN'T HAVE DONE THAT WITHOUT YOU.
SEE YOU HERE TUESDAY NIGHT?
YESSSSZZZZZZZ...
JUST LIKE THAT, YOU'RE HOOKED.

10 FACTS
about your new derby life

1. YOU WILL HAVE FUN.
2. YOU WILL GET HURT.
3. YOU WILL WANT TO QUIT THIS FOREVER. EVERY TIME.
4. YOU WON'T. BECAUSE YOU LOVE IT MORE THAN YOU'VE EVER LOVED ANYTHING IN YOUR LIFE.

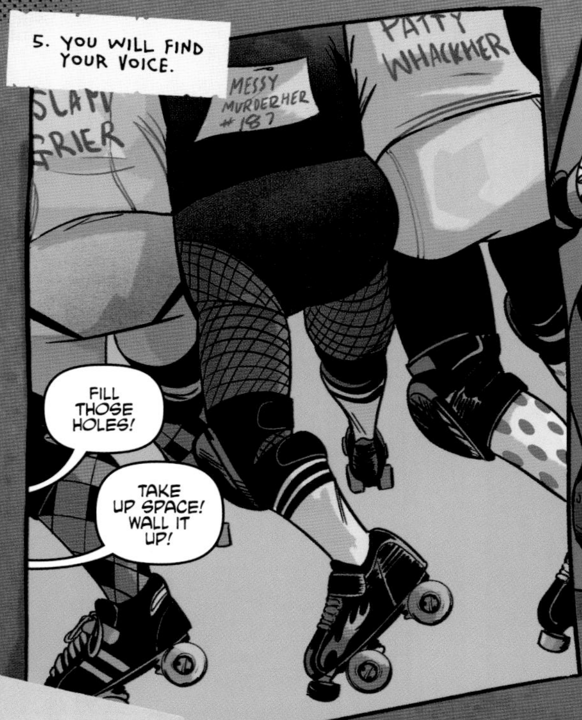
5. YOU WILL FIND YOUR VOICE.
PATTY WHACKHER
MESSY MURDERHER #187
FILL THOSE HOLES!
TAKE UP SPACE! WALL IT UP!

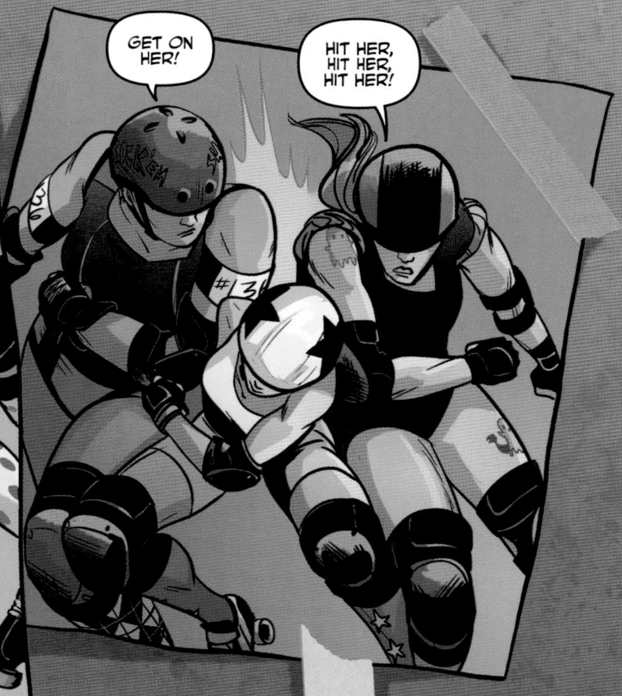
GET ON HER!
HIT HER, HIT HER, HIT HER!

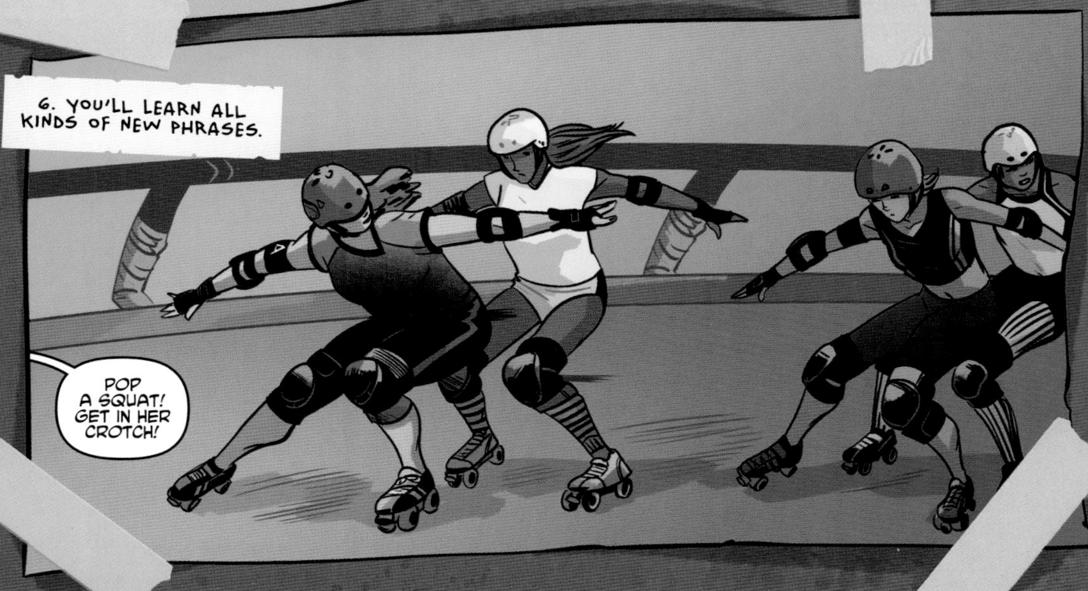
6. YOU'LL LEARN ALL KINDS OF NEW PHRASES.
POP A SQUAT! GET IN HER CROTCH!

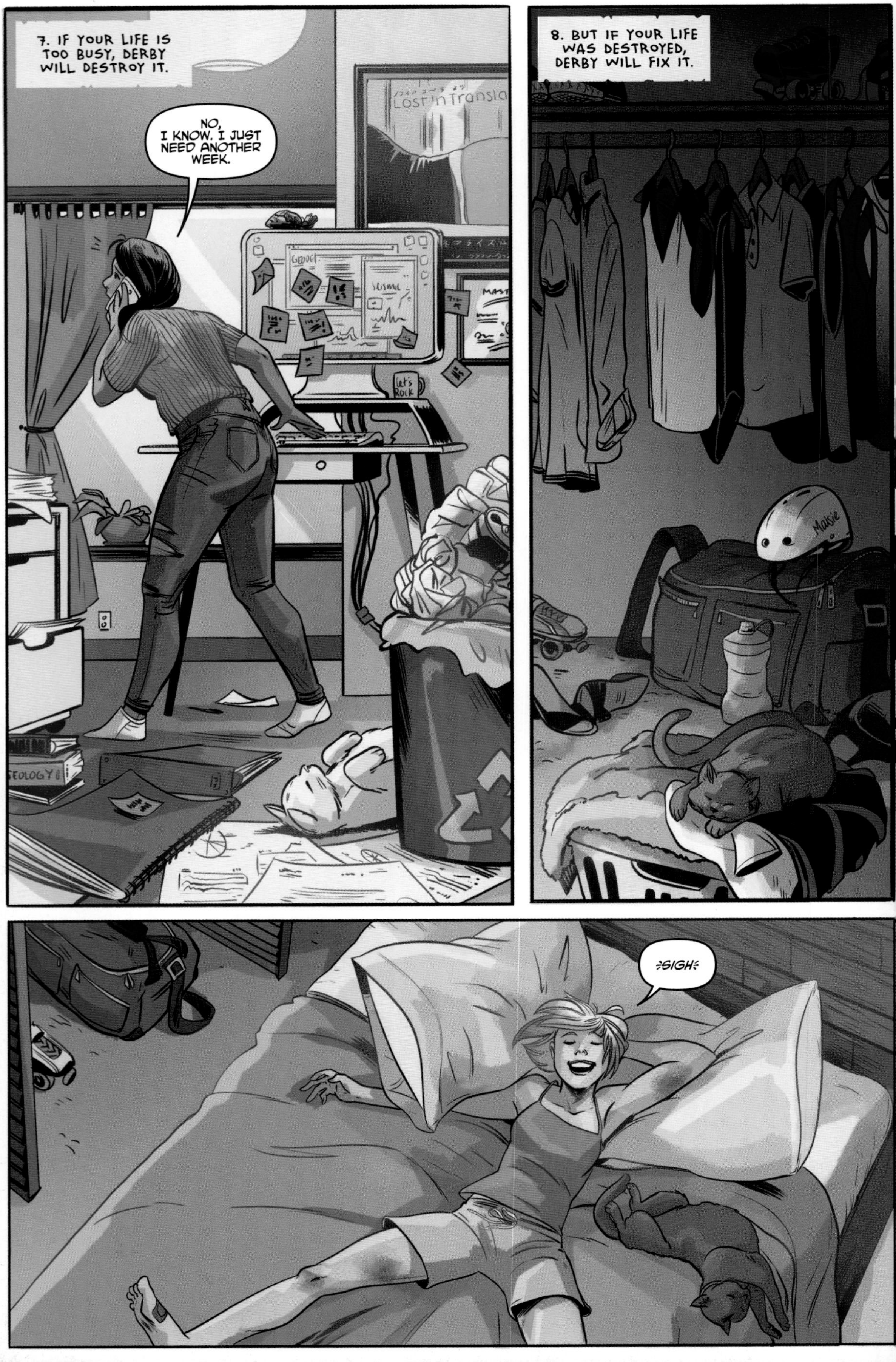

7. IF YOUR LIFE IS TOO BUSY, DERBY WILL DESTROY IT.
NO, I KNOW. I JUST NEED ANOTHER WEEK.
8. BUT IF YOUR LIFE WAS DESTROYED, DERBY WILL FIX IT.
SIGH

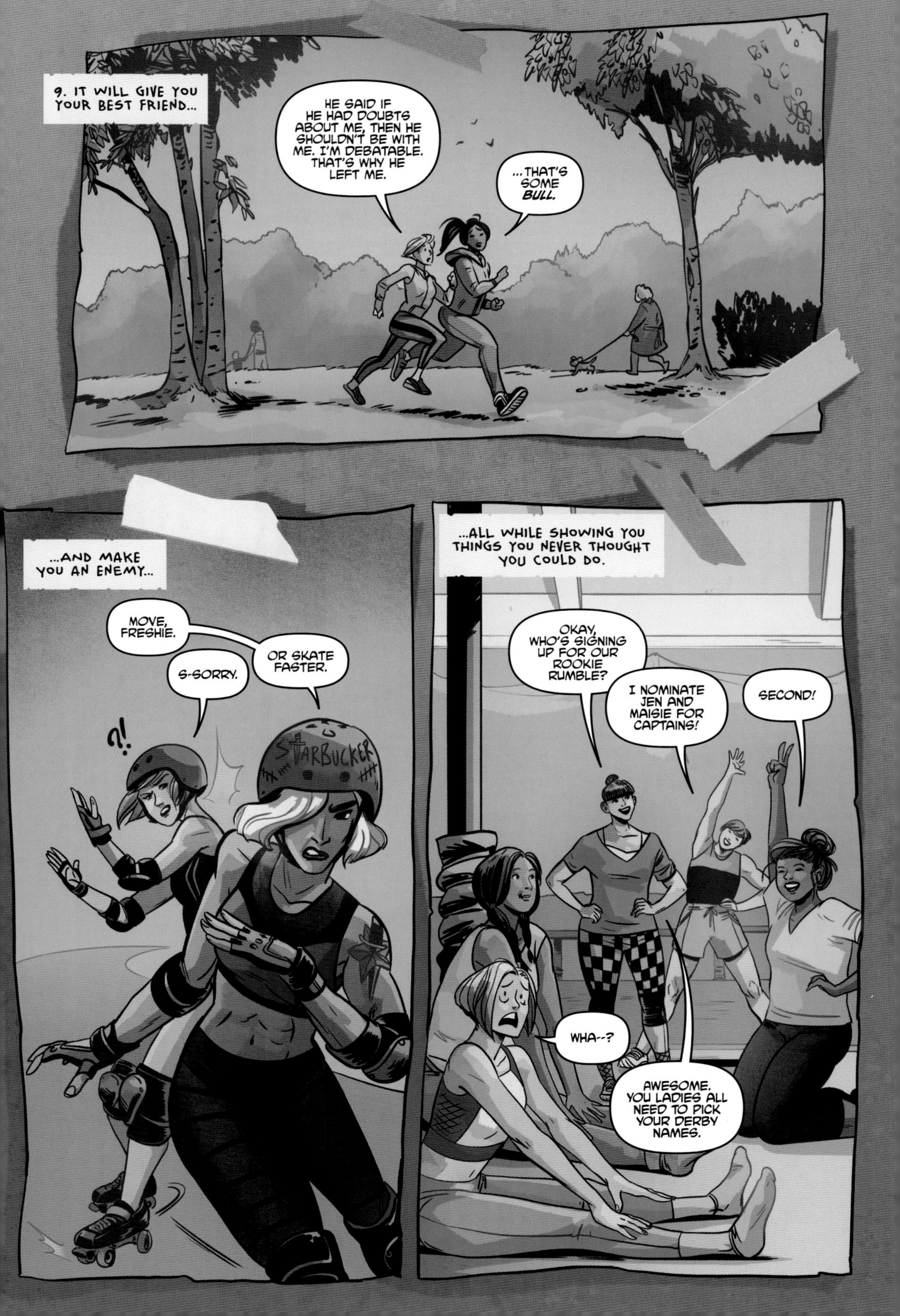
9. IT WILL GIVE YOU YOUR BEST FRIEND...
HE SAID IF HE HAD DOUBTS ABOUT ME, THEN HE SHOULDN'T BE WITH ME. I'M DEBATABLE. THAT'S WHY HE LEFT ME.
...THAT'S SOME BULL.
...AND MAKE YOU AN ENEMY...
MOVE, FRESHIE.
OR SKATE FASTER.
S-SORRY.
?!
STARBUCKER
...ALL WHILE SHOWING YOU THINGS YOU NEVER THOUGHT YOU COULD DO.
OKAY, WHO'S SIGNING UP FOR OUR ROOKIE RUMBLE?
I NOMINATE JEN AND MAISIE FOR CAPTAINS!
SECOND!
WHA--?
AWESOME. YOU LADIES ALL NEED TO PICK YOUR DERBY NAMES.

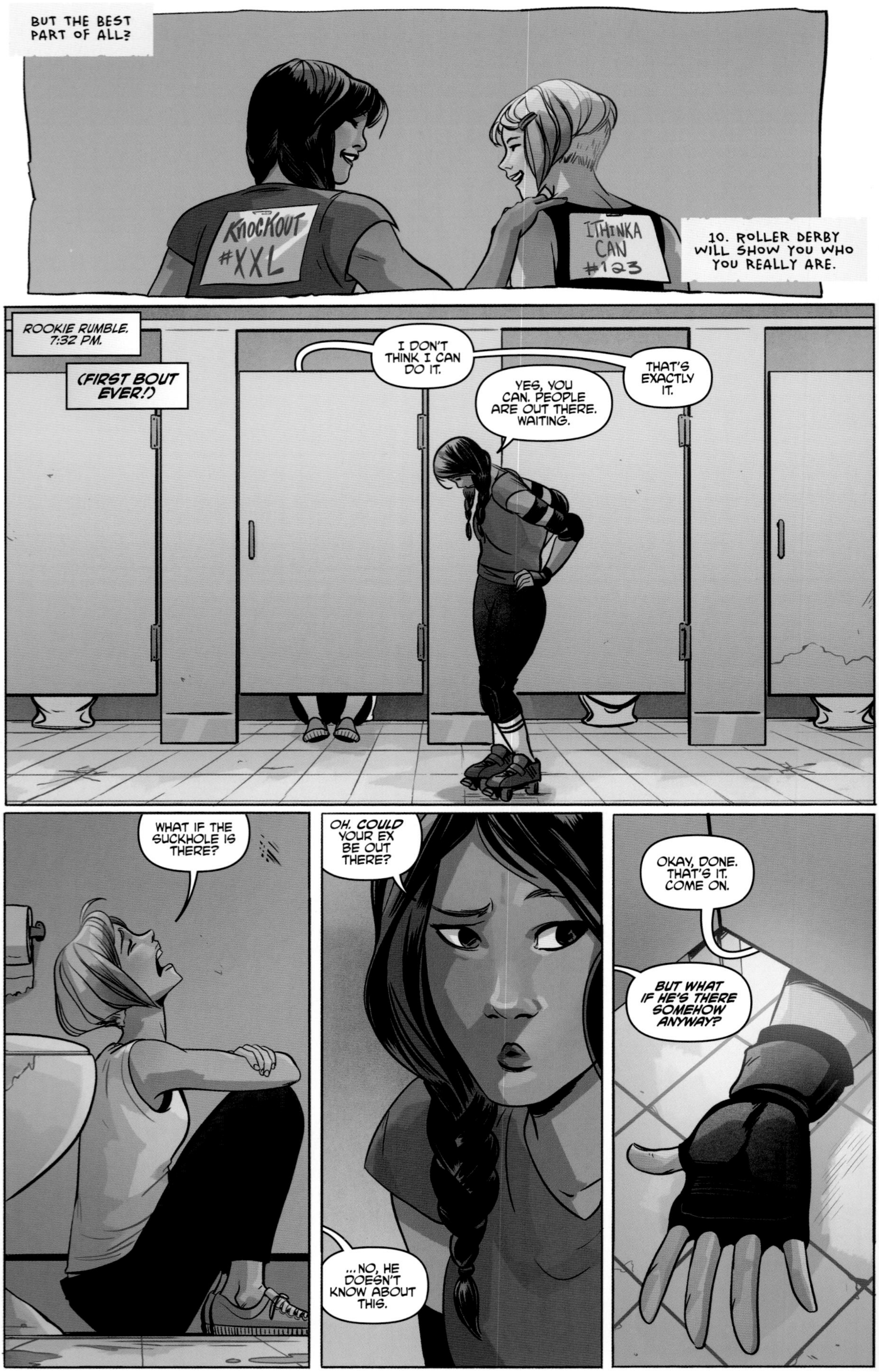
BUT THE BEST PART OF ALL?
KNOCKOUT #XXL
ITHINKA CAN #123
10. ROLLER DERBY WILL SHOW YOU WHO YOU REALLY ARE.
ROOKIE RUMBLE. 7:32 PM.
(FIRST BOUT EVER!)
I DON'T THINK I CAN DO IT.
YES, YOU CAN. PEOPLE ARE OUT THERE. WAITING.
THAT'S EXACTLY IT.
WHAT IF THE SUCKHOLE IS THERE?
OH, COULD YOUR EX BE OUT THERE?
...NO, HE DOESN'T KNOW ABOUT THIS.
OKAY, DONE. THAT'S IT. COME ON.
BUT WHAT IF HE'S THERE SOMEHOW ANYWAY?

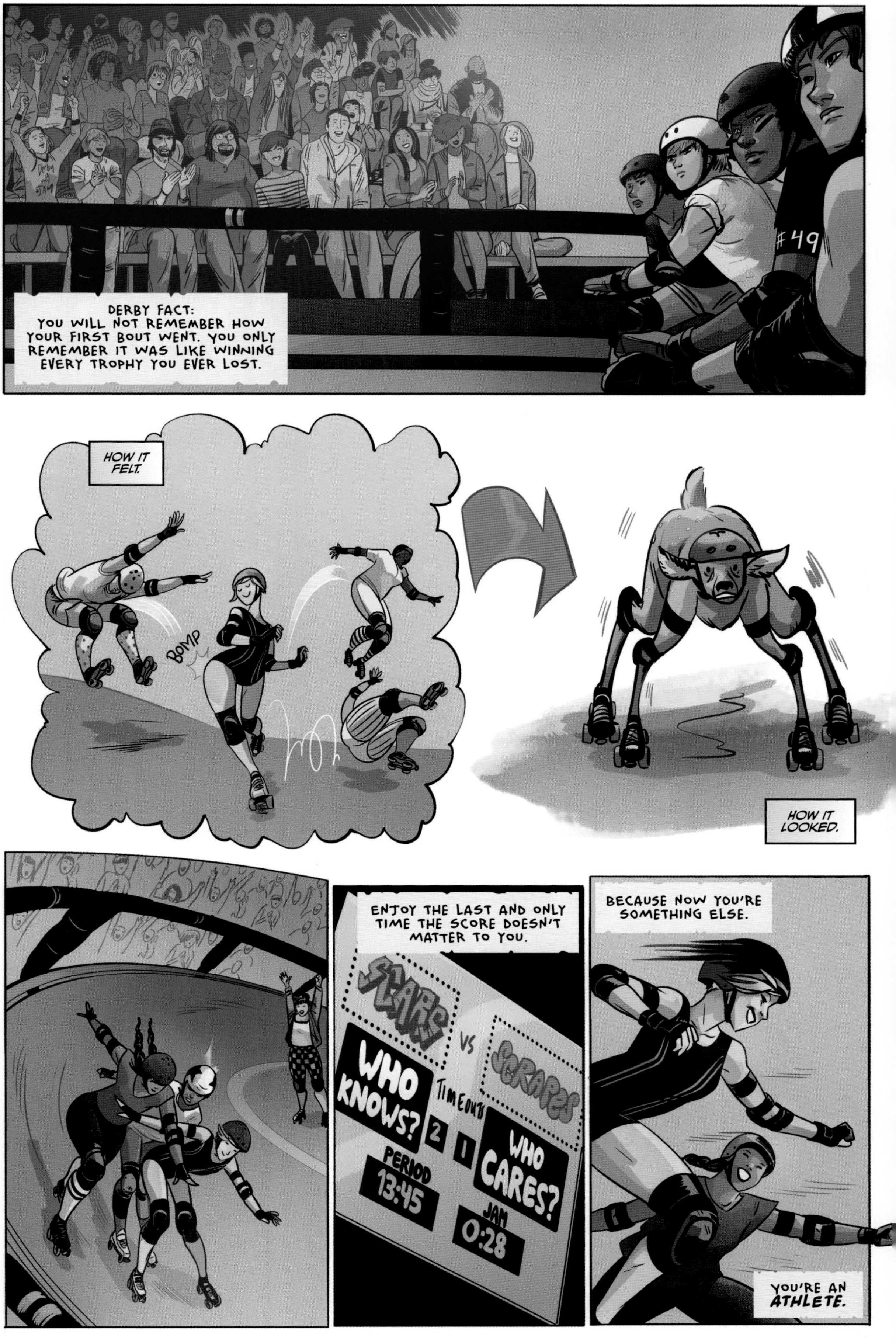
#49
DERBY FACT:
YOU WILL NOT REMEMBER HOW YOUR FIRST BOUT WENT. YOU ONLY REMEMBER IT WAS LIKE WINNING EVERY TROPHY YOU EVER LOST.
HOW IT FELT.
BOMP
HOW IT LOOKED.
ENJOY THE LAST AND ONLY TIME THE SCORE DOESN'T MATTER TO YOU.
SCARS
VS
SCRAPES
WHO KNOWS?
TIMEOUTS
2
1
WHO CARES?
PERIOD
13:45
JAM
0:28
BECAUSE NOW YOU'RE SOMETHING ELSE.
YOU'RE AN ATHLETE.

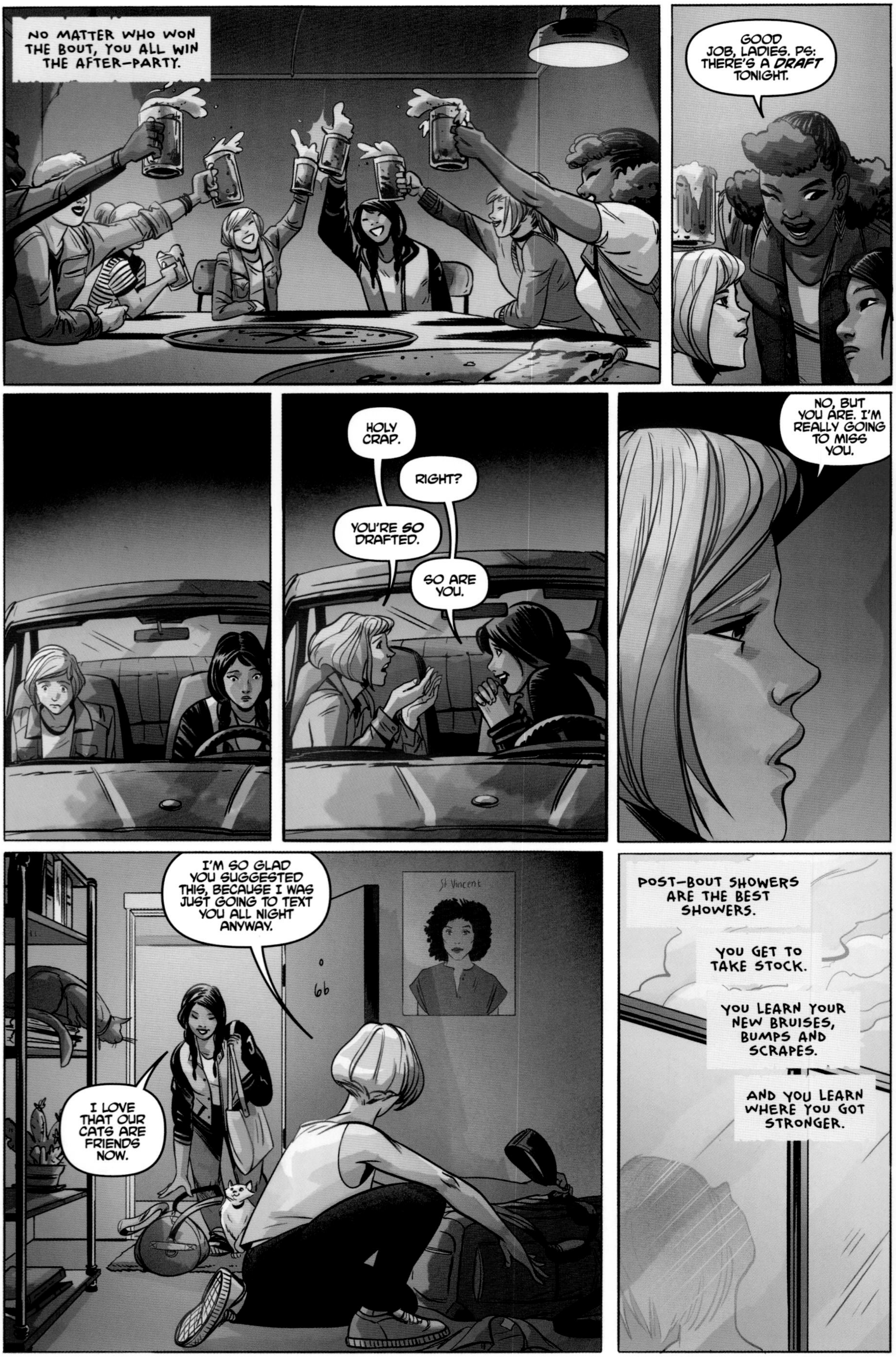
NO MATTER WHO WON THE BOUT, YOU ALL WIN THE AFTER-PARTY.
GOOD JOB, LADIES. PS: THERE'S A DRAFT TONIGHT.
HOLY CRAP.
RIGHT?
YOU'RE SO DRAFTED.
SO ARE YOU.
NO, BUT YOU ARE. I'M REALLY GOING TO MISS YOU.
I'M SO GLAD YOU SUGGESTED THIS, BECAUSE I WAS JUST GOING TO TEXT YOU ALL NIGHT ANYWAY.
I LOVE THAT OUR CATS ARE FRIENDS NOW.
St Vincent
POST-BOUT SHOWERS ARE THE BEST SHOWERS.
YOU GET TO TAKE STOCK.
YOU LEARN YOUR NEW BRUISES, BUMPS AND SCRAPES.
AND YOU LEARN WHERE YOU GOT STRONGER.

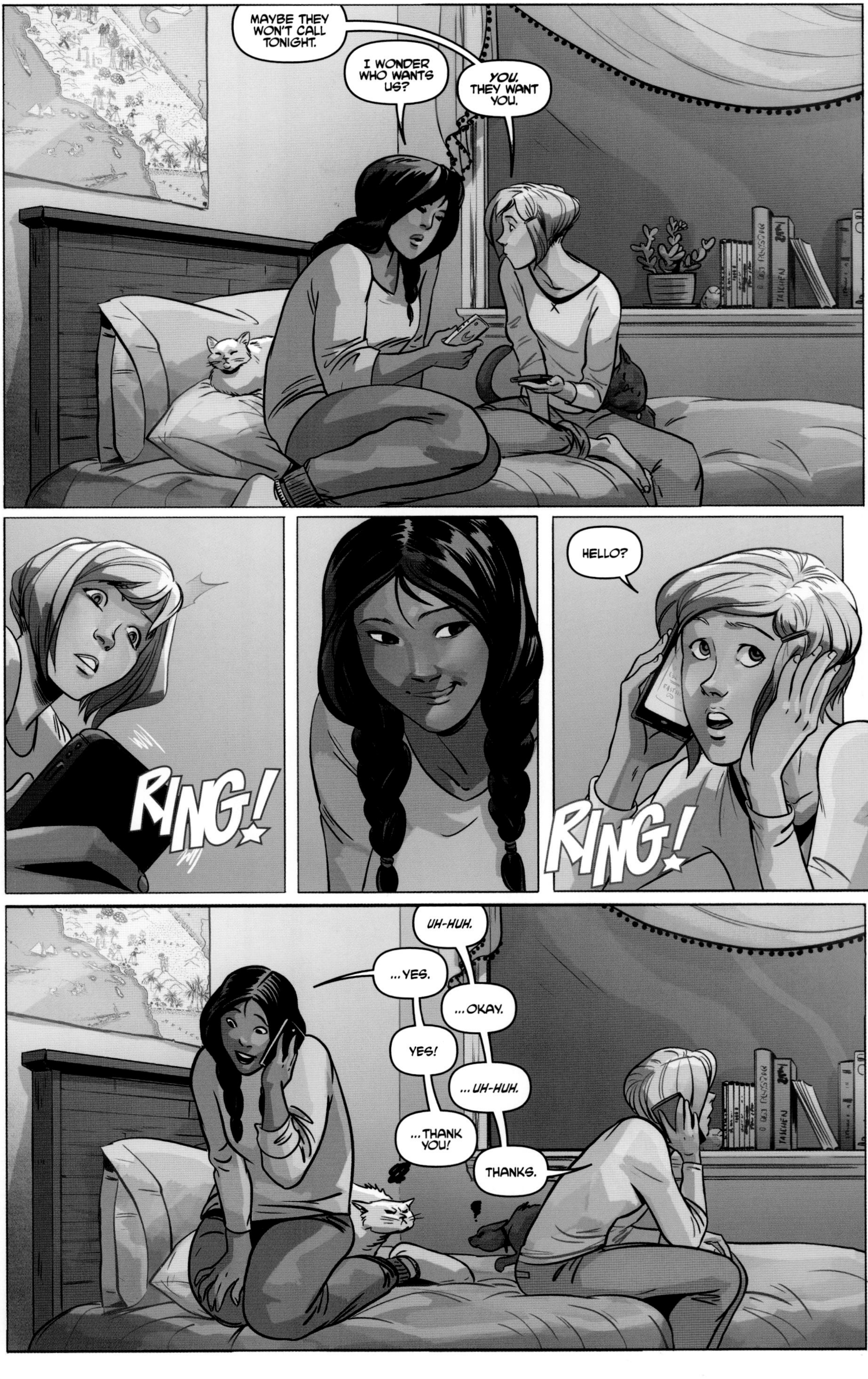
MAYBE THEY WON'T CALL TONIGHT.
I WONDER WHO WANTS US?
YOU. THEY WANT YOU.
RING!
HELLO?
RING!
UH-HUH.
...YES.
...OKAY.
YES!
...UH-HUH.
...THANK YOU!
THANKS.

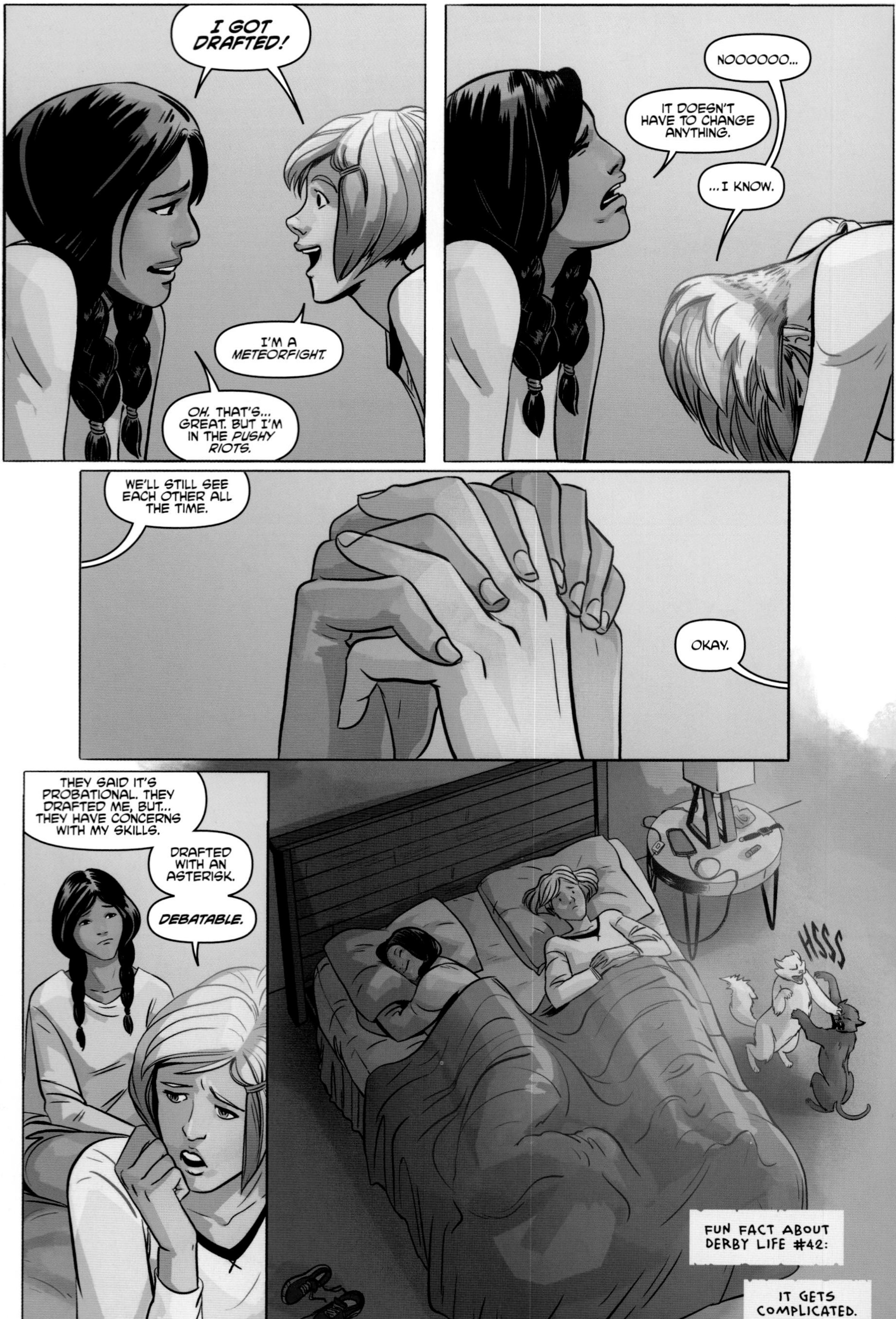
I GOT DRAFTED!
I'M A METEORFIGHT.
OH. THAT'S... GREAT. BUT I'M IN THE PUSHY RIOTS.
NOOOOOO...
IT DOESN'T HAVE TO CHANGE ANYTHING.
...I KNOW.
WE'LL STILL SEE EACH OTHER ALL THE TIME.
OKAY.
THEY SAID IT'S PROBATIONAL. THEY DRAFTED ME, BUT... THEY HAVE CONCERNS WITH MY SKILLS.
DRAFTED WITH AN ASTERISK.
DEBATABLE.
HSSS
FUN FACT ABOUT DERBY LIFE #42:
IT GETS COMPLICATED.

RIP
RIP

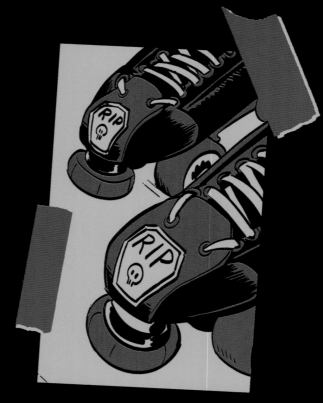

CHAPTER TWO

PUSHY RIOTS

KNOCK-OUT
EAST SIDE ROLLER GIRLS

METEORFIGHTS

ITHINKA CAN
EAST SIDE ROLLER GIRLS

CANCAN:
TODAY?!

YOU:
STRANGER?! YES.
tonight, maybe. AP?

CANCAN:
yup. practice over
@ 9:30. U?

YOU:
home. shower. i'm
gross.

CANCAN:
call me in 20?

BZ BZ

Knockout:
Home. shower. I'm
gross.

call me in 20?

BZ BZ

ZZZZ

Knockout:
U fall asleep? hello?

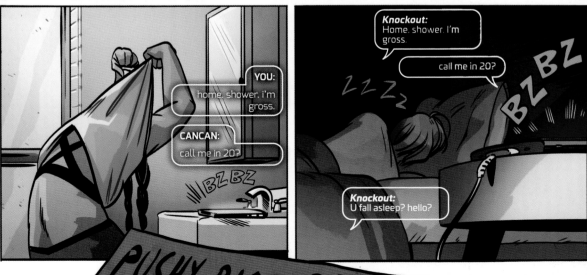

Three weeks away!

PUSHY RIOTS vs METEORFIGHTS
MAY 19TH 8PM

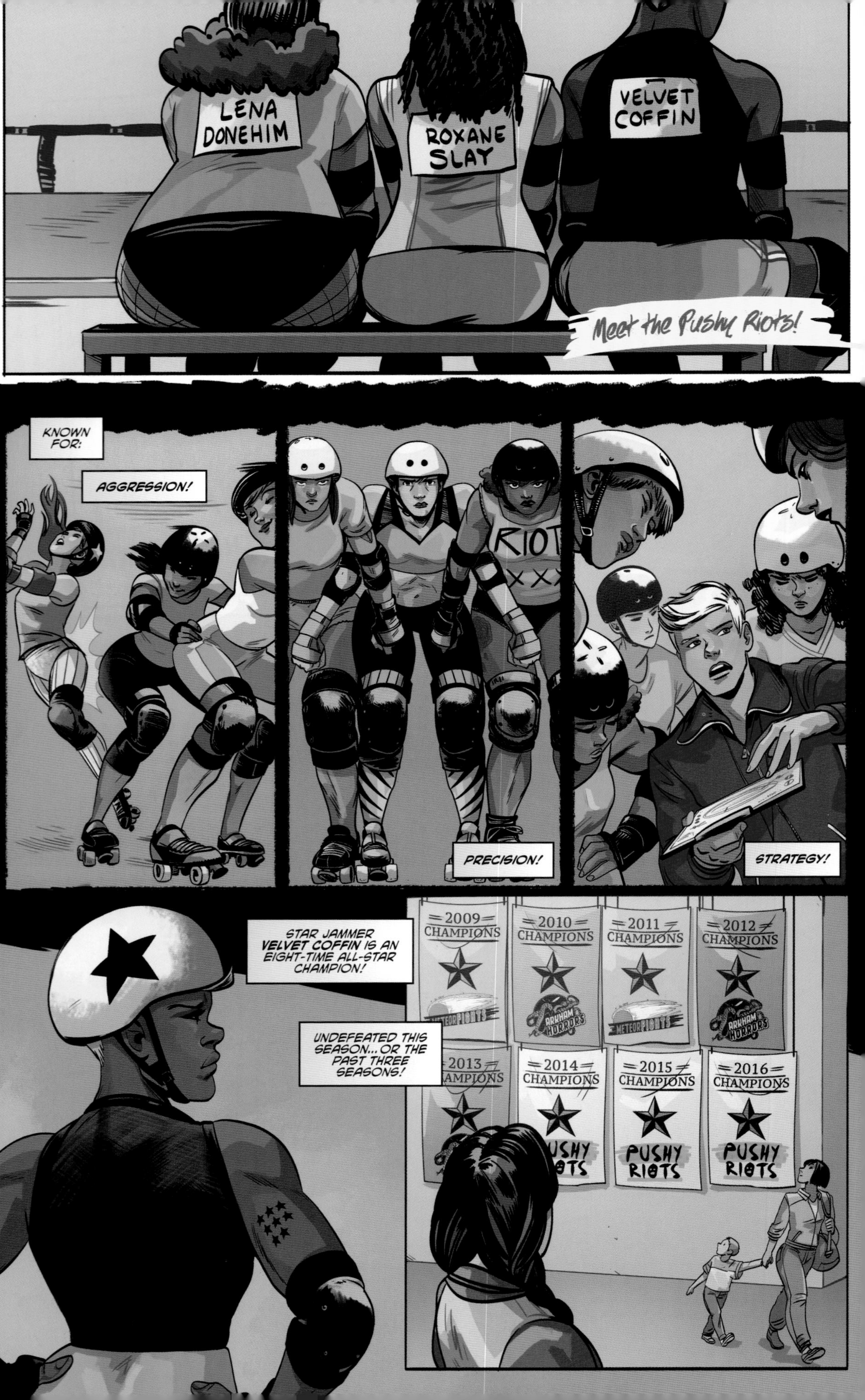
LENA DONEHIM
ROXANE SLAY
VELVET COFFIN
Meet the Pushy Riots!
KNOWN FOR:
AGGRESSION!
RIOT
PRECISION!
STRATEGY!
STAR JAMMER VELVET COFFIN IS AN EIGHT-TIME ALL-STAR CHAMPION!
UNDEFEATED THIS SEASON...OR THE PAST THREE SEASONS!
2009 CHAMPIONS
2010 CHAMPIONS
2011 CHAMPIONS
2012 CHAMPIONS
ARKHAM HORRORS
ARKHAM HORRORS
2013
2014 CHAMPIONS
2015 CHAMPIONS
2016 CHAMPIONS
PUSHY RIOTS
PUSHY RIOTS

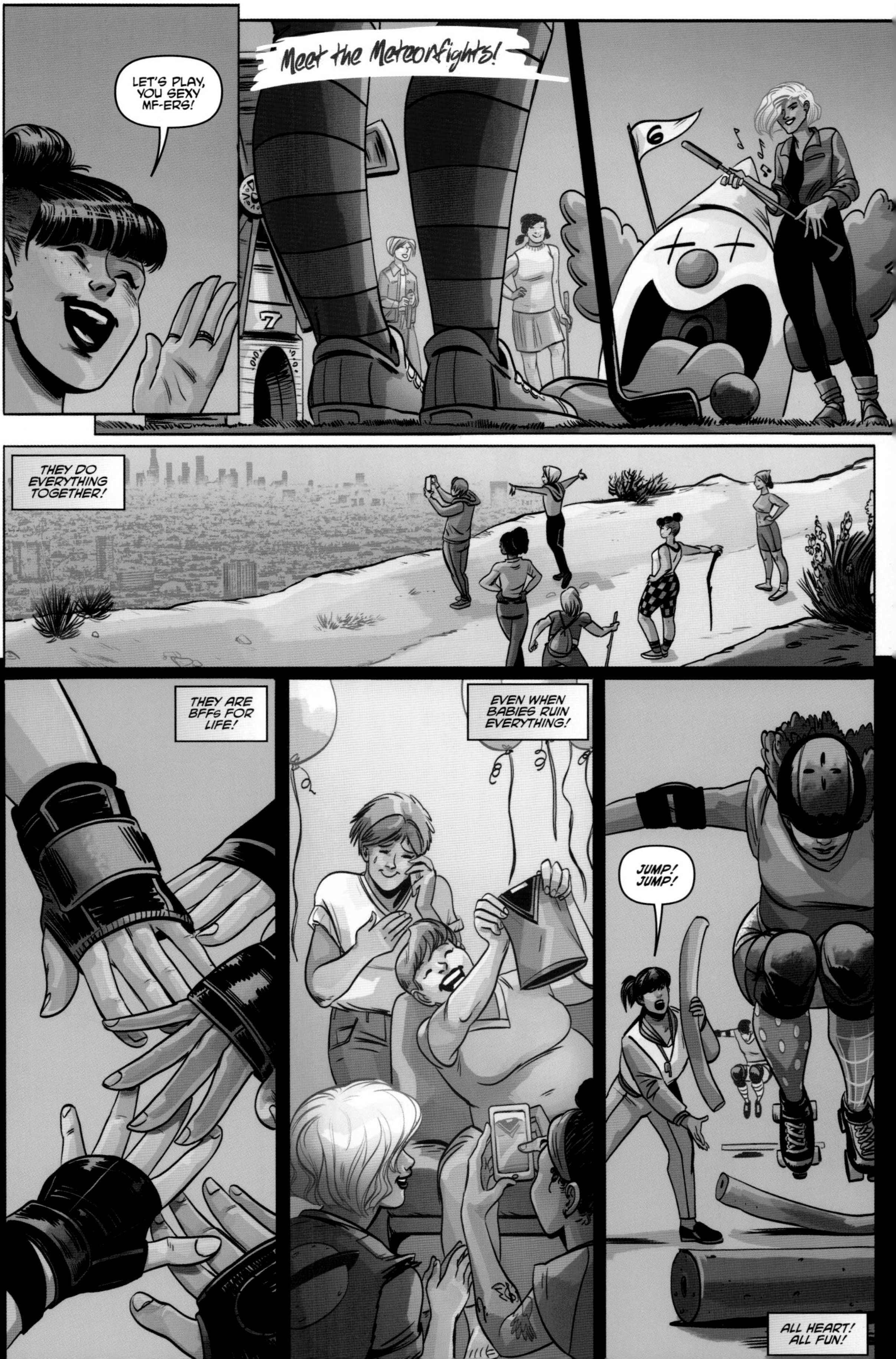
LET'S PLAY, YOU SEXY MF-ERS!
Meet the Meteorfights!
THEY DO EVERYTHING TOGETHER!
THEY ARE BFFs FOR LIFE!
EVEN WHEN BABIES RUIN EVERYTHING!
JUMP! JUMP!
ALL HEART! ALL FUN!

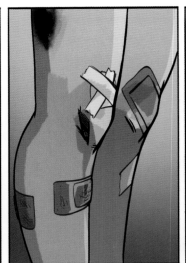

MAYBE I WON'T LET HIM GET TO SECOND BASE.

YOU HAVE DIFFERENT FIRST DATE STANDARDS THAN I DO.

MAYBE I SHOULD POSTPONE.

YOU CAN'T. THIS GUY REALLY LIKES YOU. YOU'VE PUT THIS OFF LONG ENOUGH.

HE'S PROBABLY WEIRD.

YOU'RE WEIRD.

WHAT HAPPENED HERE?

OH. VELVET.

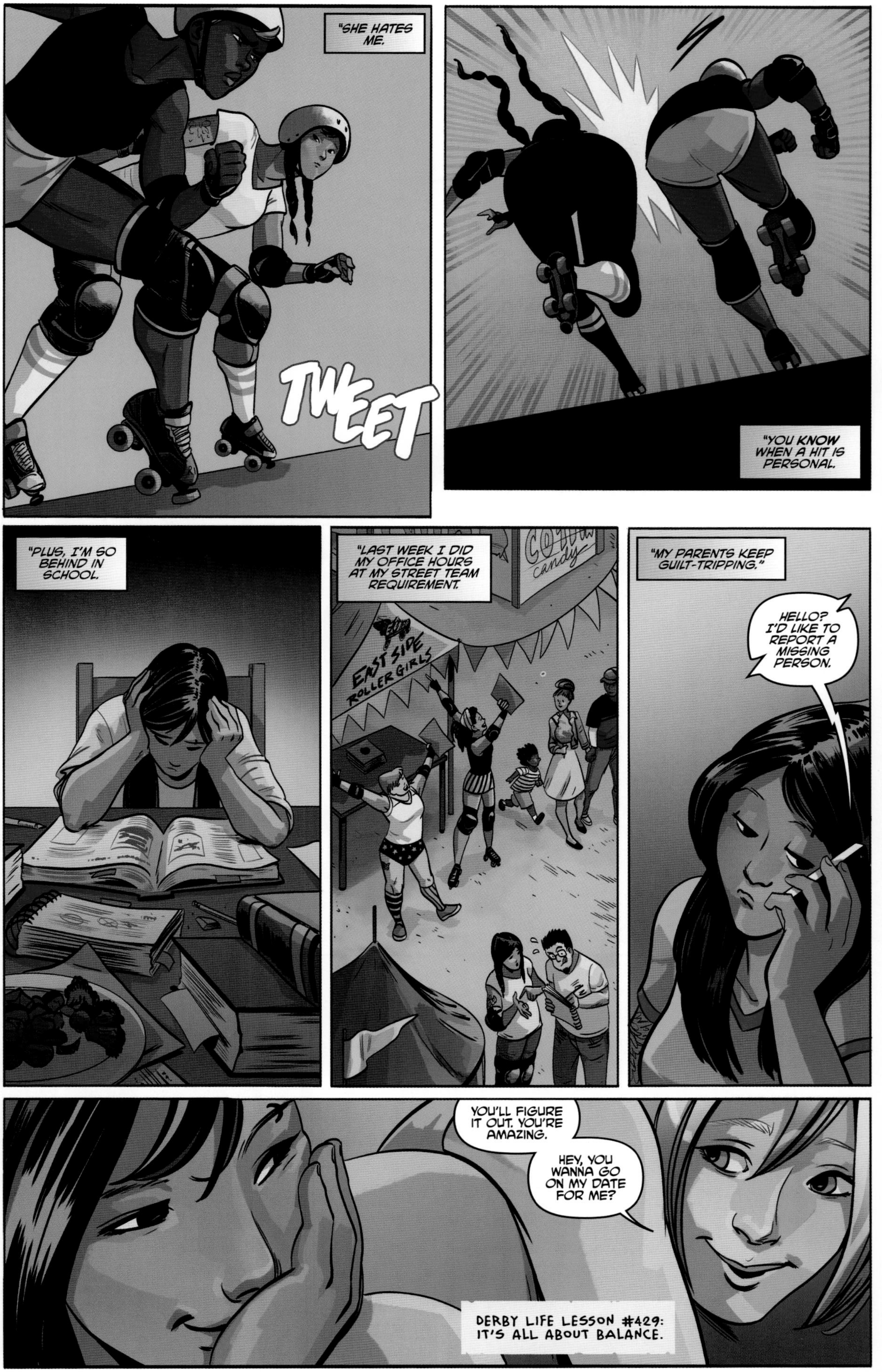
"SHE HATES ME.
TWEET
"YOU KNOW WHEN A HIT IS PERSONAL.
"PLUS, I'M SO BEHIND IN SCHOOL.
"LAST WEEK I DID MY OFFICE HOURS AT MY STREET TEAM REQUIREMENT.
EAST SIDE ROLLER GIRLS
"MY PARENTS KEEP GUILT-TRIPPING."
HELLO? I'D LIKE TO REPORT A MISSING PERSON.
YOU'LL FIGURE IT OUT. YOU'RE AMAZING.
HEY, YOU WANNA GO ON MY DATE FOR ME?
DERBY LIFE LESSON #429: IT'S ALL ABOUT BALANCE.

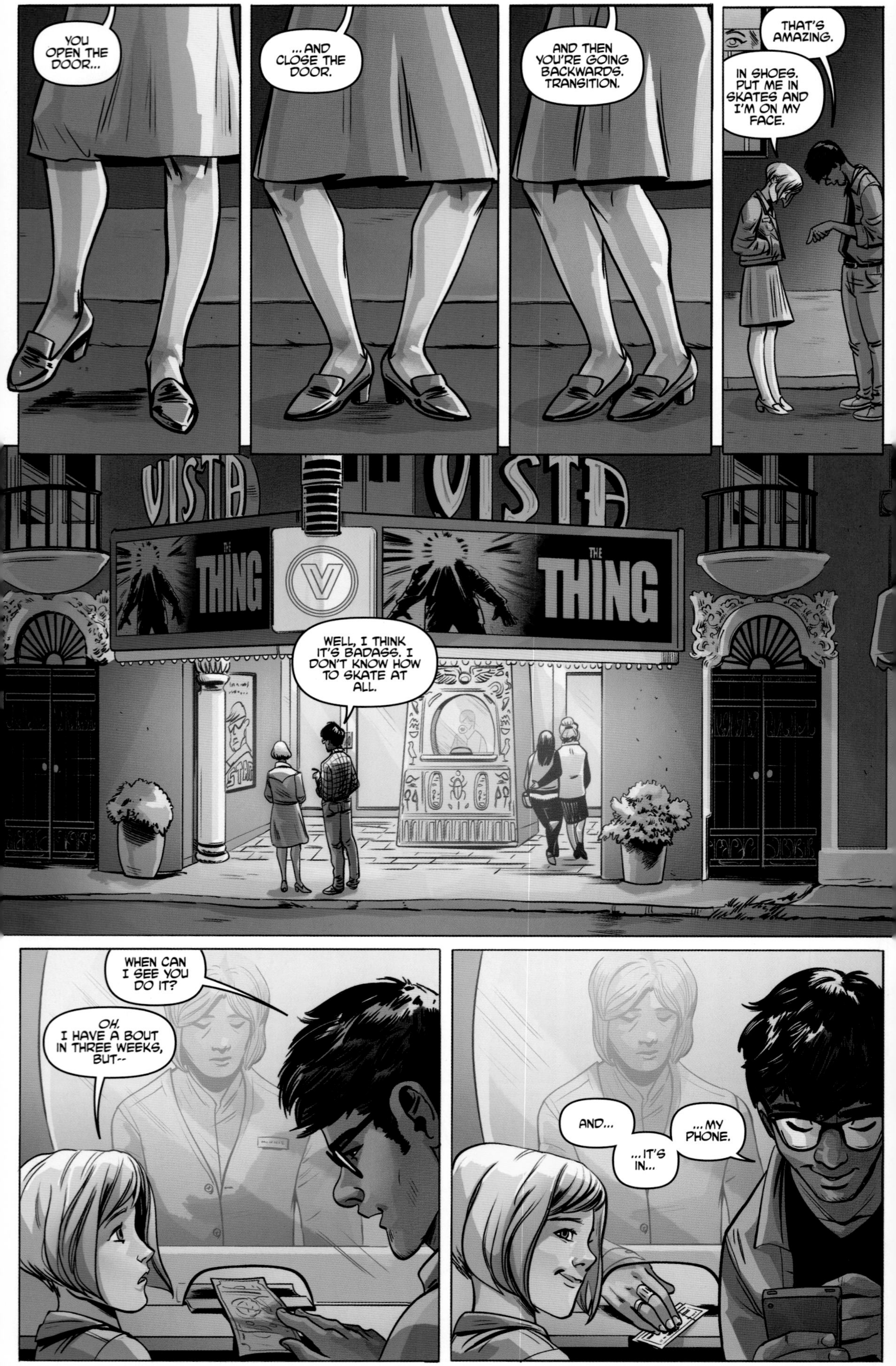

YOU OPEN THE DOOR...
...AND CLOSE THE DOOR.
AND THEN YOU'RE GOING BACKWARDS. TRANSITION.
THAT'S AMAZING.
IN SHOES. PUT ME IN SKATES AND I'M ON MY FACE.
VISTA
THE THING
THE THING
WELL, I THINK IT'S BADASS. I DON'T KNOW HOW TO SKATE AT ALL.
WHEN CAN I SEE YOU DO IT?
OH. I HAVE A BOUT IN THREE WEEKS, BUT--
AND...
...IT'S IN...
...MY PHONE.

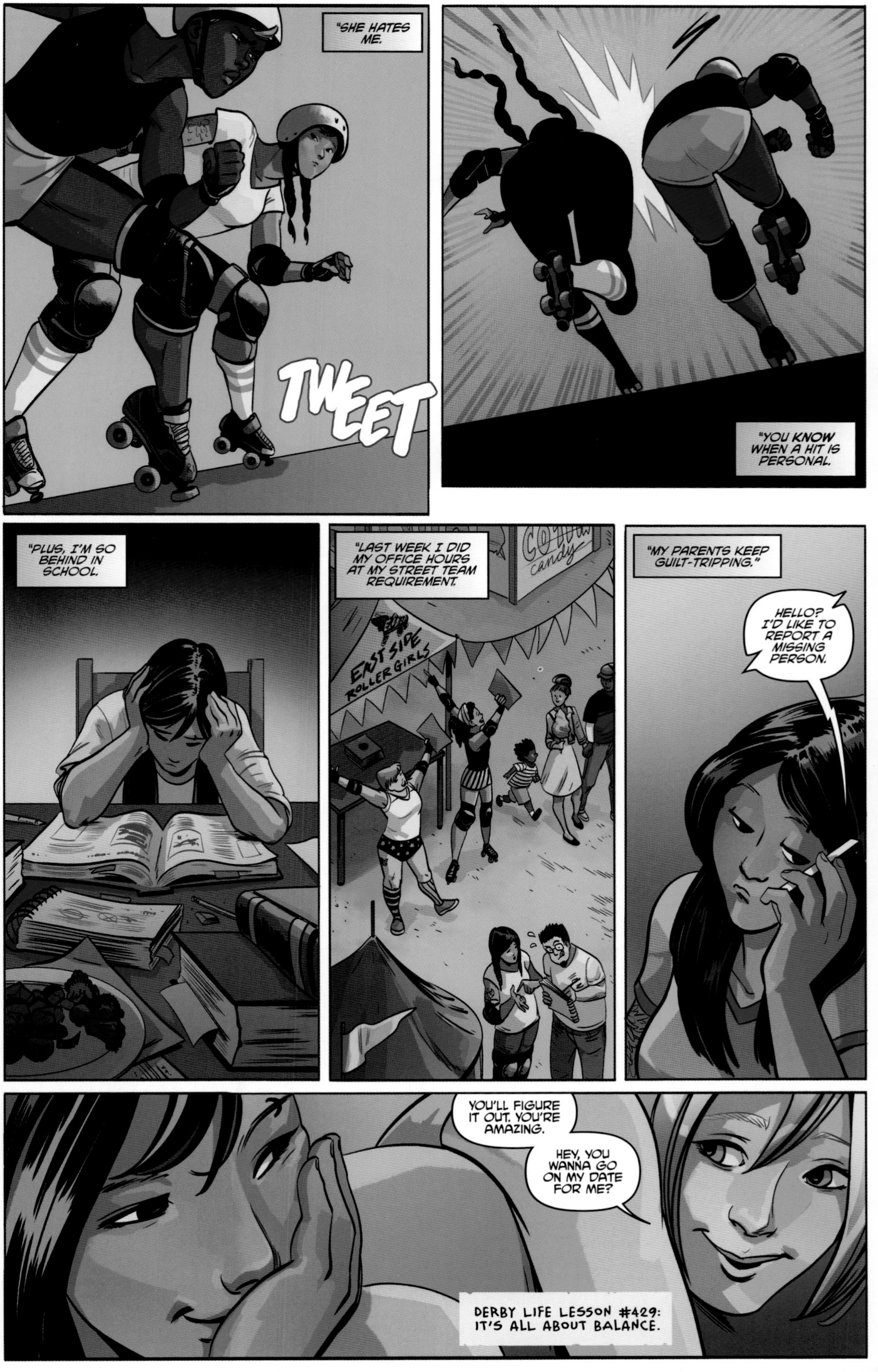
"SHE HATES ME.
TWEET
"YOU KNOW WHEN A HIT IS PERSONAL.
"PLUS, I'M SO BEHIND IN SCHOOL.
"LAST WEEK I DID MY OFFICE HOURS AT MY STREET TEAM REQUIREMENT.
EAST SIDE ROLLER GIRLS
"MY PARENTS KEEP GUILT-TRIPPING."
HELLO? I'D LIKE TO REPORT A MISSING PERSON.
YOU'LL FIGURE IT OUT. YOU'RE AMAZING.
HEY, YOU WANNA GO ON MY DATE FOR ME?
DERBY LIFE LESSON #429: IT'S ALL ABOUT BALANCE.

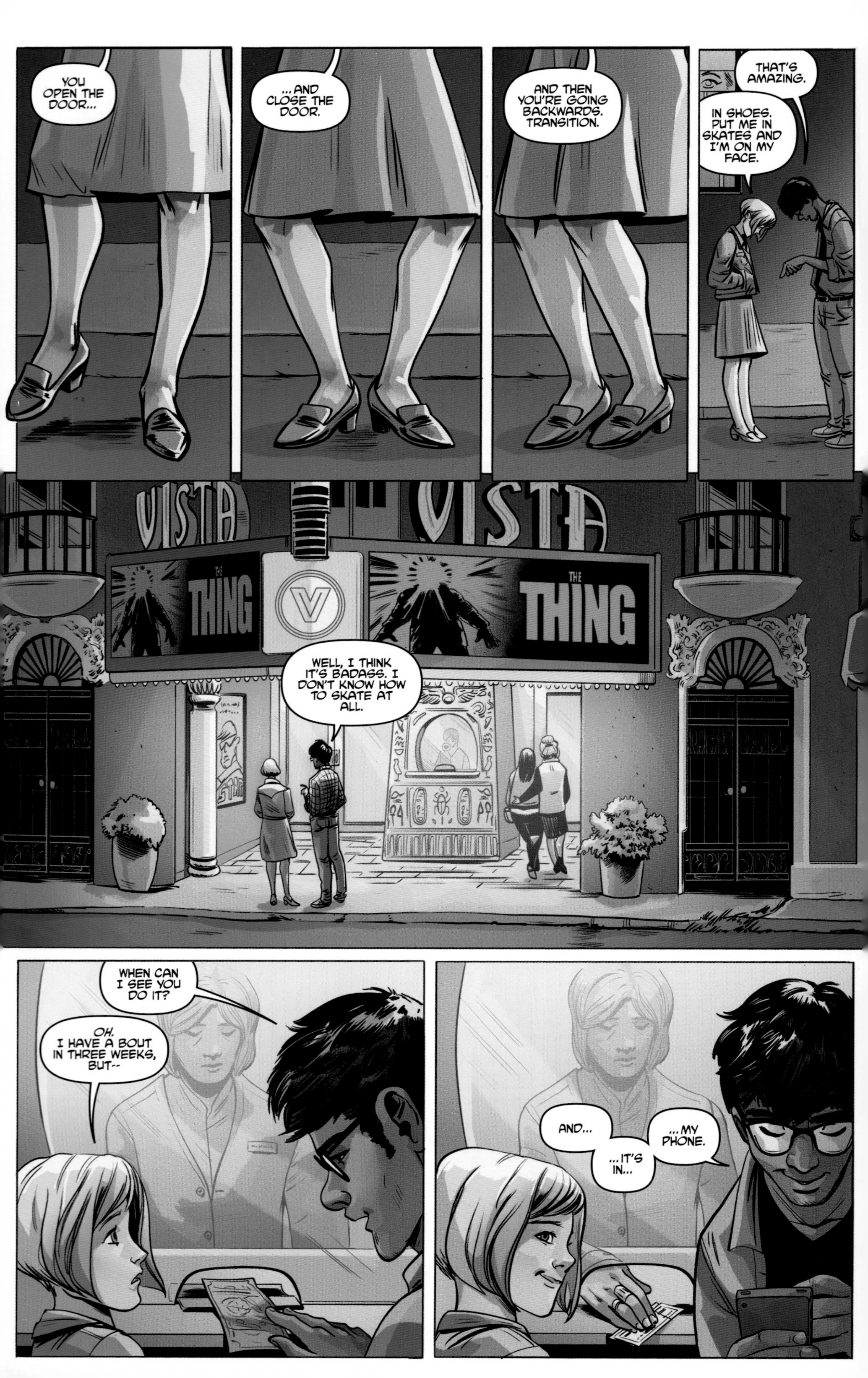
YOU OPEN THE DOOR...
...AND CLOSE THE DOOR.
AND THEN YOU'RE GOING BACKWARDS. TRANSITION.
THAT'S AMAZING.
IN SHOES. PUT ME IN SKATES AND I'M ON MY FACE.
VISTA
THE THING
THE THING
WELL, I THINK IT'S BADASS. I DON'T KNOW HOW TO SKATE AT ALL.
WHEN CAN I SEE YOU DO IT?
OH. I HAVE A BOUT IN THREE WEEKS, BUT--
AND...
...IT'S IN...
...MY PHONE.

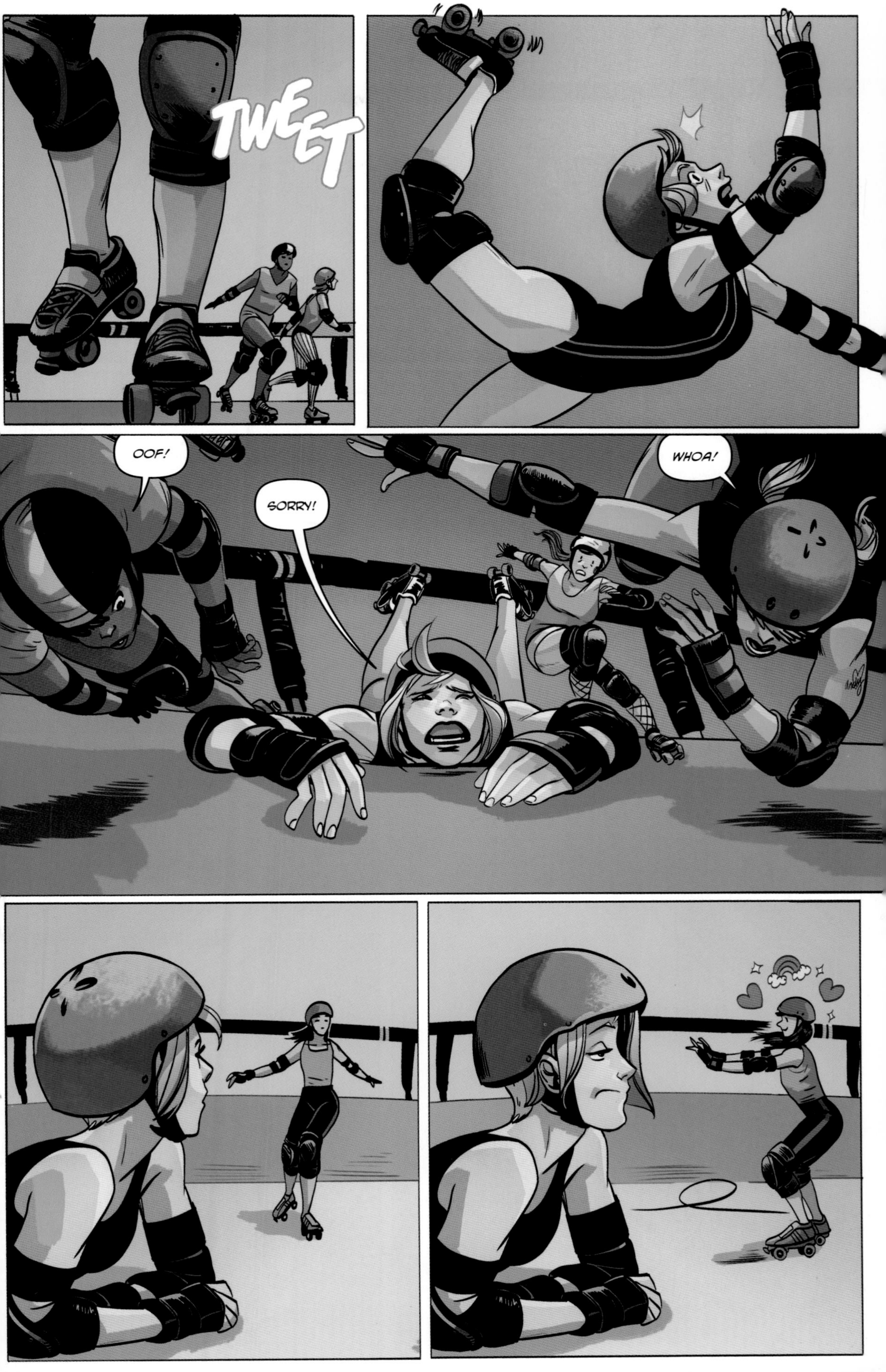
TWEET
OOF!
SORRY!
WHOA!

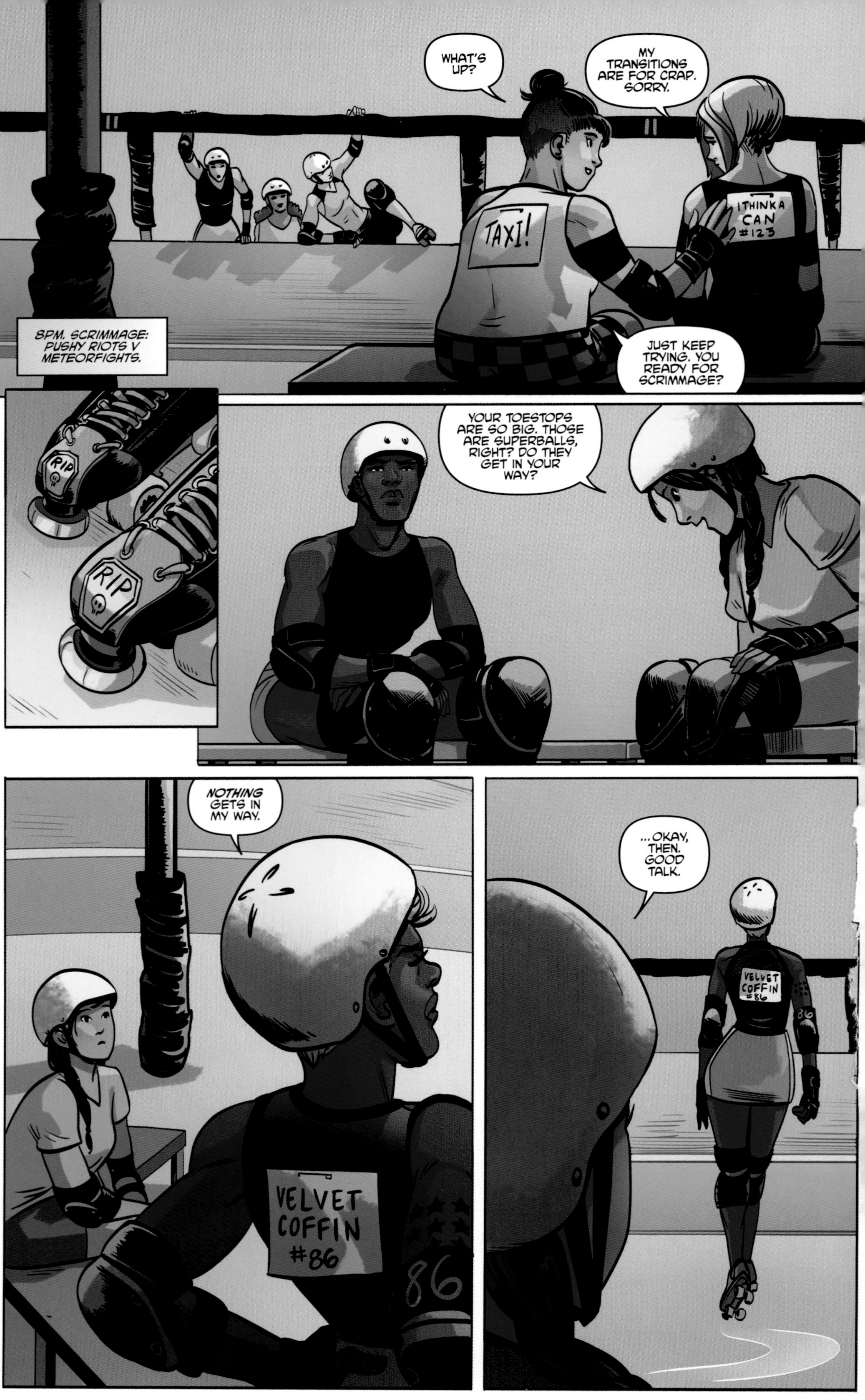
WHAT'S UP?
MY TRANSITIONS ARE FOR CRAP. SORRY.
TAXI!
ITHINKA CAN #123
8PM. SCRIMMAGE: PUSHY RIOTS V METEORFIGHTS.
JUST KEEP TRYING. YOU READY FOR SCRIMMAGE?
RIP
RIP
YOUR TOESTOPS ARE SO BIG. THOSE ARE SUPERBALLS, RIGHT? DO THEY GET IN YOUR WAY?
NOTHING GETS IN MY WAY.
VELVET COFFIN #86
86
...OKAY, THEN. GOOD TALK.
VELVET COFFIN #86
86

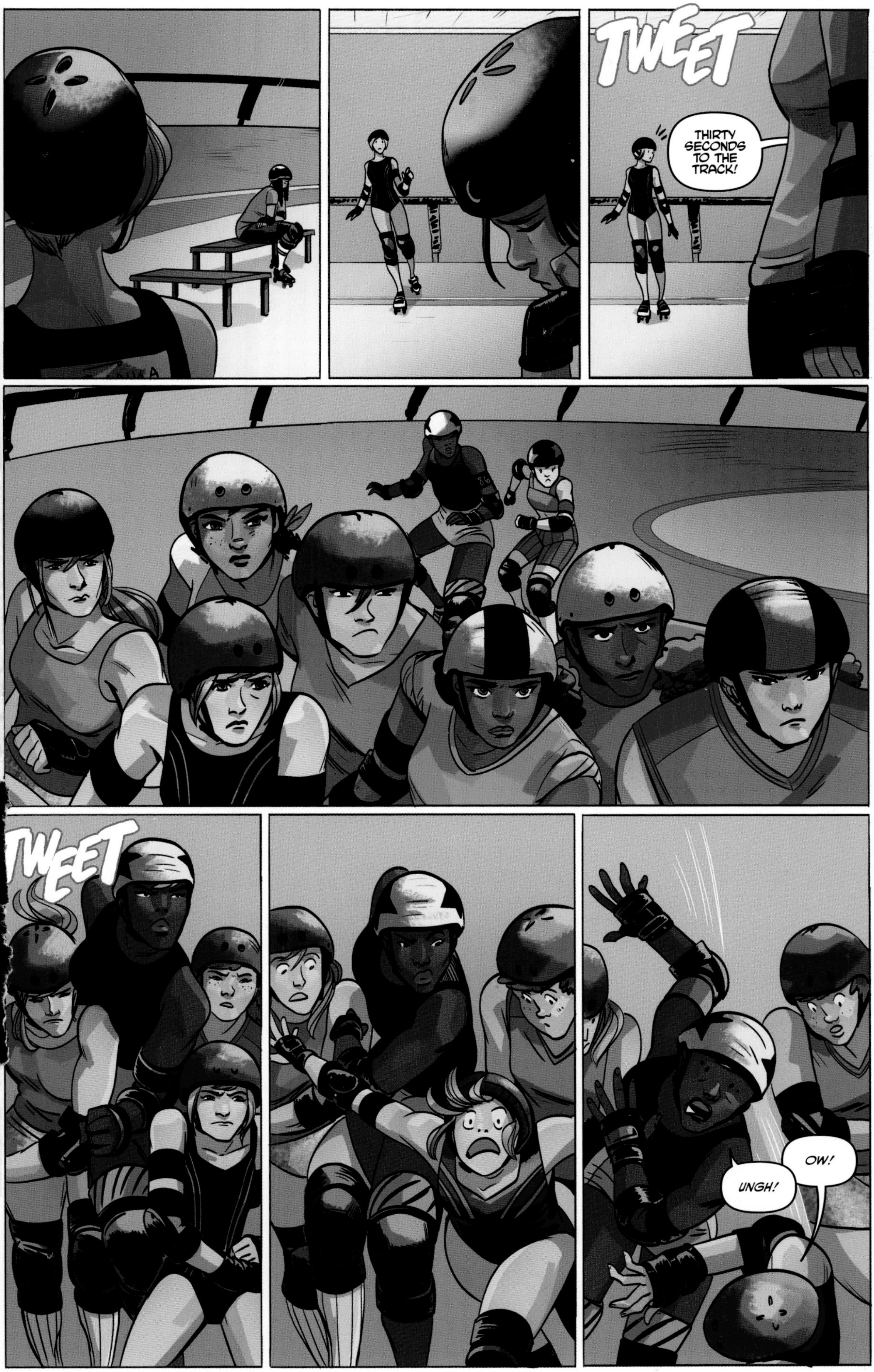
TWEET
THIRTY SECONDS TO THE TRACK!
TWEET
UNGH!
OW!

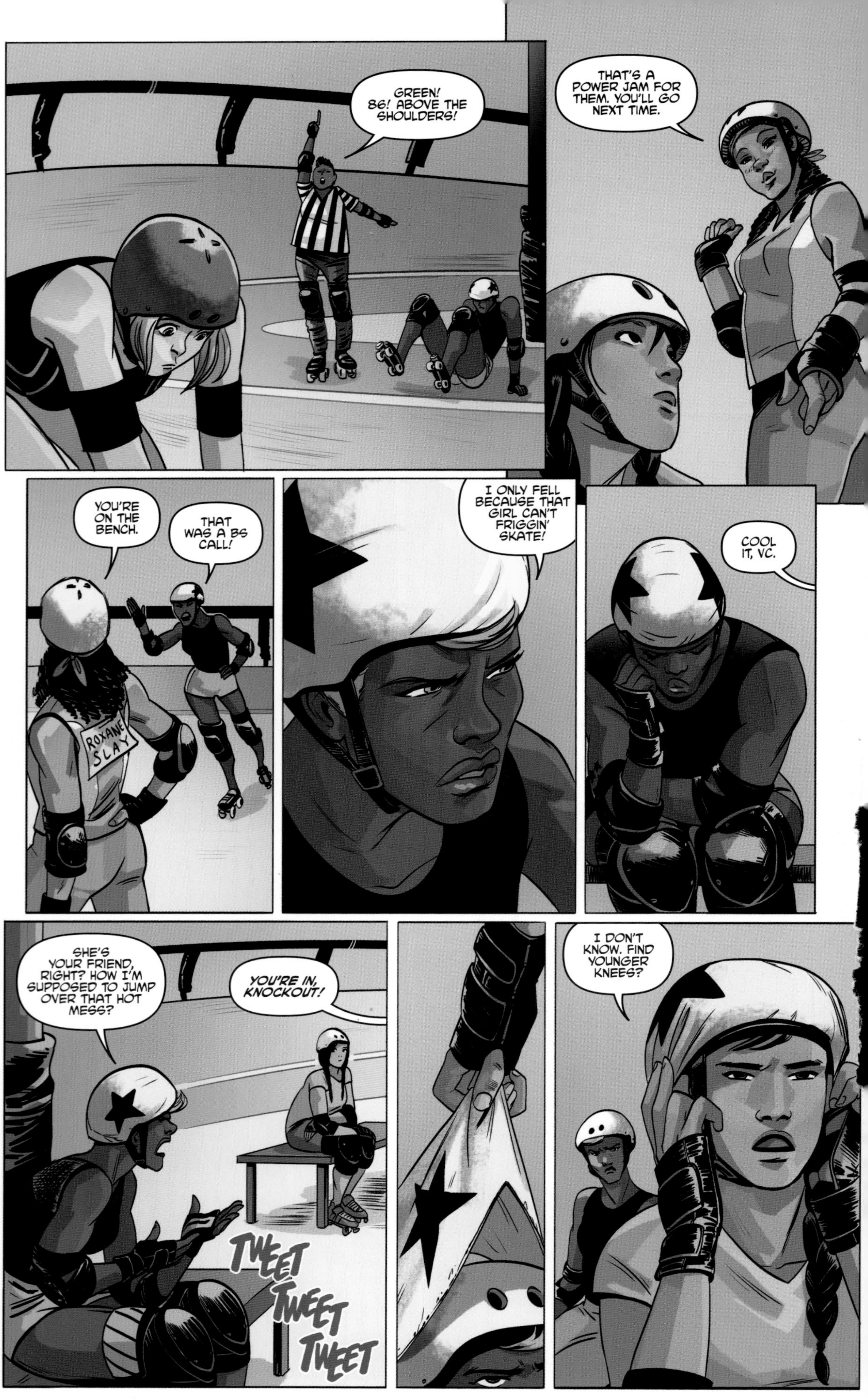
GREEN! 86! ABOVE THE SHOULDERS!
THAT'S A POWER JAM FOR THEM. YOU'LL GO NEXT TIME.
YOU'RE ON THE BENCH.
THAT WAS A BS CALL!
ROXANE SLAY
I ONLY FELL BECAUSE THAT GIRL CAN'T FRIGGIN' SKATE!
COOL IT, VC.
SHE'S YOUR FRIEND, RIGHT? HOW I'M SUPPOSED TO JUMP OVER THAT HOT MESS?
YOU'RE IN, KNOCKOUT!
TWEET TWEET TWEET
I DON'T KNOW. FIND YOUNGER KNEES?

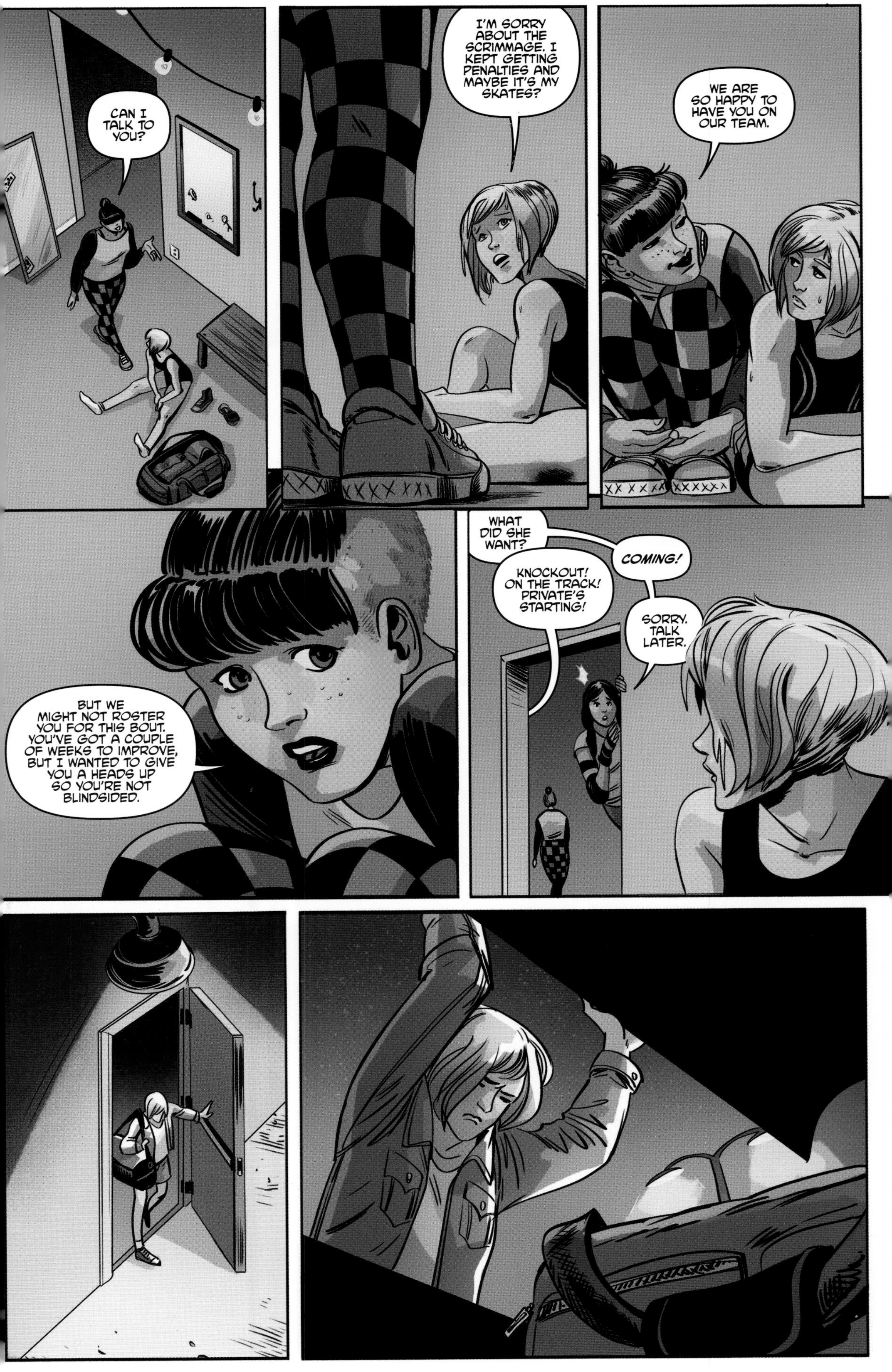
CAN I TALK TO YOU?
I'M SORRY ABOUT THE SCRIMMAGE. I KEPT GETTING PENALTIES AND MAYBE IT'S MY SKATES?
WE ARE SO HAPPY TO HAVE YOU ON OUR TEAM.
BUT WE MIGHT NOT ROSTER YOU FOR THIS BOUT. YOU'VE GOT A COUPLE OF WEEKS TO IMPROVE, BUT I WANTED TO GIVE YOU A HEADS UP SO YOU'RE NOT BLINDSIDED.
WHAT DID SHE WANT?
KNOCKOUT! ON THE TRACK! PRIVATE'S STARTING!
COMING!
SORRY. TALK LATER.

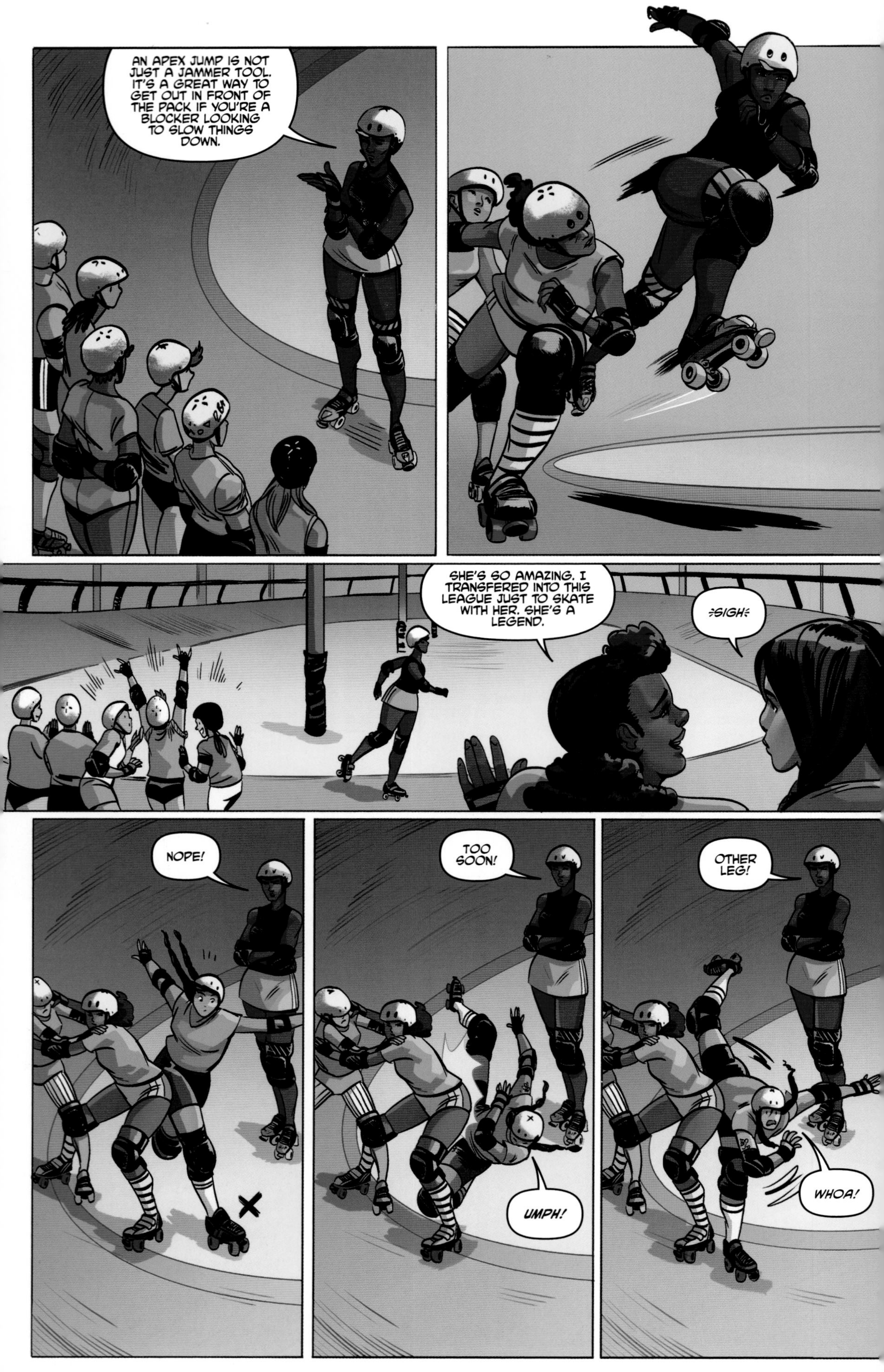
AN APEX JUMP IS NOT JUST A JAMMER TOOL. IT'S A GREAT WAY TO GET OUT IN FRONT OF THE PACK IF YOU'RE A BLOCKER LOOKING TO SLOW THINGS DOWN.
SHE'S SO AMAZING. I TRANSFERED INTO THIS LEAGUE JUST TO SKATE WITH HER. SHE'S A LEGEND.
SIGH
NOPE!
TOO SOON!
UMPH!
OTHER LEG!
WHOA!

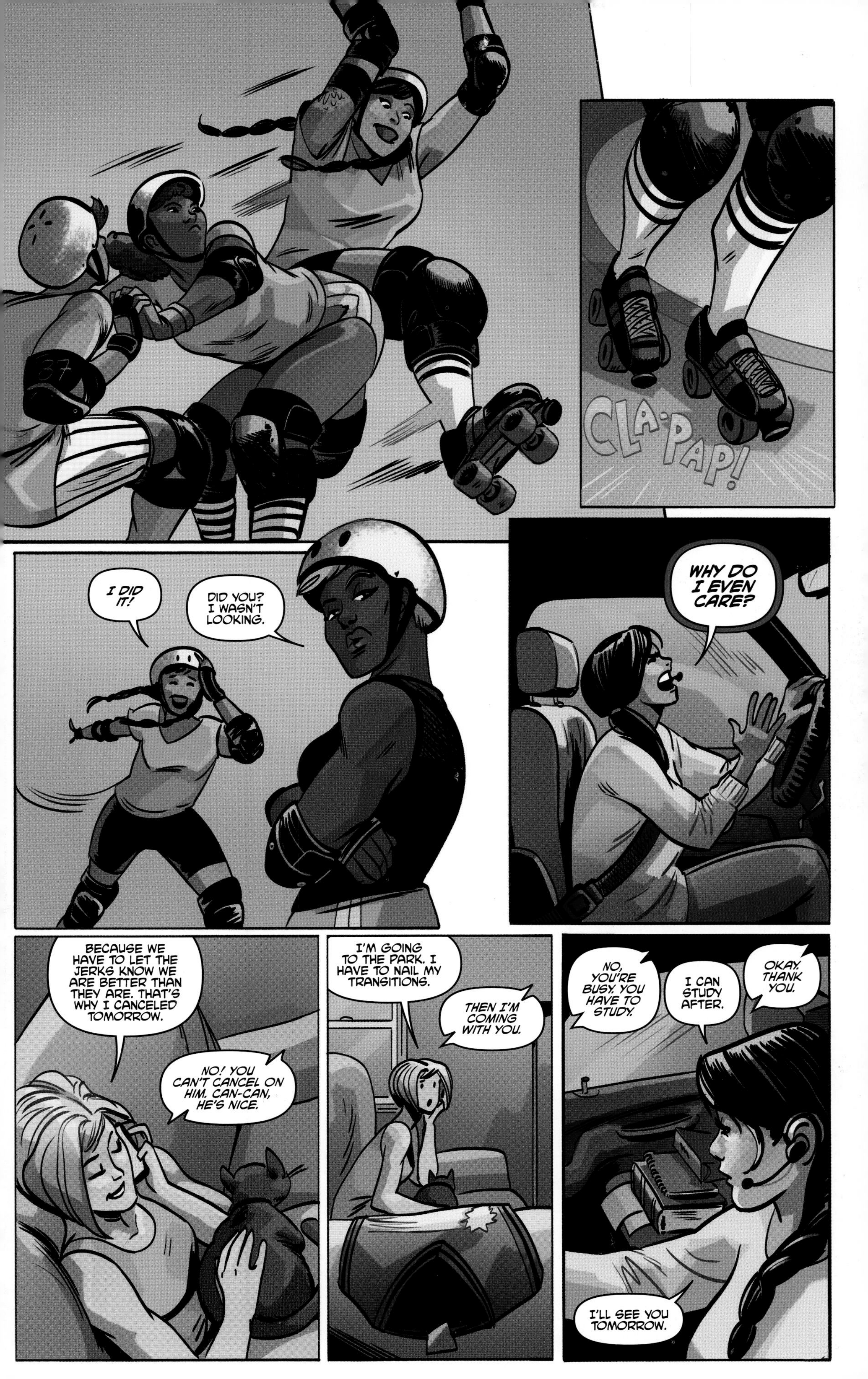
CLA-PAP!
I DID IT!
DID YOU? I WASN'T LOOKING.
WHY DO I EVEN CARE?
BECAUSE WE HAVE TO LET THE JERKS KNOW WE ARE BETTER THAN THEY ARE. THAT'S WHY I CANCELED TOMORROW.
NO! YOU CAN'T CANCEL ON HIM. CAN-CAN, HE'S NICE.
I'M GOING TO THE PARK. I HAVE TO NAIL MY TRANSITIONS.
THEN I'M COMING WITH YOU.
NO, YOU'RE BUSY. YOU HAVE TO STUDY.
I CAN STUDY AFTER.
OKAY. THANK YOU.
I'LL SEE YOU TOMORROW.

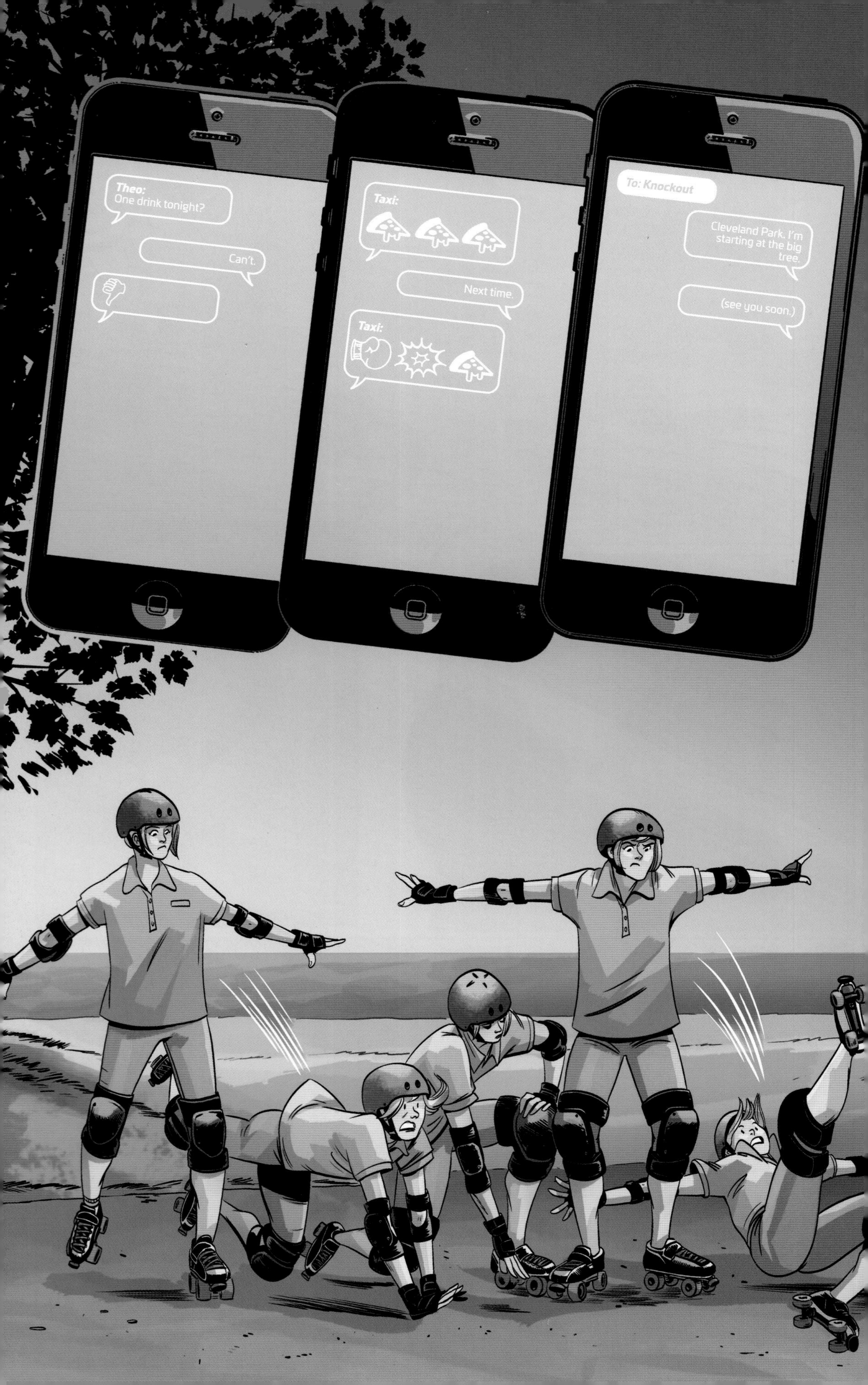

Theo:
One drink tonight?
Can't.
Taxi:
Next time.
Taxi:
To: Knockout
Cleveland Park. I'm starting at the big tree.
(see you soon.)

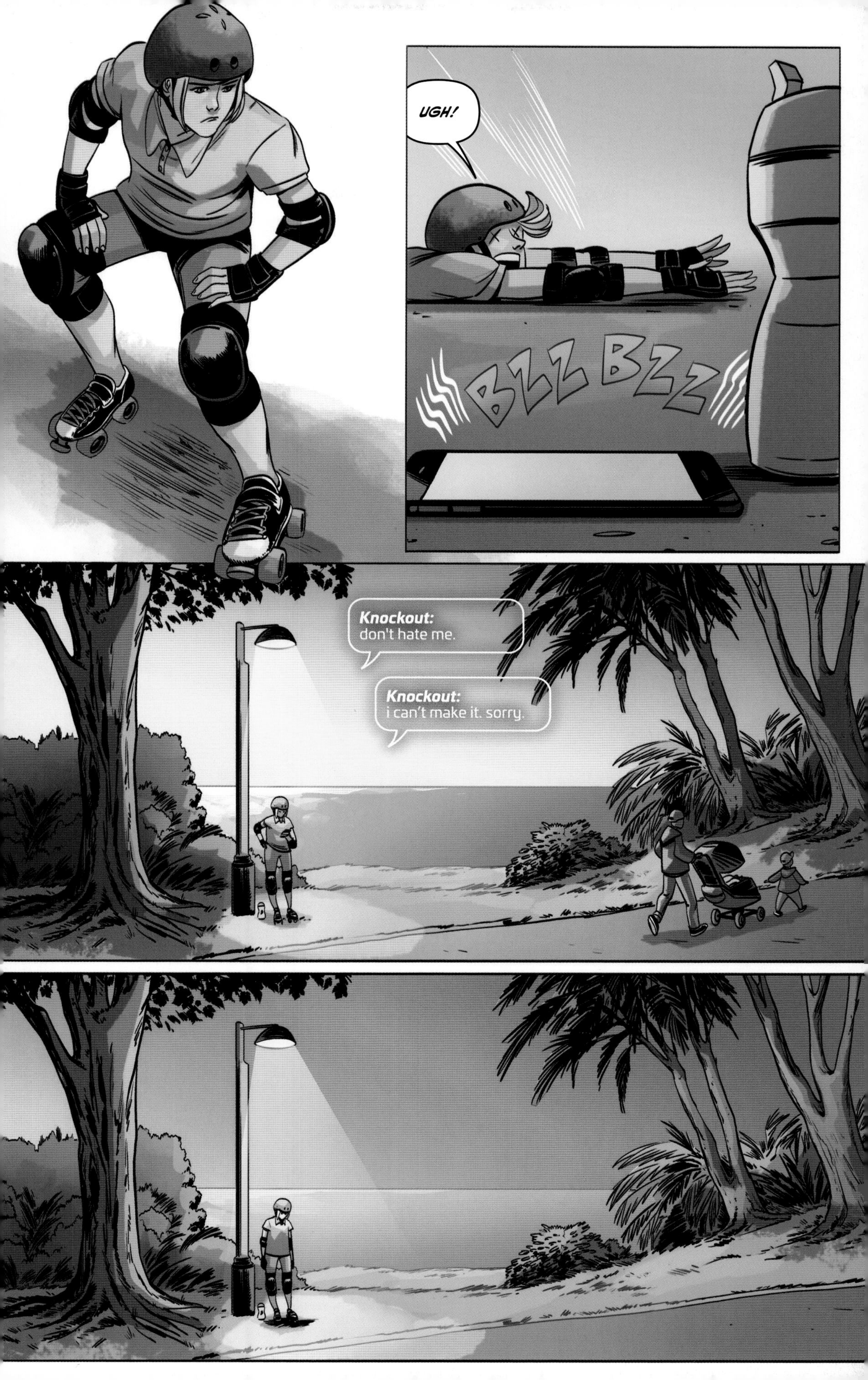
UGH!
BZZ BZZ
Knockout: don't hate me.
Knockout: i can't make it. sorry.

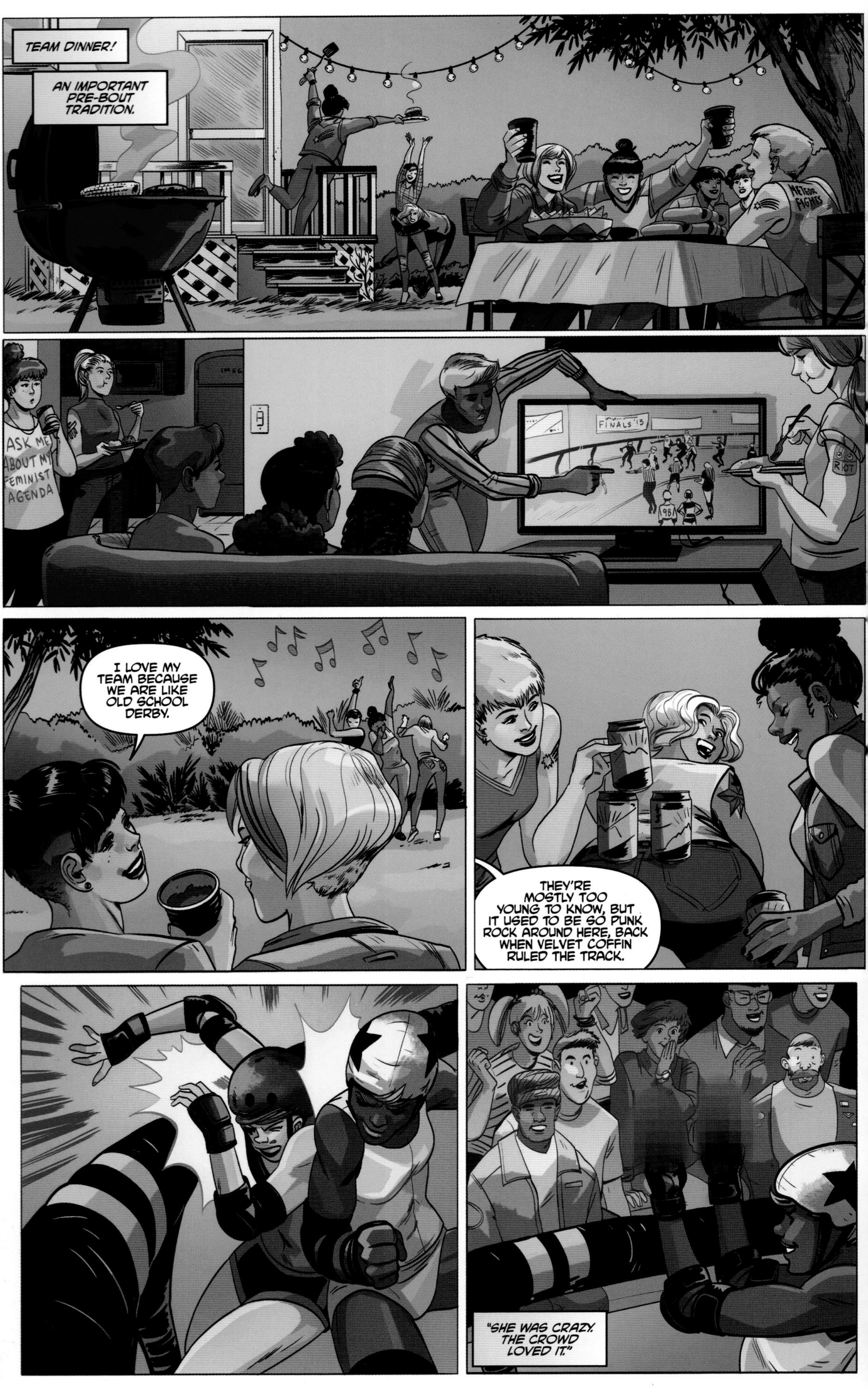
TEAM DINNER!
AN IMPORTANT PRE-BOUT TRADITION.
METEOR FIGHTS
ASK ME ABOUT MY FEMINIST AGENDA
FINALS '15
RIOT
I LOVE MY TEAM BECAUSE WE ARE LIKE OLD SCHOOL DERBY.
THEY'RE MOSTLY TOO YOUNG TO KNOW, BUT IT USED TO BE SO PUNK ROCK AROUND HERE, BACK WHEN VELVET COFFIN RULED THE TRACK.
"SHE WAS CRAZY. THE CROWD LOVED IT."

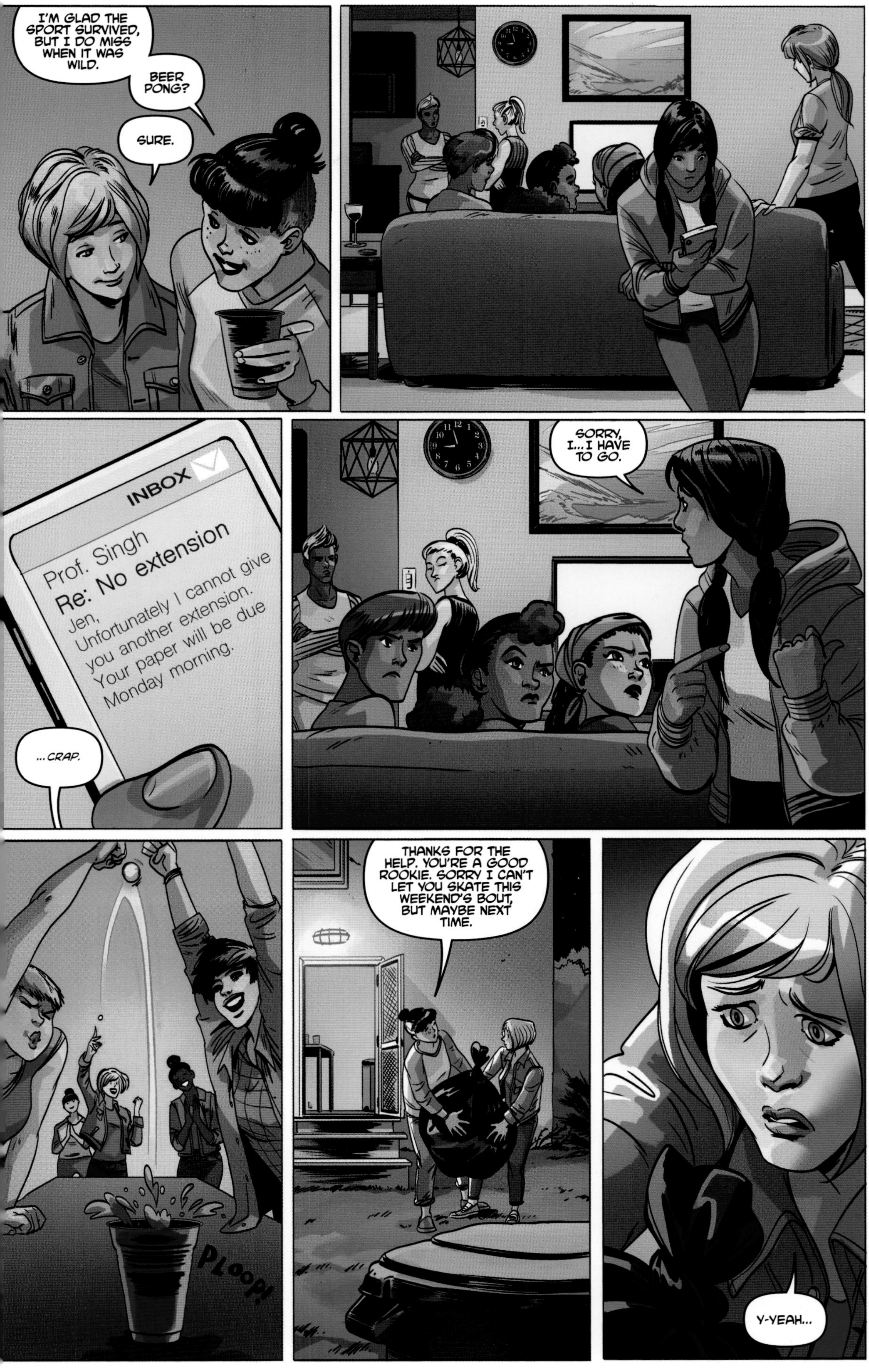

I'M GLAD THE SPORT SURVIVED, BUT I DO MISS WHEN IT WAS WILD.
BEER PONG?
SURE.
INBOX
Prof. Singh
Re: No extension
Jen,
Unfortunately I cannot give you another extension. Your paper will be due Monday morning.
...CRAP.
SORRY, I...I HAVE TO GO.
PLOOP!
THANKS FOR THE HELP. YOU'RE A GOOD ROOKIE. SORRY I CAN'T LET YOU SKATE THIS WEEKEND'S BOUT, BUT MAYBE NEXT TIME.
Y-YEAH...

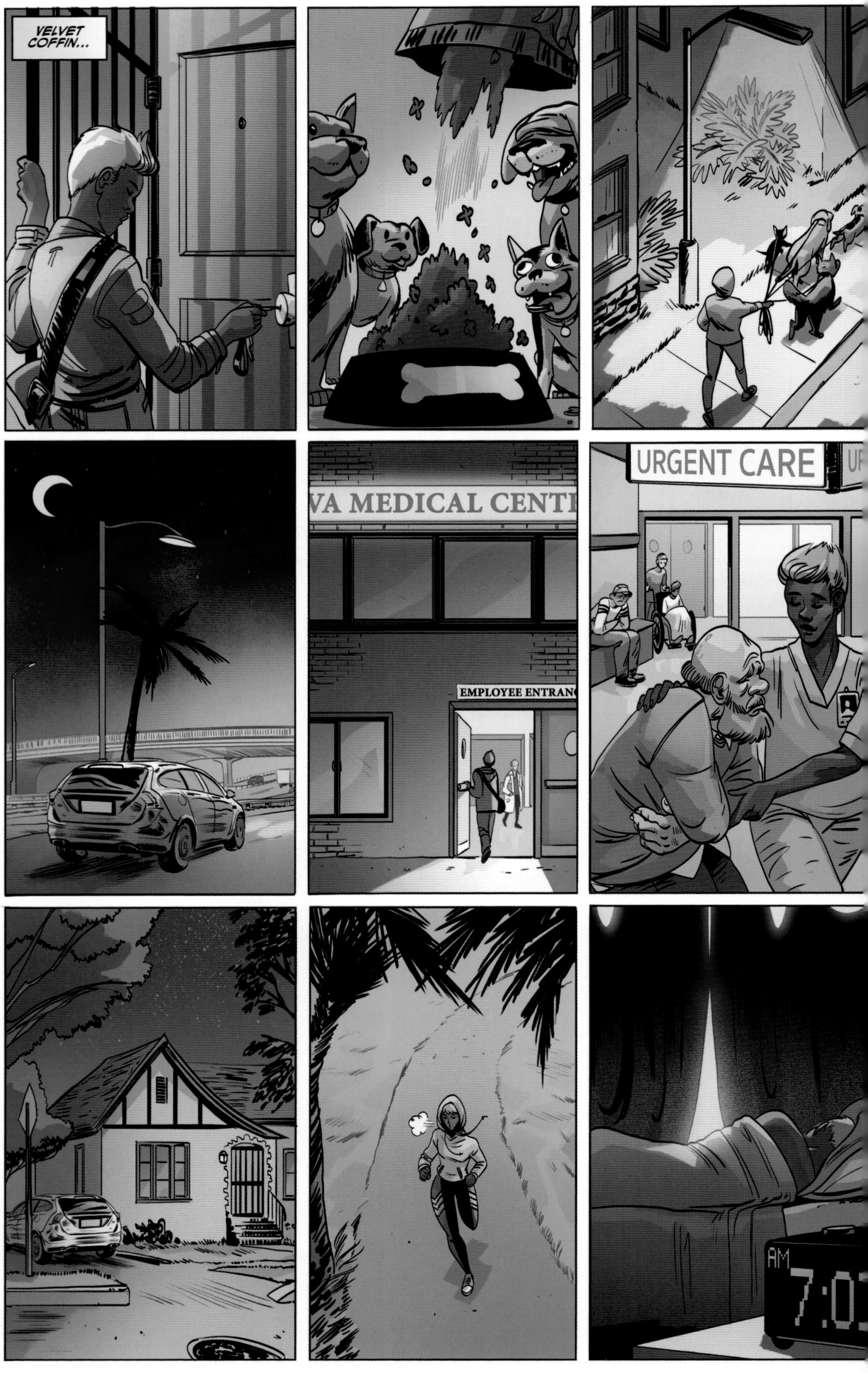
VELVET COFFIN...
URGENT CARE
VA MEDICAL CENT
EMPLOYEE ENTRANC
AM
7:0

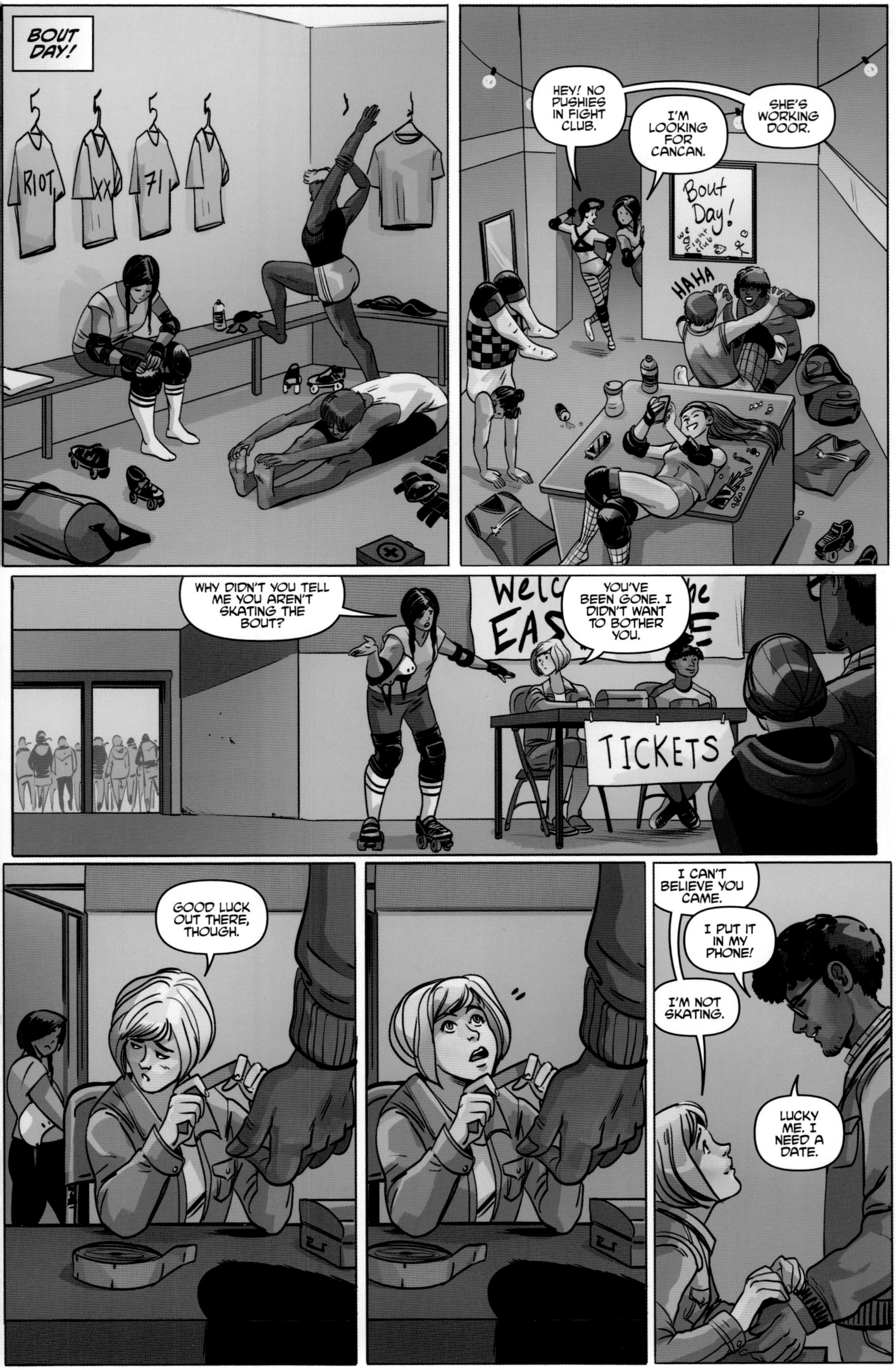
BOUT DAY!
RIOT
XX
71
HEY! NO PUSHIES IN FIGHT CLUB.
I'M LOOKING FOR CANCAN.
SHE'S WORKING DOOR.
Bout Day!
HAHA
WHY DIDN'T YOU TELL ME YOU AREN'T SKATING THE BOUT?
YOU'VE BEEN GONE. I DIDN'T WANT TO BOTHER YOU.
TICKETS
GOOD LUCK OUT THERE, THOUGH.
I CAN'T BELIEVE YOU CAME.
I PUT IT IN MY PHONE!
I'M NOT SKATING.
LUCKY ME. I NEED A DATE.

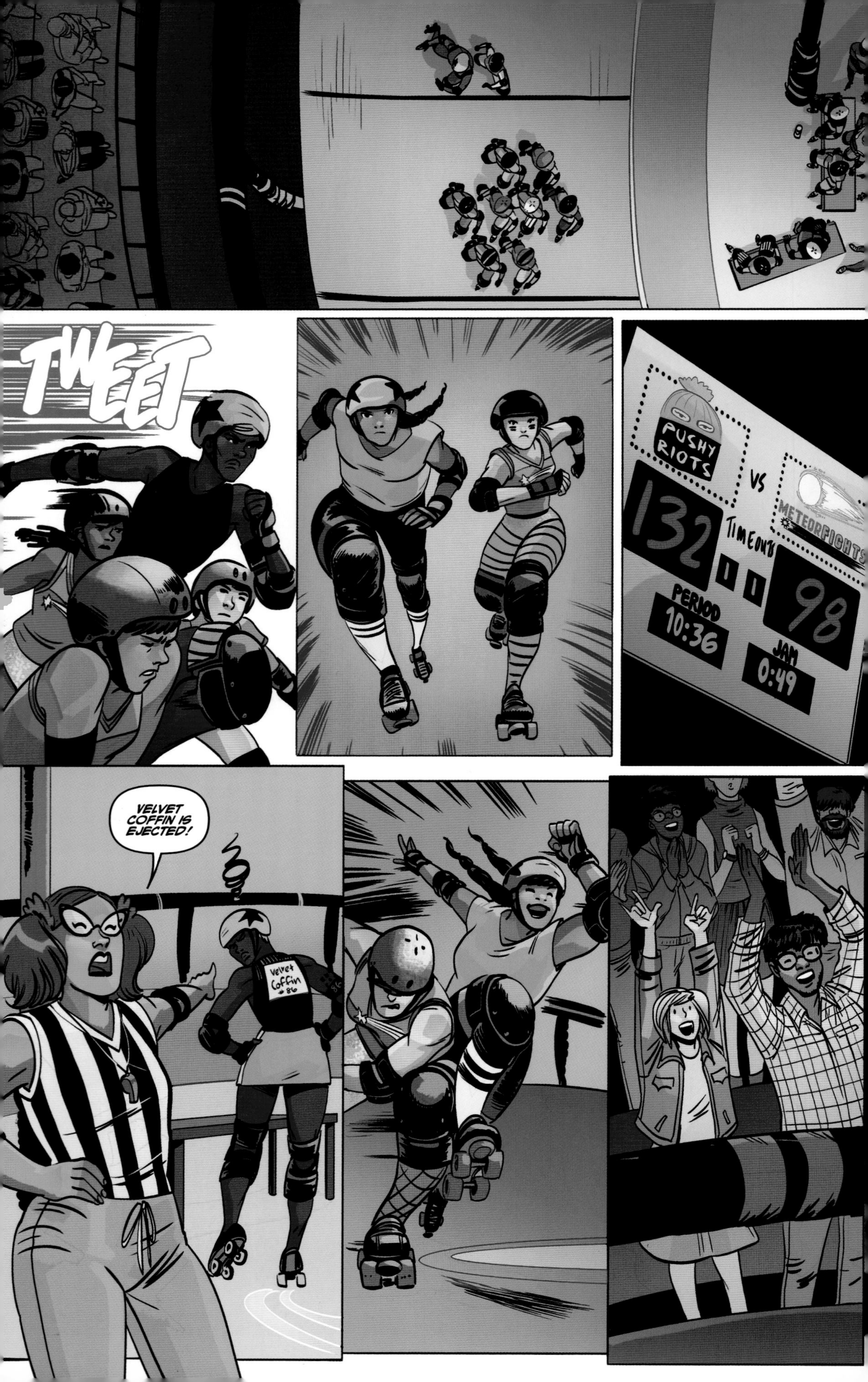
TWEET
PUSHY RIOTS
VS
METEORFIGHTS
132
TIMEOUTS
98
PERIOD
10:36
JAM
0:49
VELVET COFFIN IS EJECTED!
Velvet Coffin #86

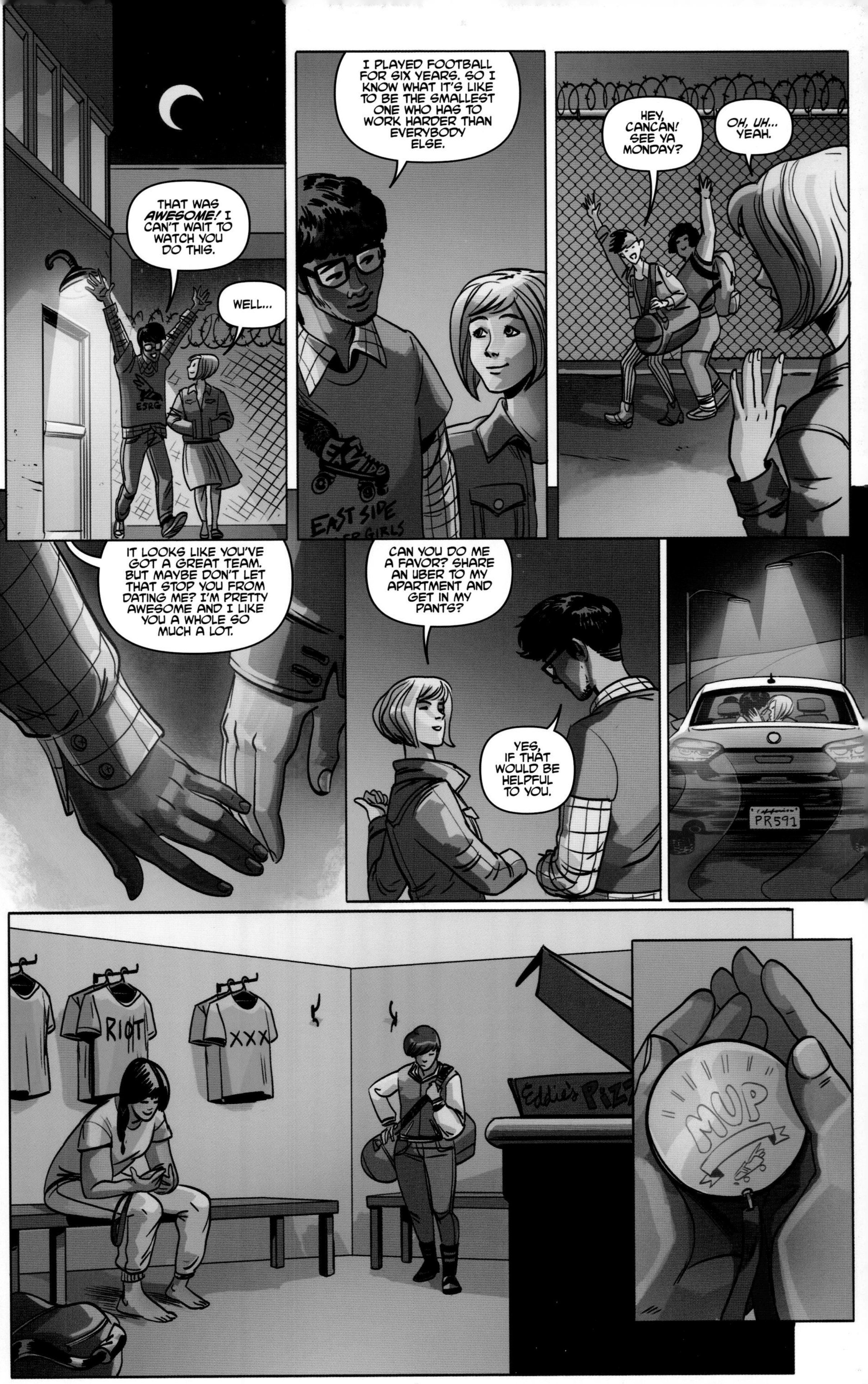
THAT WAS *AWESOME!* I CAN'T WAIT TO WATCH YOU DO THIS.
WELL...
I PLAYED FOOTBALL FOR SIX YEARS. SO I KNOW WHAT IT'S LIKE TO BE THE SMALLEST ONE WHO HAS TO WORK HARDER THAN EVERYBODY ELSE.
ESRG
EAST SIDE
HEY, CANCAN! SEE YA MONDAY?
OH, UH... YEAH.
IT LOOKS LIKE YOU'VE GOT A GREAT TEAM. BUT MAYBE DON'T LET THAT STOP YOU FROM DATING ME? I'M PRETTY AWESOME AND I LIKE YOU A WHOLE SO MUCH A LOT.
CAN YOU DO ME A FAVOR? SHARE AN UBER TO MY APARTMENT AND GET IN MY PANTS?
YES, IF THAT WOULD BE HELPFUL TO YOU.
PR591
RIOT
XXX
MUP

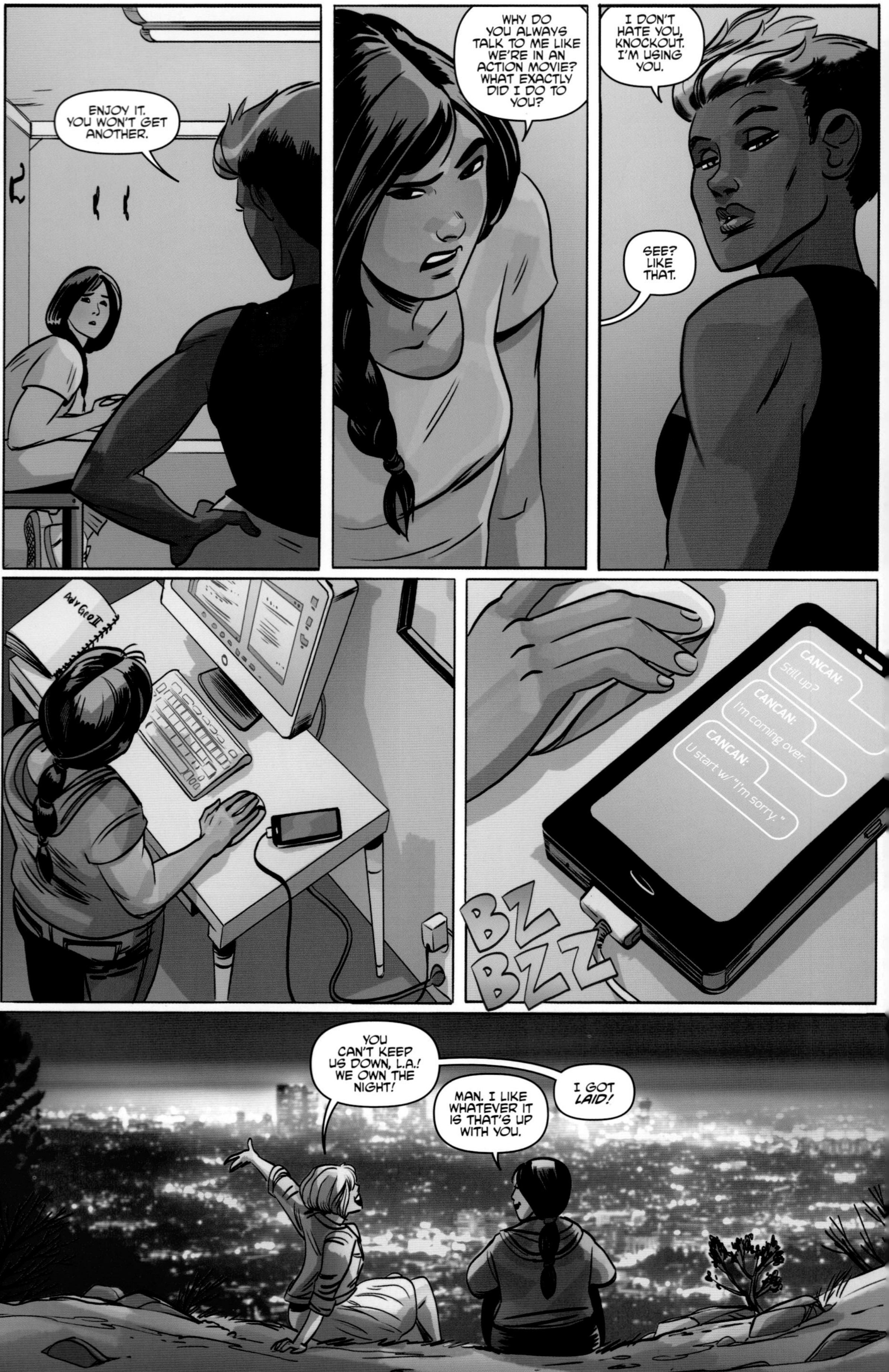
ENJOY IT. YOU WON'T GET ANOTHER.
WHY DO YOU ALWAYS TALK TO ME LIKE WE'RE IN AN ACTION MOVIE? WHAT EXACTLY DID I DO TO YOU?
I DON'T HATE YOU, KNOCKOUT. I'M USING YOU.
SEE? LIKE THAT.
Adv Geo II
CANCAN: Still up?
CANCAN: I'm coming over.
CANCAN: U start w/ "I'm sorry."
BZ BZZ
YOU CAN'T KEEP US DOWN, L.A.! WE OWN THE NIGHT!
I GOT LAID!
MAN. I LIKE WHATEVER IT IS THAT'S UP WITH YOU.

CHAPTER
THREE

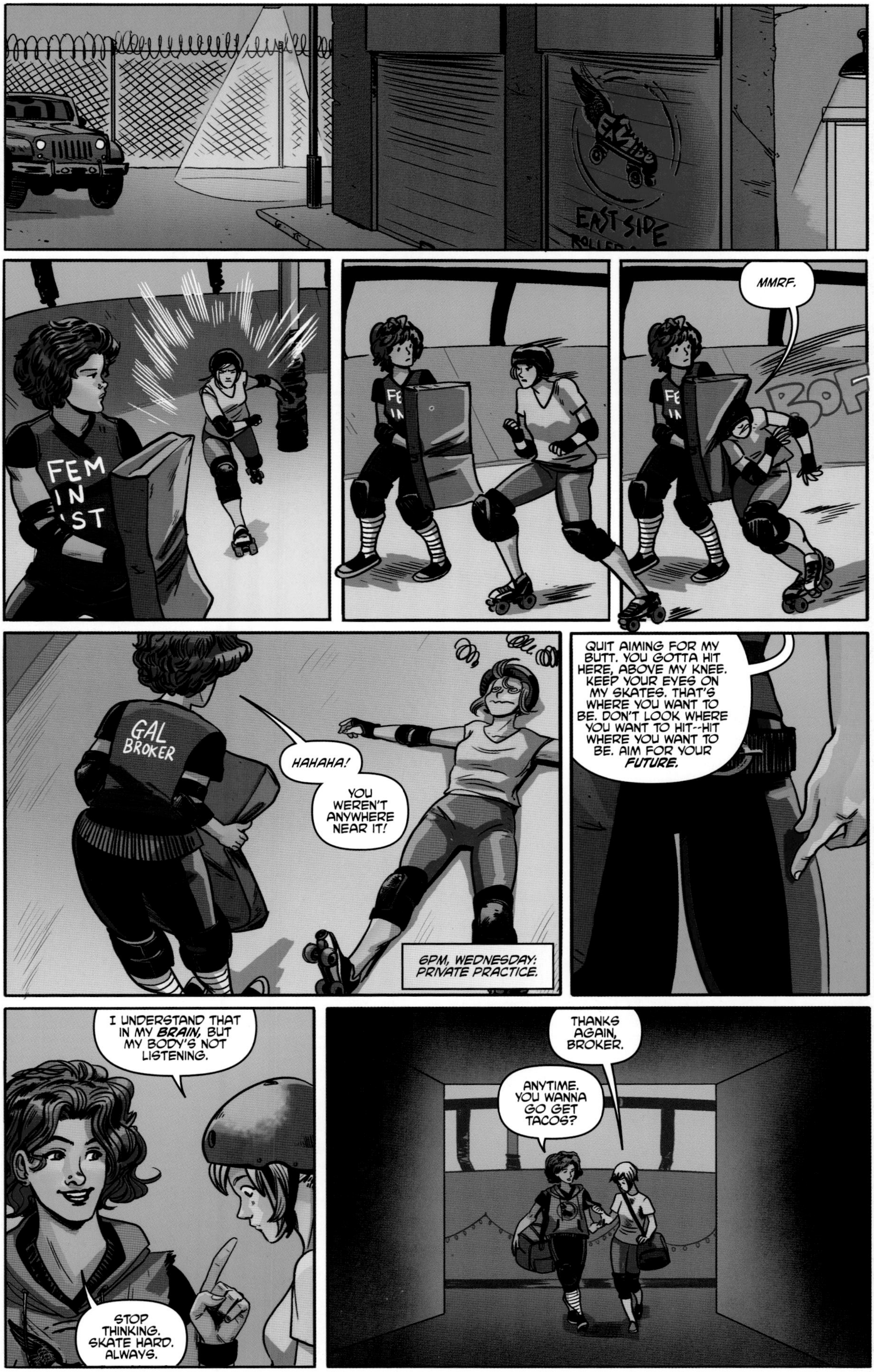

EAST SIDE
FEM IN IST
MMRF.
BOF
GAL BROKER
HAHAHA!
YOU WEREN'T ANYWHERE NEAR IT!
6PM, WEDNESDAY: PRIVATE PRACTICE.
QUIT AIMING FOR MY BUTT. YOU GOTTA HIT HERE, ABOVE MY KNEE. KEEP YOUR EYES ON MY SKATES. THAT'S WHERE YOU WANT TO BE. DON'T LOOK WHERE YOU WANT TO HIT--HIT WHERE YOU WANT TO BE. AIM FOR YOUR *FUTURE.*
I UNDERSTAND THAT IN MY *BRAIN,* BUT MY BODY'S NOT LISTENING.
STOP THINKING. SKATE HARD. ALWAYS.
THANKS AGAIN, BROKER.
ANYTIME. YOU WANNA GO GET TACOS?

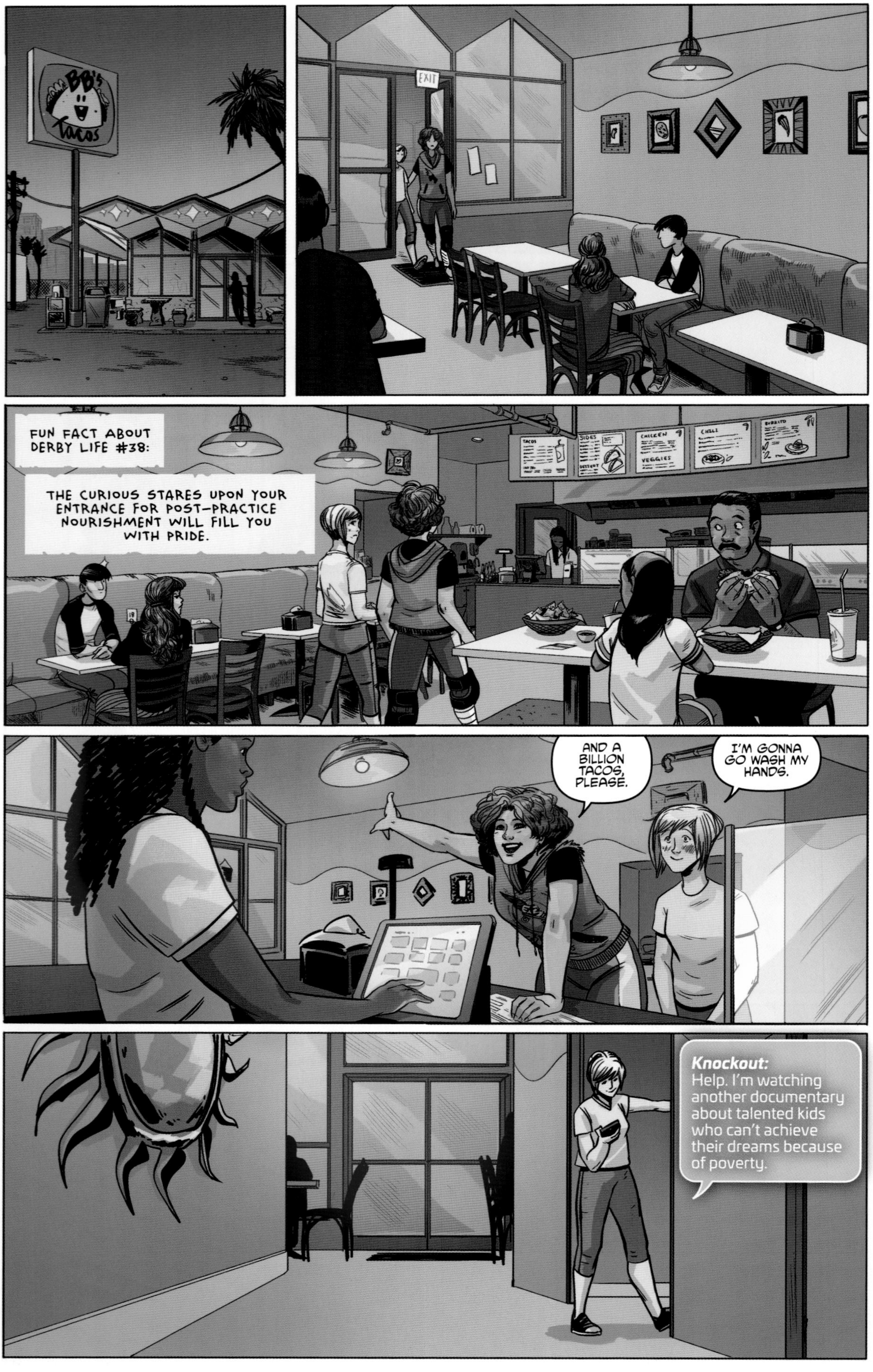
BB's Tacos
EXIT
FUN FACT ABOUT DERBY LIFE #38:
THE CURIOUS STARES UPON YOUR ENTRANCE FOR POST-PRACTICE NOURISHMENT WILL FILL YOU WITH PRIDE.
TACOS
SIDES
DESSERT
CHICKEN
VEGGIES
CHILI
BURRITO
AND A BILLION TACOS, PLEASE.
I'M GONNA GO WASH MY HANDS.
Knockout:
Help. I'm watching another documentary about talented kids who can't achieve their dreams because of poverty.

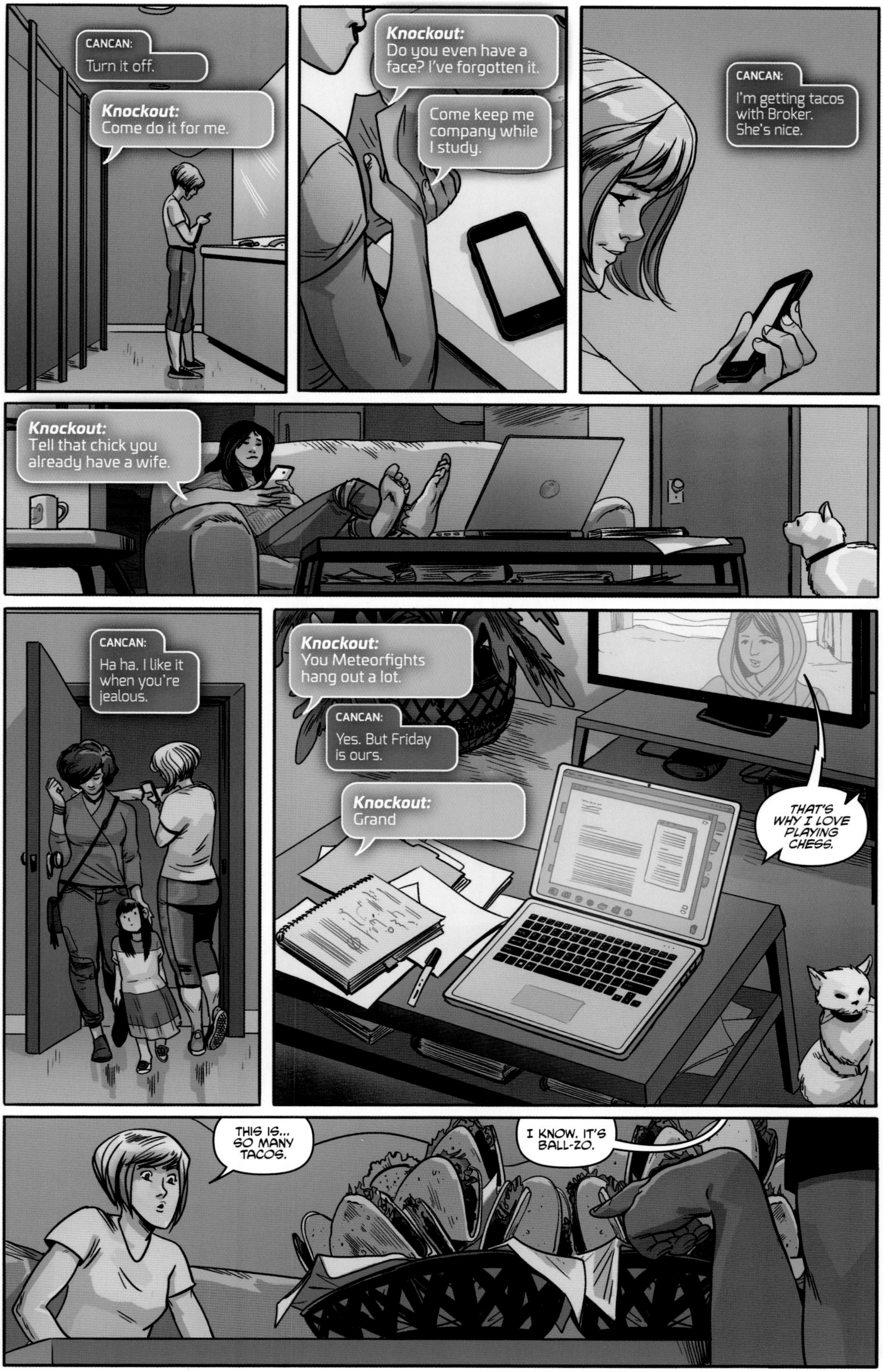
CANCAN:
Turn it off.
Knockout:
Come do it for me.
Knockout:
Do you even have a face? I've forgotten it.
Come keep me company while I study.
CANCAN:
I'm getting tacos with Broker. She's nice.
Knockout:
Tell that chick you already have a wife.
CANCAN:
Ha ha. I like it when you're jealous.
Knockout:
You Meteorfights hang out a lot.
CANCAN:
Yes. But Friday is ours.
Knockout:
Grand
THAT'S WHY I LOVE PLAYING CHESS.
THIS IS... SO MANY TACOS.
I KNOW. IT'S BALL-ZO.

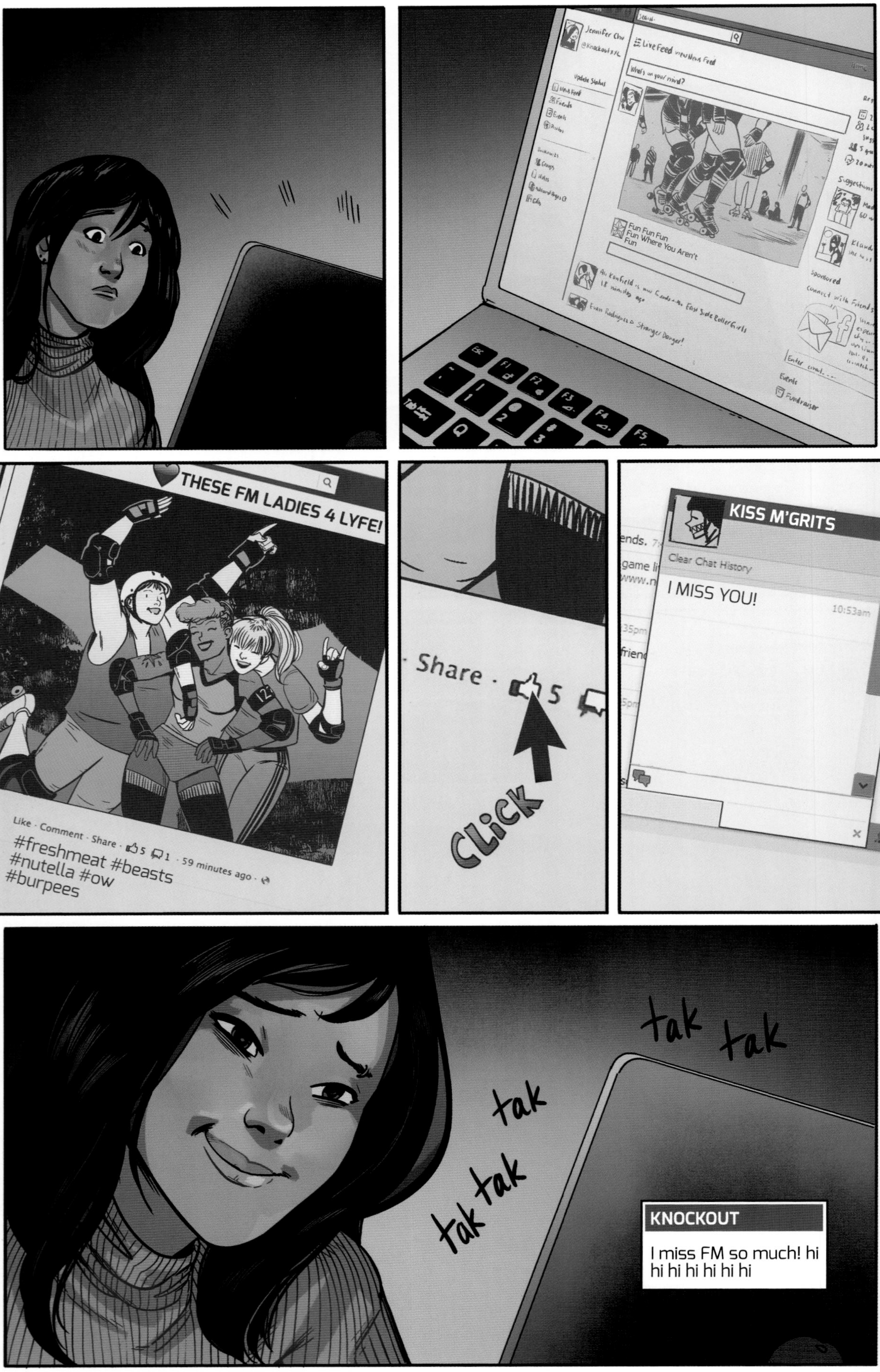
Jennifer Chu
Live Feed
Fun Fun Fun
Fun Where You Aren't
Fun
THESE FM LADIES 4 LYFE!
Like · Comment · Share · 5 1 · 59 minutes ago ·
#freshmeat #beasts
#nutella #ow
#burpees
Share · 5
CLICK
KISS M'GRITS
Clear Chat History
I MISS YOU!
10:53am
tak tak
tak
tak tak
KNOCKOUT
I miss FM so much! hi hi hi hi hi hi hi

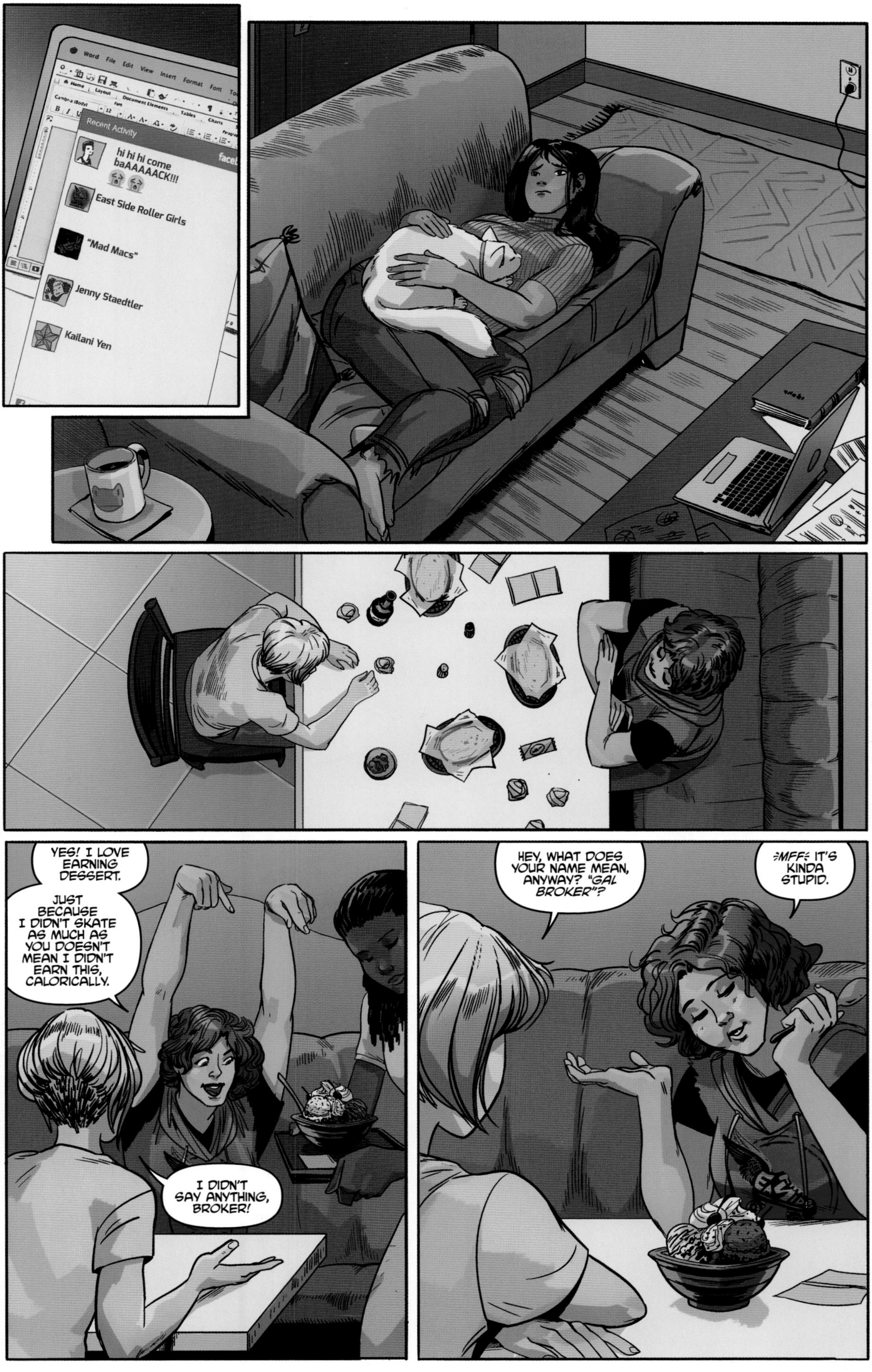
Word File Edit View Insert Format Font
Recent Activity
hi hi hi come baAAAAACK!!!
East Side Roller Girls
"Mad Macs"
Jenny Staedtler
Kailani Yen
YES! I LOVE EARNING DESSERT.
JUST BECAUSE I DIDN'T SKATE AS MUCH AS YOU DOESN'T MEAN I DIDN'T EARN THIS, CALORICALLY.
I DIDN'T SAY ANYTHING, BROKER!
HEY, WHAT DOES YOUR NAME MEAN, ANYWAY? "GAL BROKER"?
MFF IT'S KINDA STUPID.

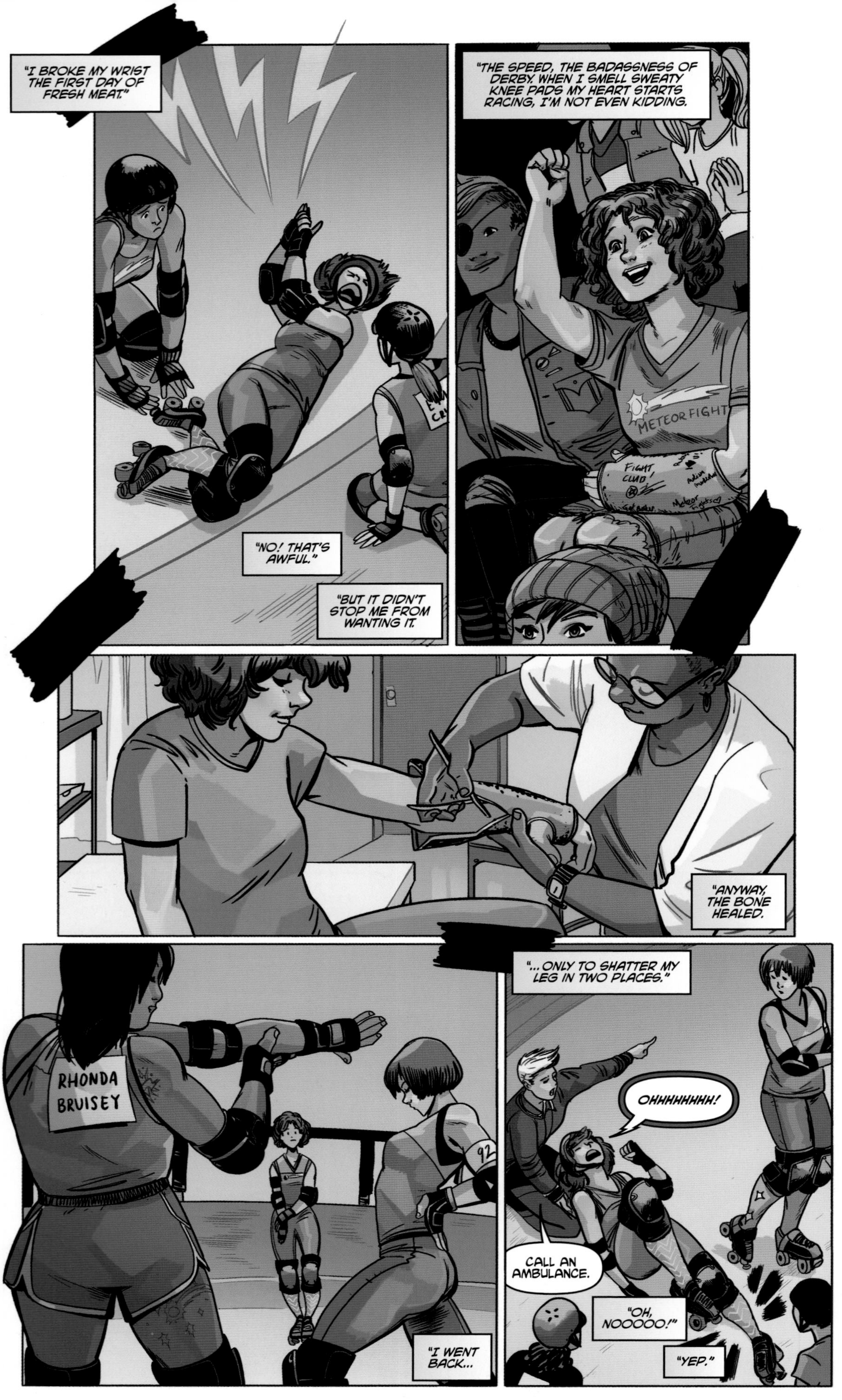
"I BROKE MY WRIST THE FIRST DAY OF FRESH MEAT."
"NO! THAT'S AWFUL."
"BUT IT DIDN'T STOP ME FROM WANTING IT.
"THE SPEED, THE BADASSNESS OF DERBY. WHEN I SMELL SWEATY KNEE PADS MY HEART STARTS RACING, I'M NOT EVEN KIDDING.
METEOR FIGHT
"ANYWAY, THE BONE HEALED.
RHONDA BRUISEY
92
"I WENT BACK...
"...ONLY TO SHATTER MY LEG IN TWO PLACES."
OHHHHHHHH!
CALL AN AMBULANCE.
"OH, NOOOOO!"
"YEP."

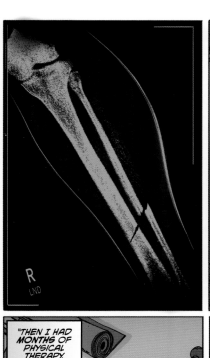

"I HAD SURGERY. PINS.

"THE GIRLS IN THE LEAGUE WERE SO SUPPORTIVE.

"THEN I HAD MONTHS OF PHYSICAL THERAPY.

"ONE YEAR TO THE DAY I FIRST BROKE MY WRIST... I WENT BACK.

"AND THIS TIME I DIDN'T BREAK ANYTHING.

"IT WAS JUST AS INCREDIBLE AS I KNEW IT WAS GOING TO BE.

"SO, ANYWAY, AL ROKER/ GAL BROKER. NOT A GREAT PUN, BUT I DON'T CARE. I EARNED IT."

YOU. ARE. AMAZING.

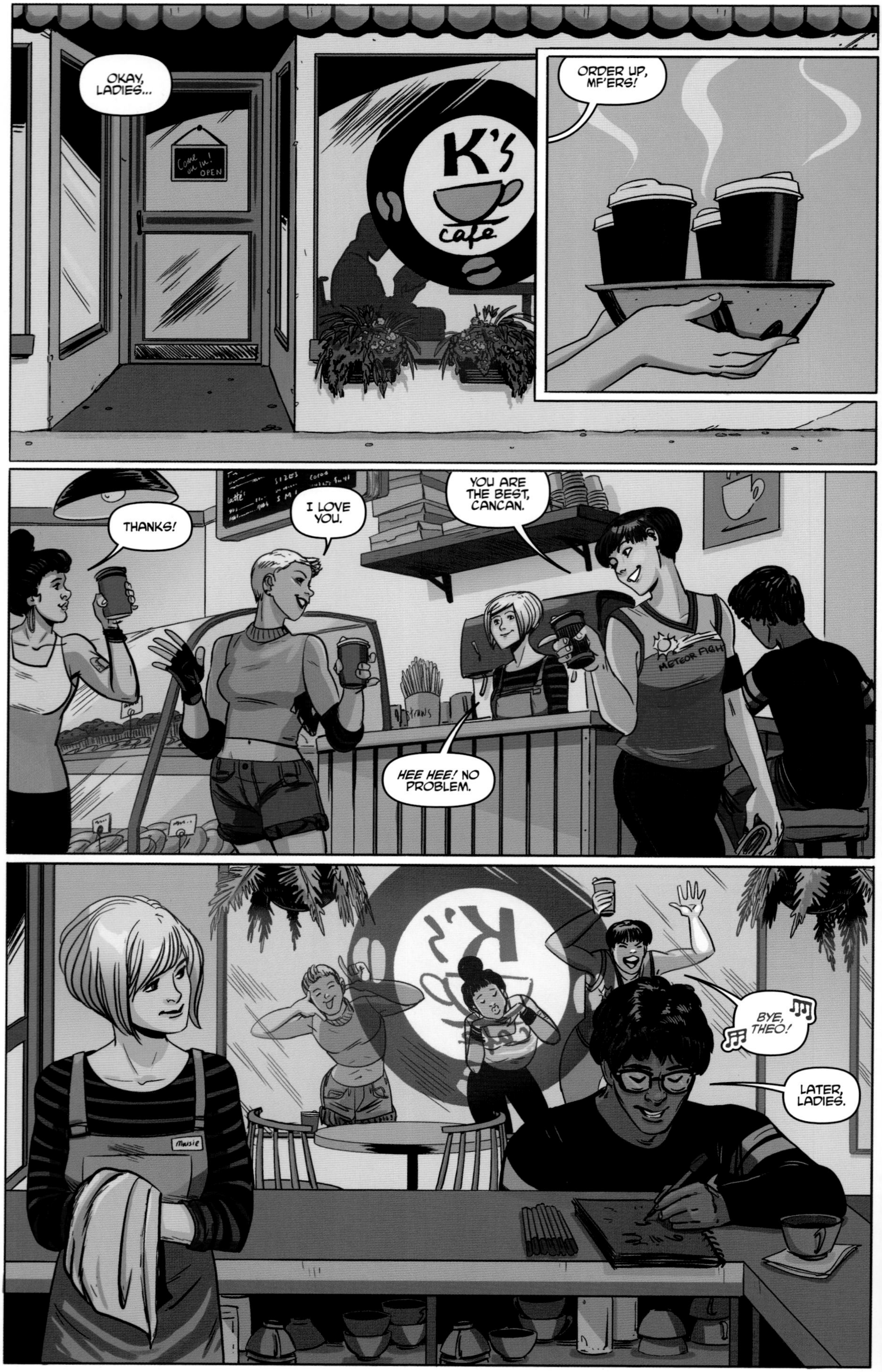
OKAY, LADIES...
Come on in! OPEN
K's cafe
ORDER UP, MF'ERS!
THANKS!
I LOVE YOU.
YOU ARE THE BEST, CANCAN.
HEE HEE! NO PROBLEM.
METEOR FIGH
BYE, THEO!
LATER, LADIES.

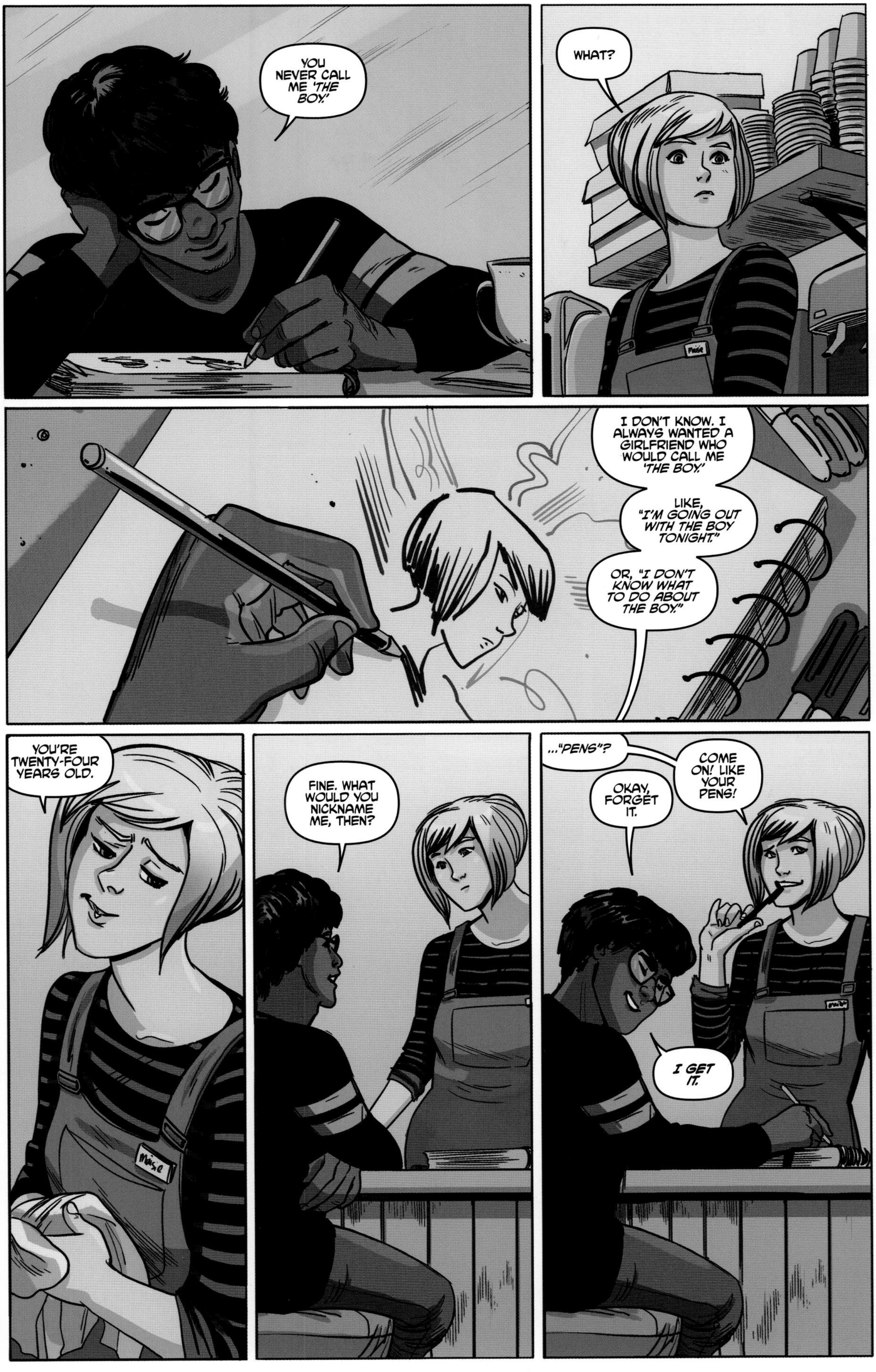
YOU NEVER CALL ME 'THE BOY.'
WHAT?
I DON'T KNOW. I ALWAYS WANTED A GIRLFRIEND WHO WOULD CALL ME 'THE BOY.'
LIKE, "I'M GOING OUT WITH THE BOY TONIGHT."
OR, "I DON'T KNOW WHAT TO DO ABOUT THE BOY."
YOU'RE TWENTY-FOUR YEARS OLD.
FINE. WHAT WOULD YOU NICKNAME ME, THEN?
COME ON! LIKE YOUR PENS!
..."PENS"?
OKAY, FORGET IT.
I GET IT.

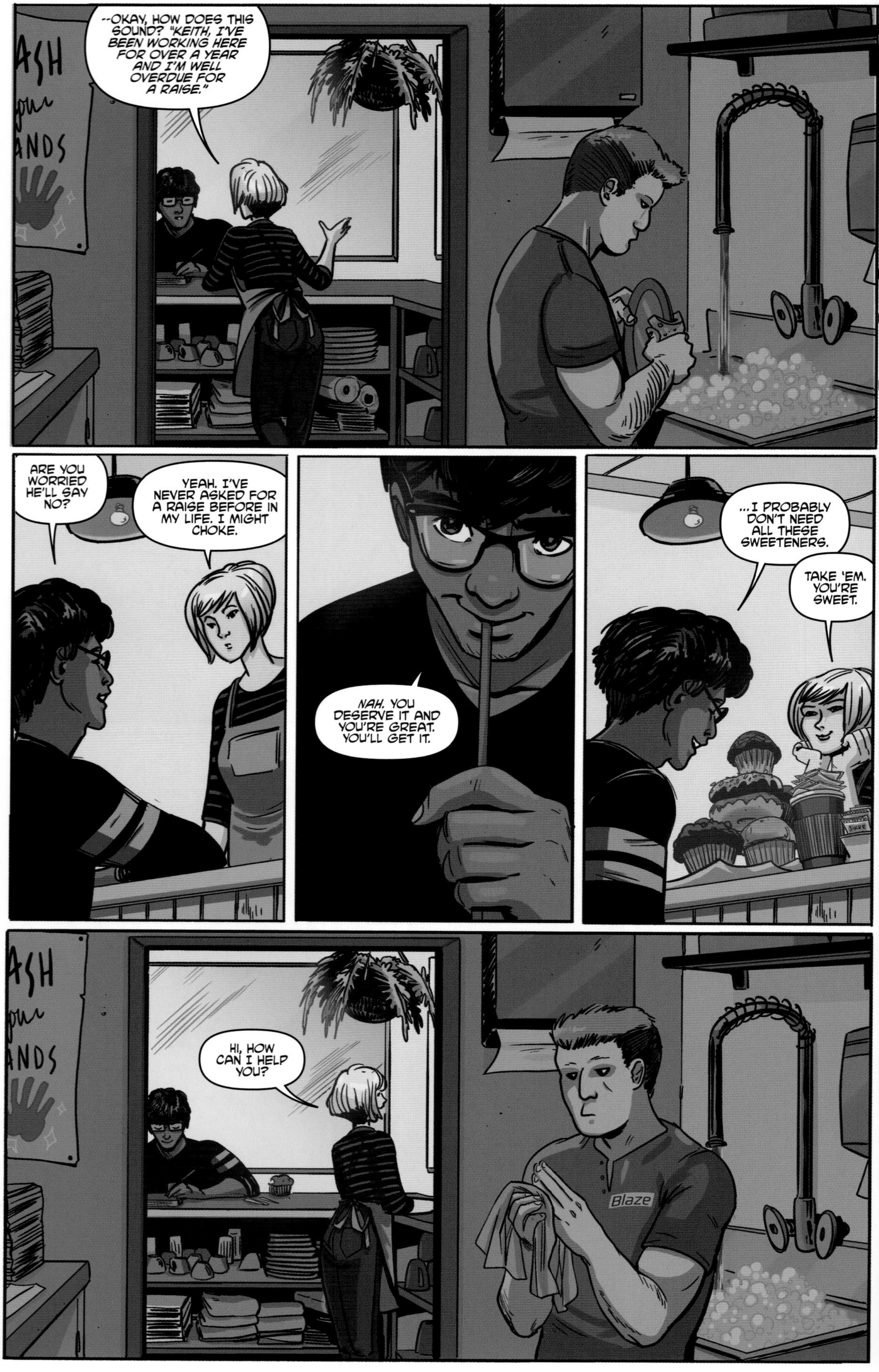

ASH your ANDS
--OKAY, HOW DOES THIS SOUND? "KEITH, I'VE BEEN WORKING HERE FOR OVER A YEAR AND I'M WELL OVERDUE FOR A RAISE."
ARE YOU WORRIED HE'LL SAY NO?
YEAH. I'VE NEVER ASKED FOR A RAISE BEFORE IN MY LIFE. I MIGHT CHOKE.
NAH. YOU DESERVE IT AND YOU'RE GREAT. YOU'LL GET IT.
...I PROBABLY DON'T NEED ALL THESE SWEETENERS.
TAKE 'EM. YOU'RE SWEET.
ASH your ANDS
HI, HOW CAN I HELP YOU?
Blaze

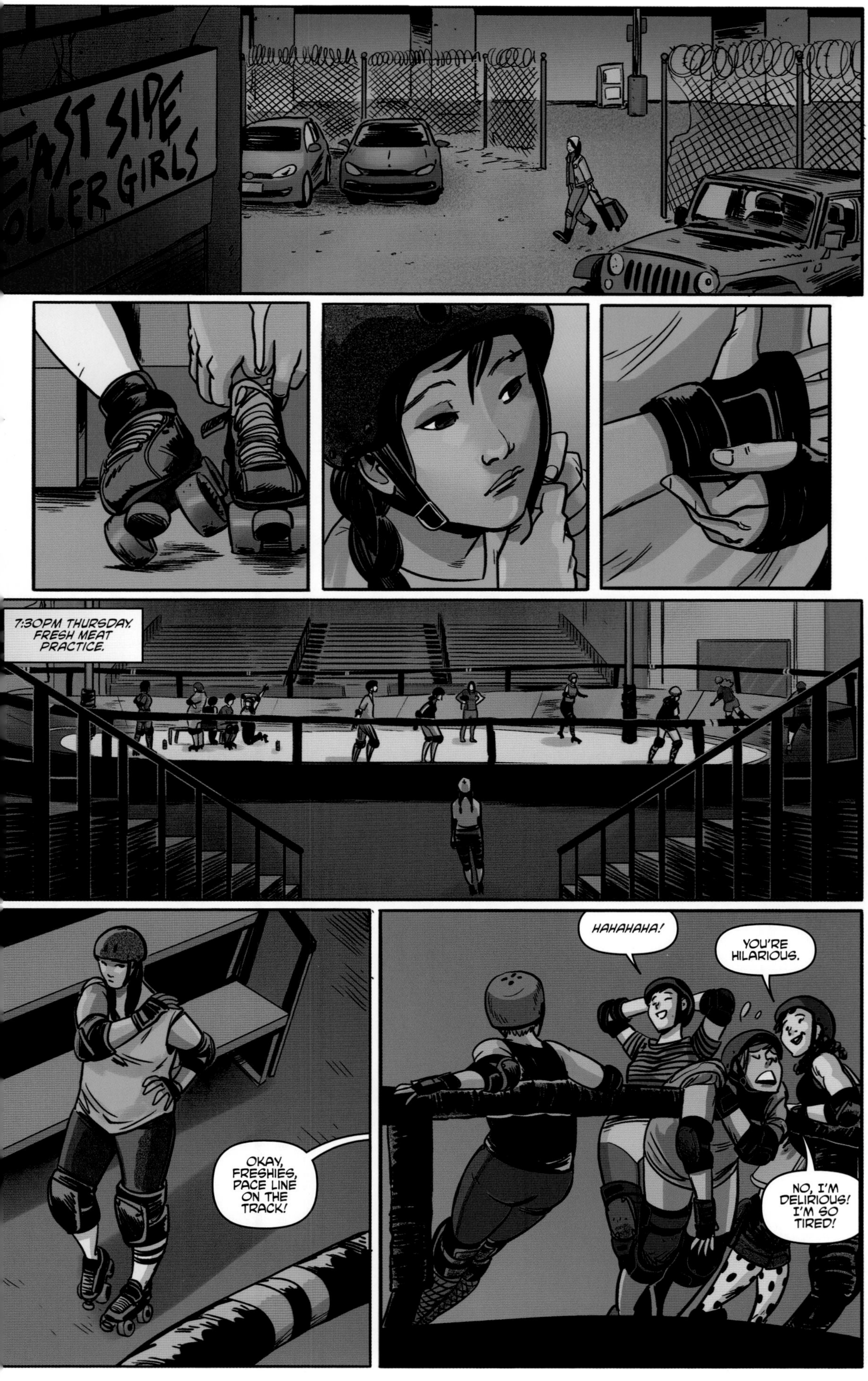
EAST SIDE ROLLER GIRLS
7:30PM THURSDAY. FRESH MEAT PRACTICE.
OKAY, FRESHIES, PACE LINE ON THE TRACK!
HAHAHAHA!
YOU'RE HILARIOUS.
NO, I'M DELIRIOUS! I'M SO TIRED!

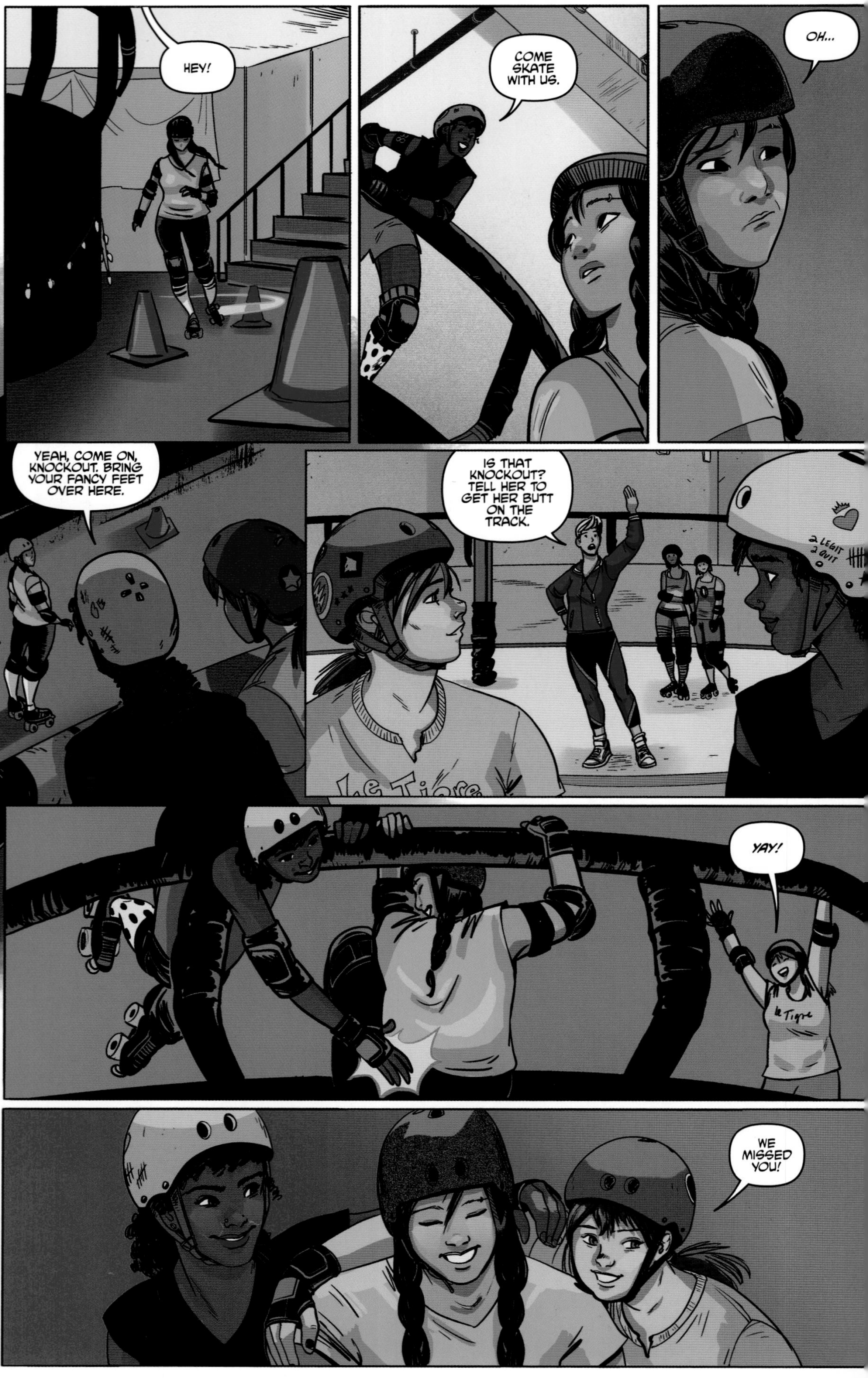
HEY!
COME SKATE WITH US.
OH...
YEAH, COME ON, KNOCKOUT. BRING YOUR FANCY FEET OVER HERE.
IS THAT KNOCKOUT? TELL HER TO GET HER BUTT ON THE TRACK.
2 LEGIT 2 QUIT
YAY!
WE MISSED YOU!

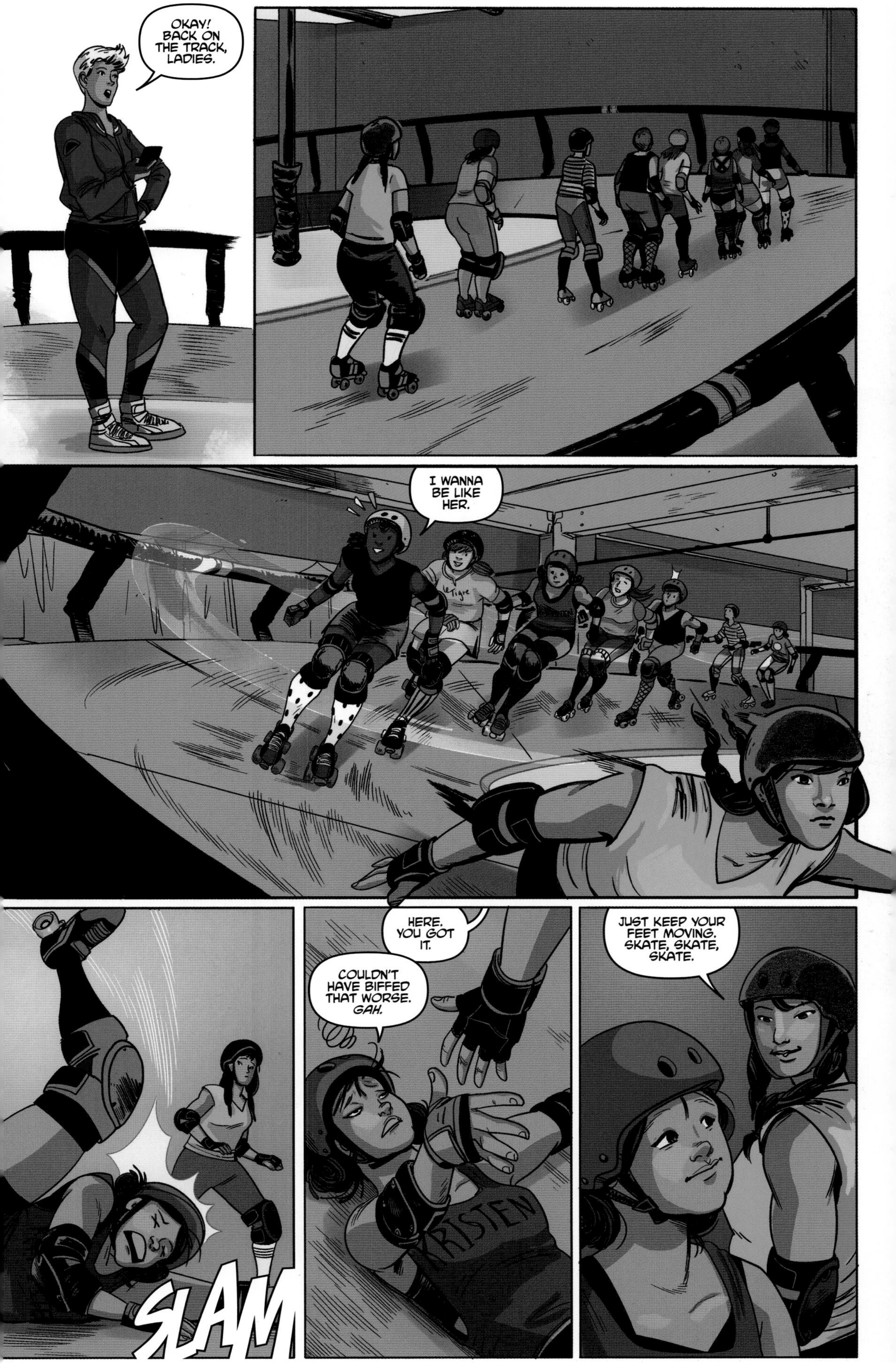
OKAY! BACK ON THE TRACK, LADIES.
I WANNA BE LIKE HER.
le Tigre
SLAM
HERE. YOU GOT IT.
COULDN'T HAVE BIFFED THAT WORSE. GAH.
KRISTEN
JUST KEEP YOUR FEET MOVING. SKATE, SKATE, SKATE.

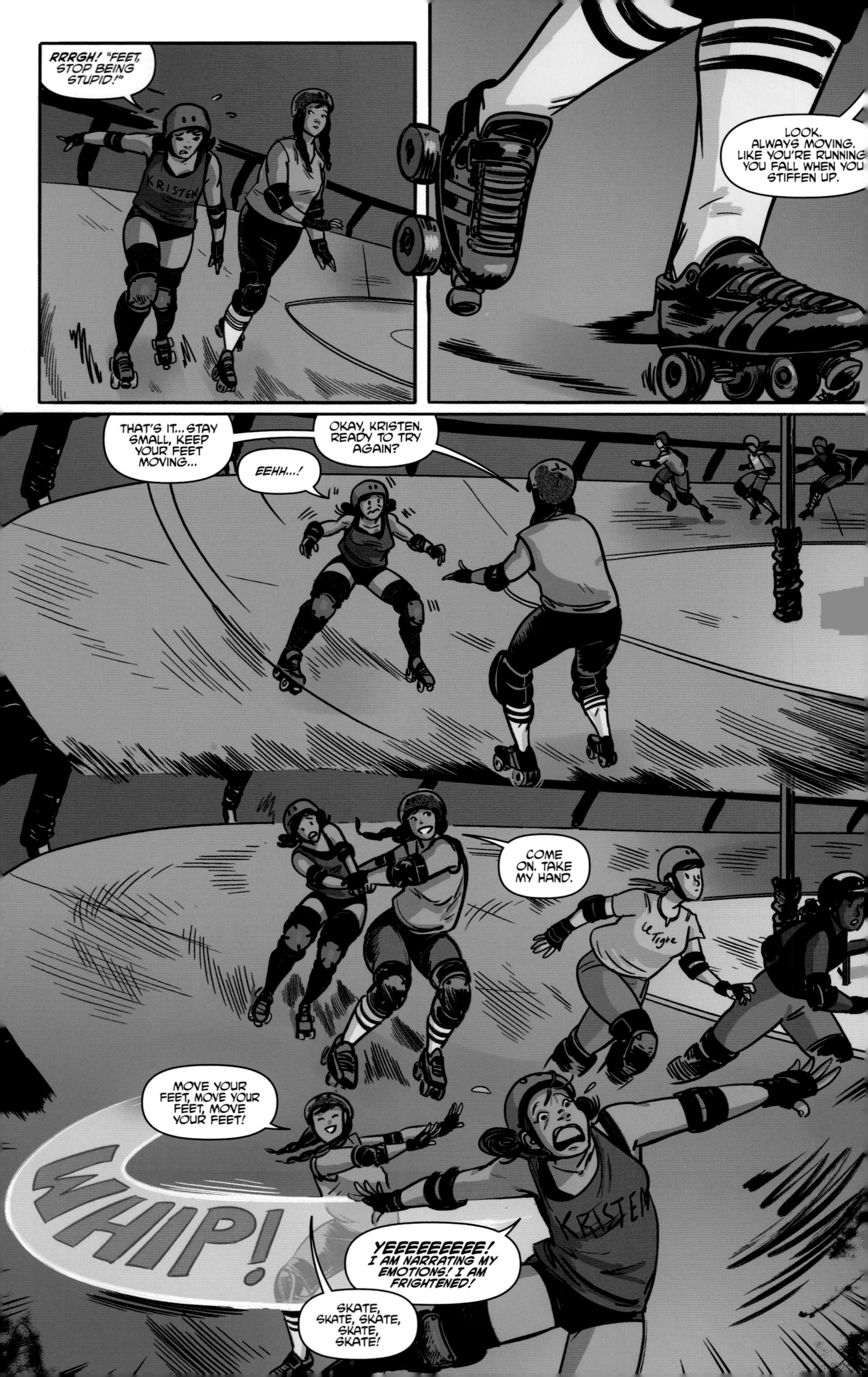
RRRGH! "FEET, STOP BEING STUPID!"
KRISTEN
LOOK. ALWAYS MOVING. LIKE YOU'RE RUNNING. YOU FALL WHEN YOU STIFFEN UP.
THAT'S IT... STAY SMALL, KEEP YOUR FEET MOVING...
OKAY, KRISTEN. READY TO TRY AGAIN?
EEHH...!
COME ON. TAKE MY HAND.
MOVE YOUR FEET, MOVE YOUR FEET, MOVE YOUR FEET!
WHIP!
YEEEEEEEEE! I AM NARRATING MY EMOTIONS! I AM FRIGHTENED!
KRISTEN
SKATE, SKATE, SKATE, SKATE, SKATE!

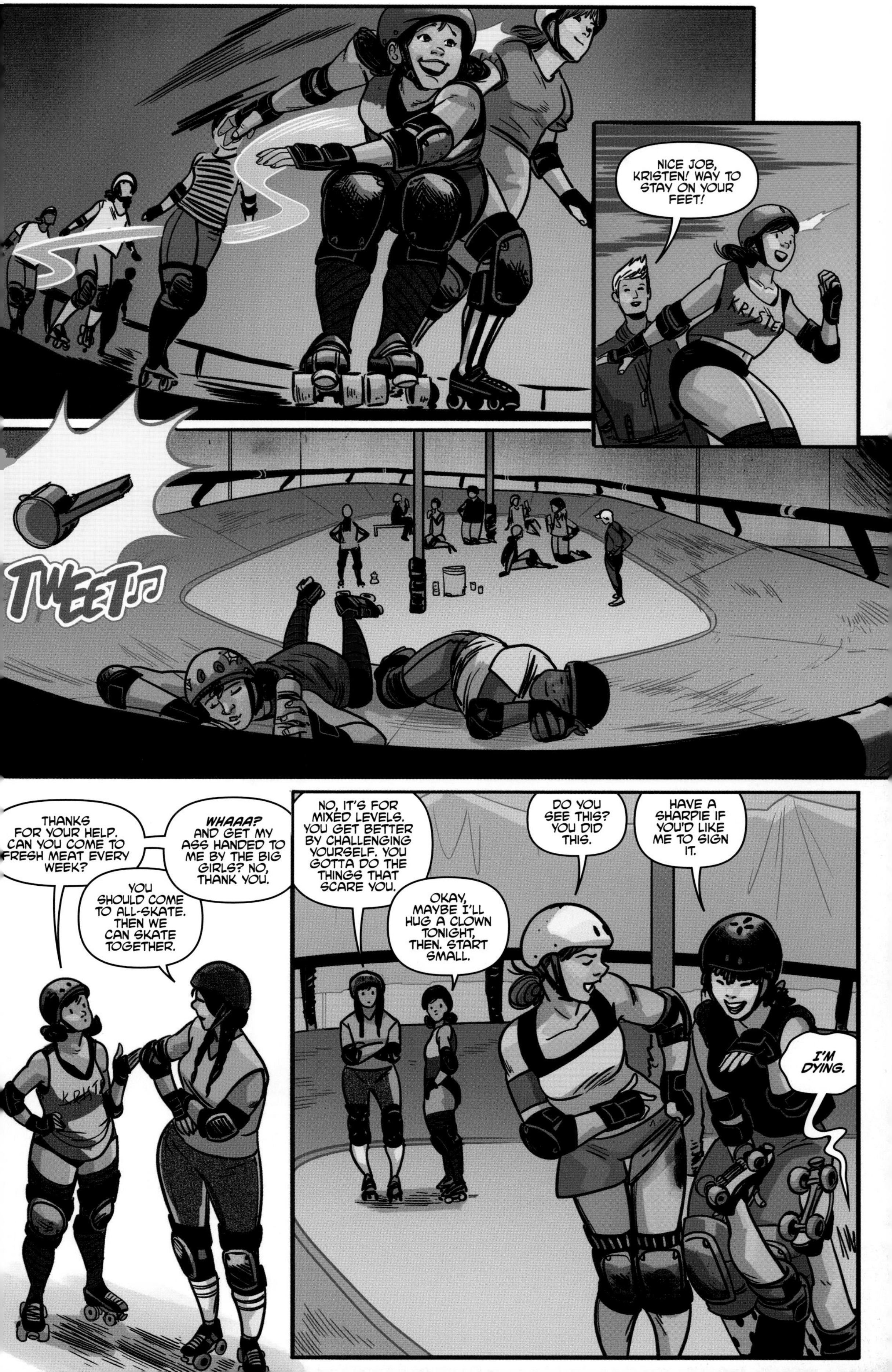
NICE JOB, KRISTEN! WAY TO STAY ON YOUR FEET!
TWEET
THANKS FOR YOUR HELP. CAN YOU COME TO FRESH MEAT EVERY WEEK?
WHAAA? AND GET MY ASS HANDED TO ME BY THE BIG GIRLS? NO, THANK YOU.
YOU SHOULD COME TO ALL-SKATE. THEN WE CAN SKATE TOGETHER.
NO, IT'S FOR MIXED LEVELS. YOU GET BETTER BY CHALLENGING YOURSELF. YOU GOTTA DO THE THINGS THAT SCARE YOU.
OKAY, MAYBE I'LL HUG A CLOWN TONIGHT, THEN. START SMALL.
DO YOU SEE THIS? YOU DID THIS.
HAVE A SHARPIE IF YOU'D LIKE ME TO SIGN IT.
I'M DYING.

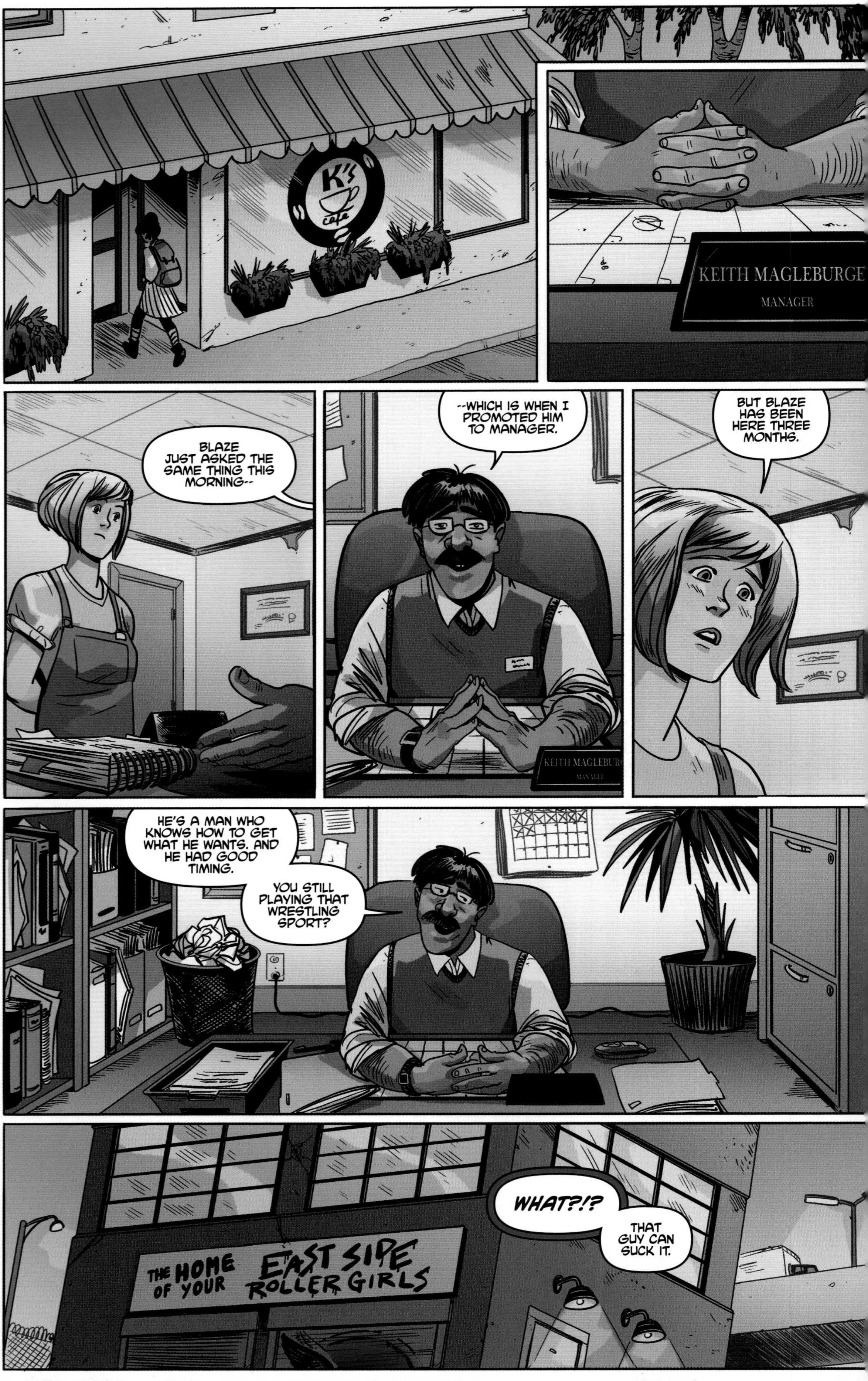
K's cafe
KEITH MAGLEBURGE
MANAGER
BLAZE JUST ASKED THE SAME THING THIS MORNING--
--WHICH IS WHEN I PROMOTED HIM TO MANAGER.
KEITH MAGLEBUR
MANAGER
BUT BLAZE HAS BEEN HERE THREE MONTHS.
HE'S A MAN WHO KNOWS HOW TO GET WHAT HE WANTS. AND HE HAD GOOD TIMING.
YOU STILL PLAYING THAT WRESTLING SPORT?
THE HOME OF YOUR EAST SIDE ROLLER GIRLS
WHAT?!?
THAT GUY CAN SUCK IT.

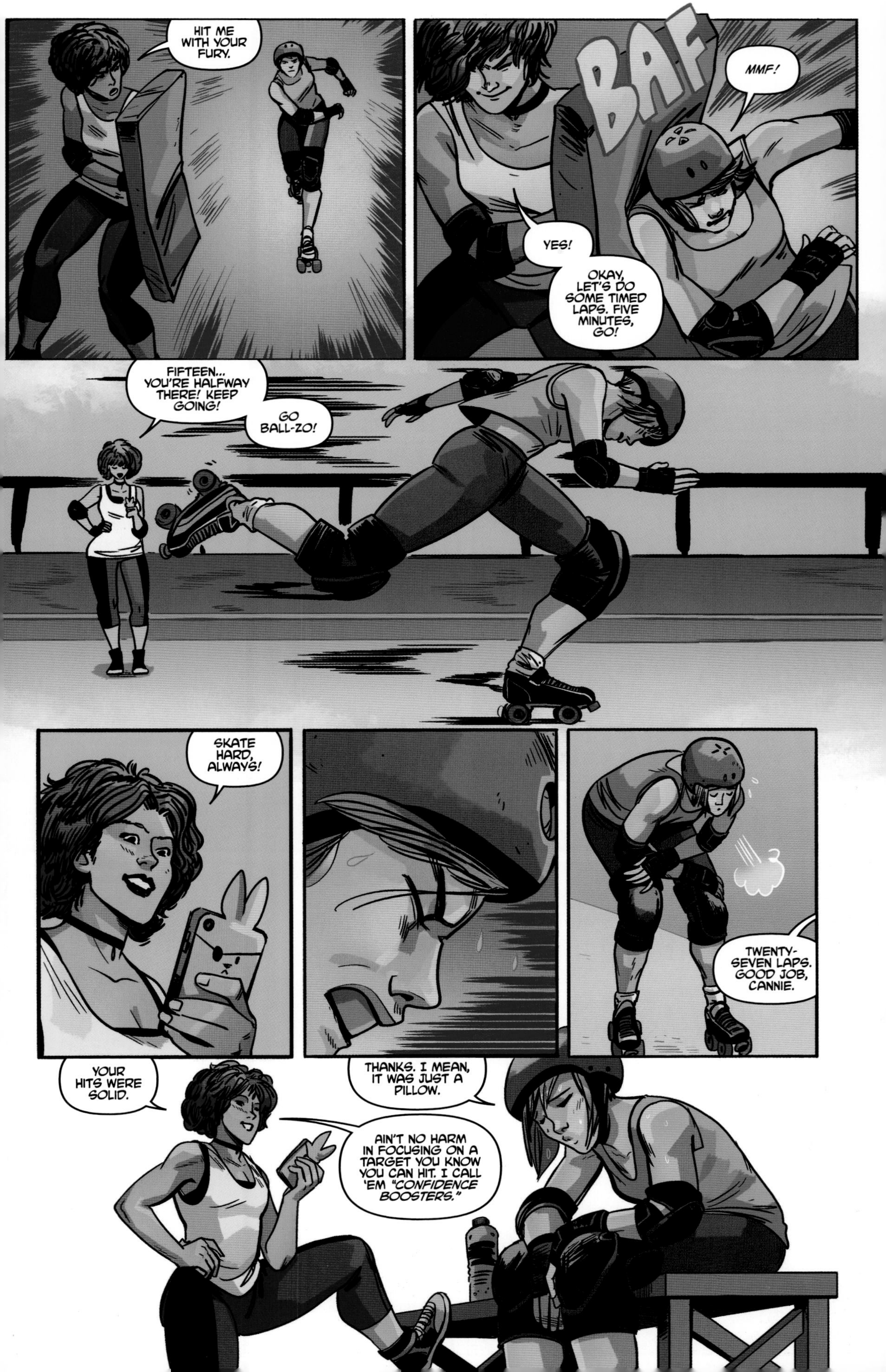

HIT ME WITH YOUR FURY.
BAF
MMF!
YES!
OKAY, LET'S DO SOME TIMED LAPS. FIVE MINUTES, GO!
FIFTEEN... YOU'RE HALFWAY THERE! KEEP GOING!
GO BALL-ZO!
SKATE HARD, ALWAYS!
TWENTY-SEVEN LAPS. GOOD JOB, CANNIE.
YOUR HITS WERE SOLID.
THANKS. I MEAN, IT WAS JUST A PILLOW.
AIN'T NO HARM IN FOCUSING ON A TARGET YOU KNOW YOU CAN HIT. I CALL 'EM *"CONFIDENCE BOOSTERS."*

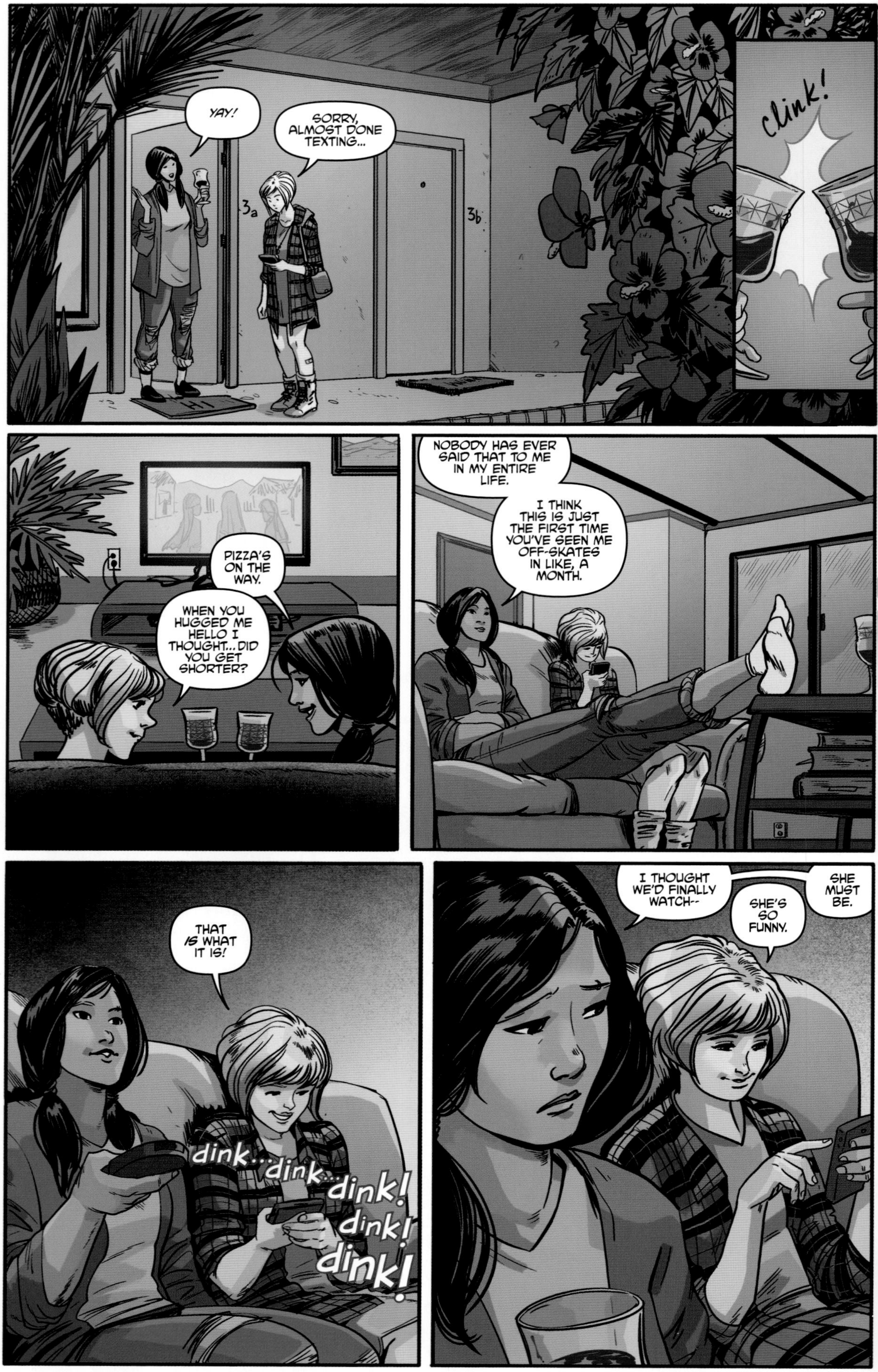
YAY!
SORRY, ALMOST DONE TEXTING...
3a
3b
clink!
PIZZA'S ON THE WAY.
WHEN YOU HUGGED ME HELLO I THOUGHT...DID YOU GET SHORTER?
NOBODY HAS EVER SAID THAT TO ME IN MY ENTIRE LIFE.
I THINK THIS IS JUST THE FIRST TIME YOU'VE SEEN ME OFF-SKATES IN LIKE, A MONTH.
THAT IS WHAT IT IS!
dink...dink...dink! dink! dink!
I THOUGHT WE'D FINALLY WATCH--
SHE'S SO FUNNY.
SHE MUST BE.

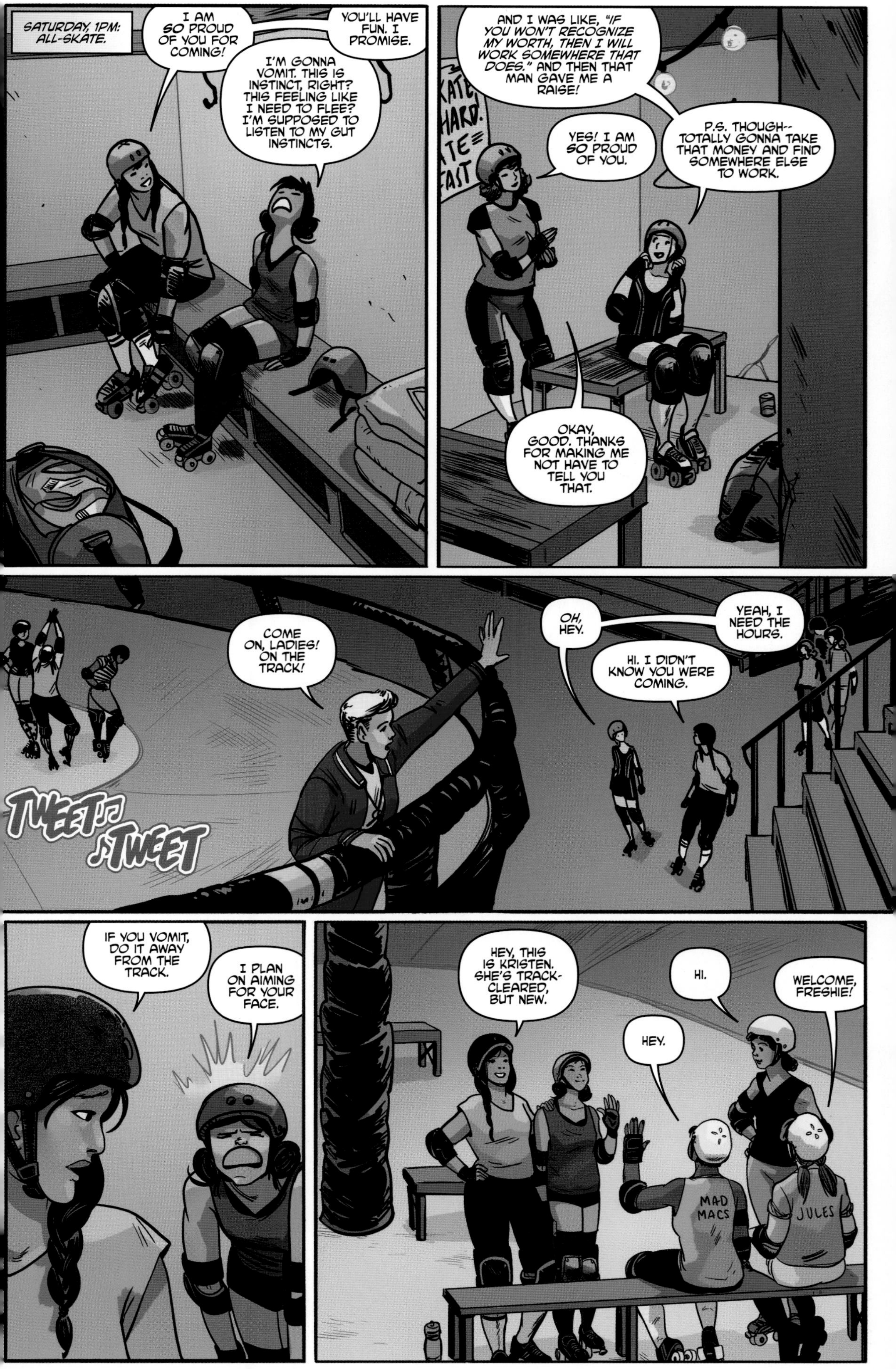
SATURDAY, 1PM: ALL-SKATE.
I AM SO PROUD OF YOU FOR COMING!
YOU'LL HAVE FUN. I PROMISE.
I'M GONNA VOMIT. THIS IS INSTINCT, RIGHT? THIS FEELING LIKE I NEED TO FLEE? I'M SUPPOSED TO LISTEN TO MY GUT INSTINCTS.
AND I WAS LIKE, "IF YOU WON'T RECOGNIZE MY WORTH, THEN I WILL WORK SOMEWHERE THAT DOES." AND THEN THAT MAN GAVE ME A RAISE!
YES! I AM SO PROUD OF YOU.
P.S. THOUGH-- TOTALLY GONNA TAKE THAT MONEY AND FIND SOMEWHERE ELSE TO WORK.
OKAY, GOOD. THANKS FOR MAKING ME NOT HAVE TO TELL YOU THAT.
COME ON, LADIES! ON THE TRACK!
TWEET TWEET
OH, HEY.
YEAH, I NEED THE HOURS.
HI. I DIDN'T KNOW YOU WERE COMING.
IF YOU VOMIT, DO IT AWAY FROM THE TRACK.
I PLAN ON AIMING FOR YOUR FACE.
HEY, THIS IS KRISTEN. SHE'S TRACK-CLEARED, BUT NEW.
HI.
WELCOME, FRESHIE!
HEY.
MAD MACS
JULES

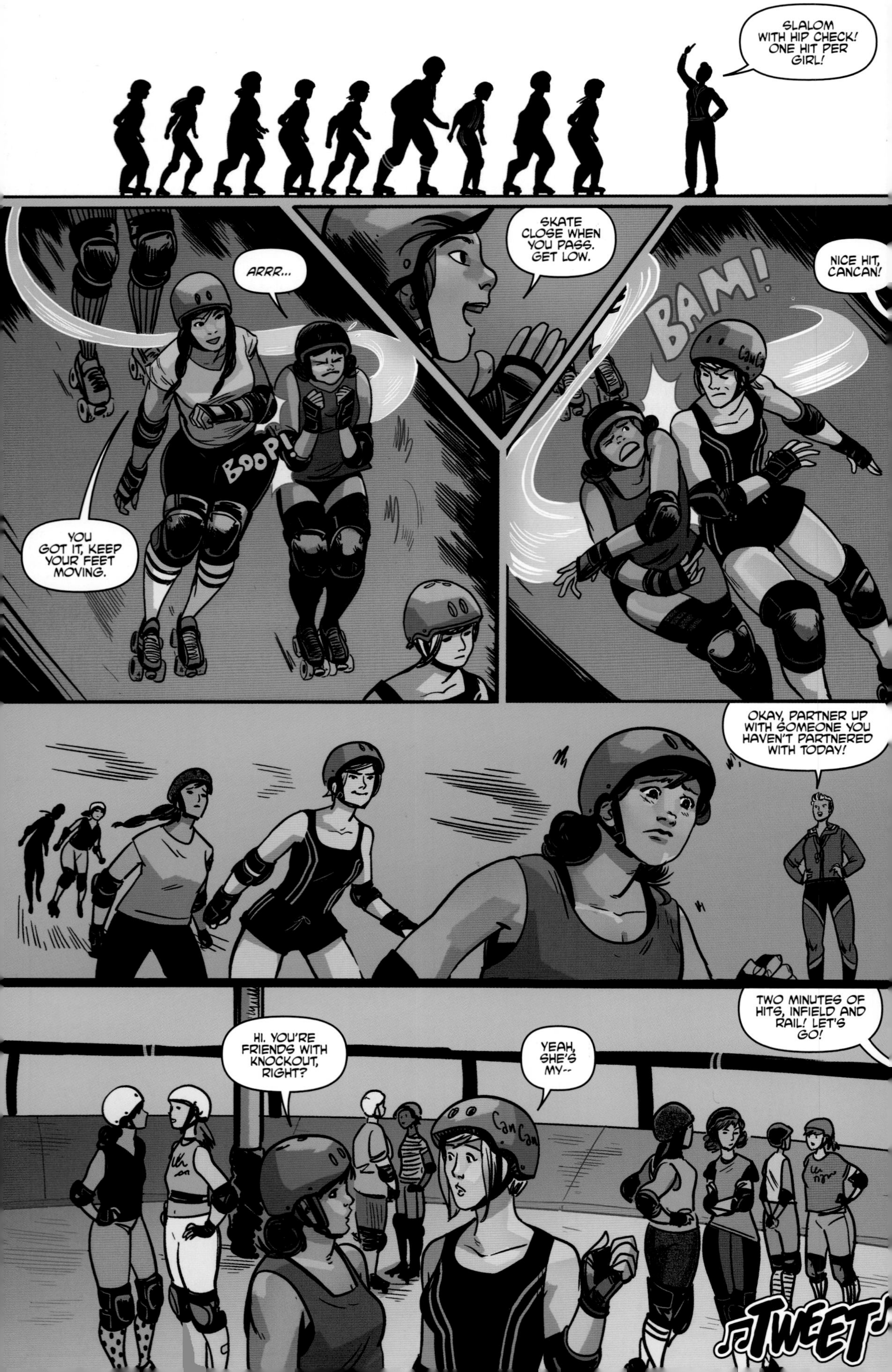
SLALOM WITH HIP CHECK! ONE HIT PER GIRL!
ARRR...
BOOP!
YOU GOT IT, KEEP YOUR FEET MOVING.
SKATE CLOSE WHEN YOU PASS. GET LOW.
BAM!
NICE HIT, CANCAN!
OKAY, PARTNER UP WITH SOMEONE YOU HAVEN'T PARTNERED WITH TODAY!
HI. YOU'RE FRIENDS WITH KNOCKOUT, RIGHT?
YEAH, SHE'S MY--
TWO MINUTES OF HITS, INFIELD AND RAIL! LET'S GO!
TWEET

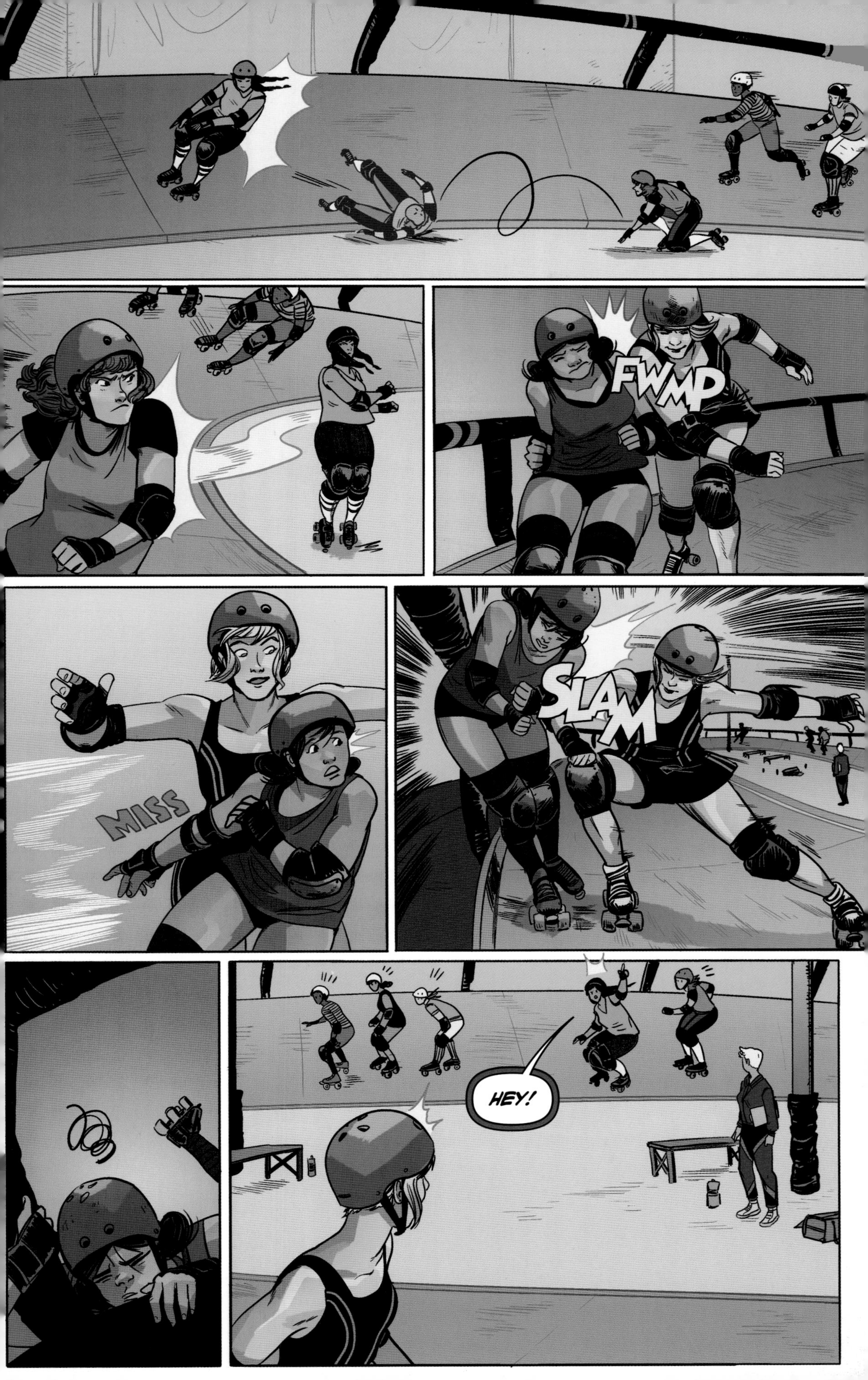
FWMP
MISS
SLAM
HEY!

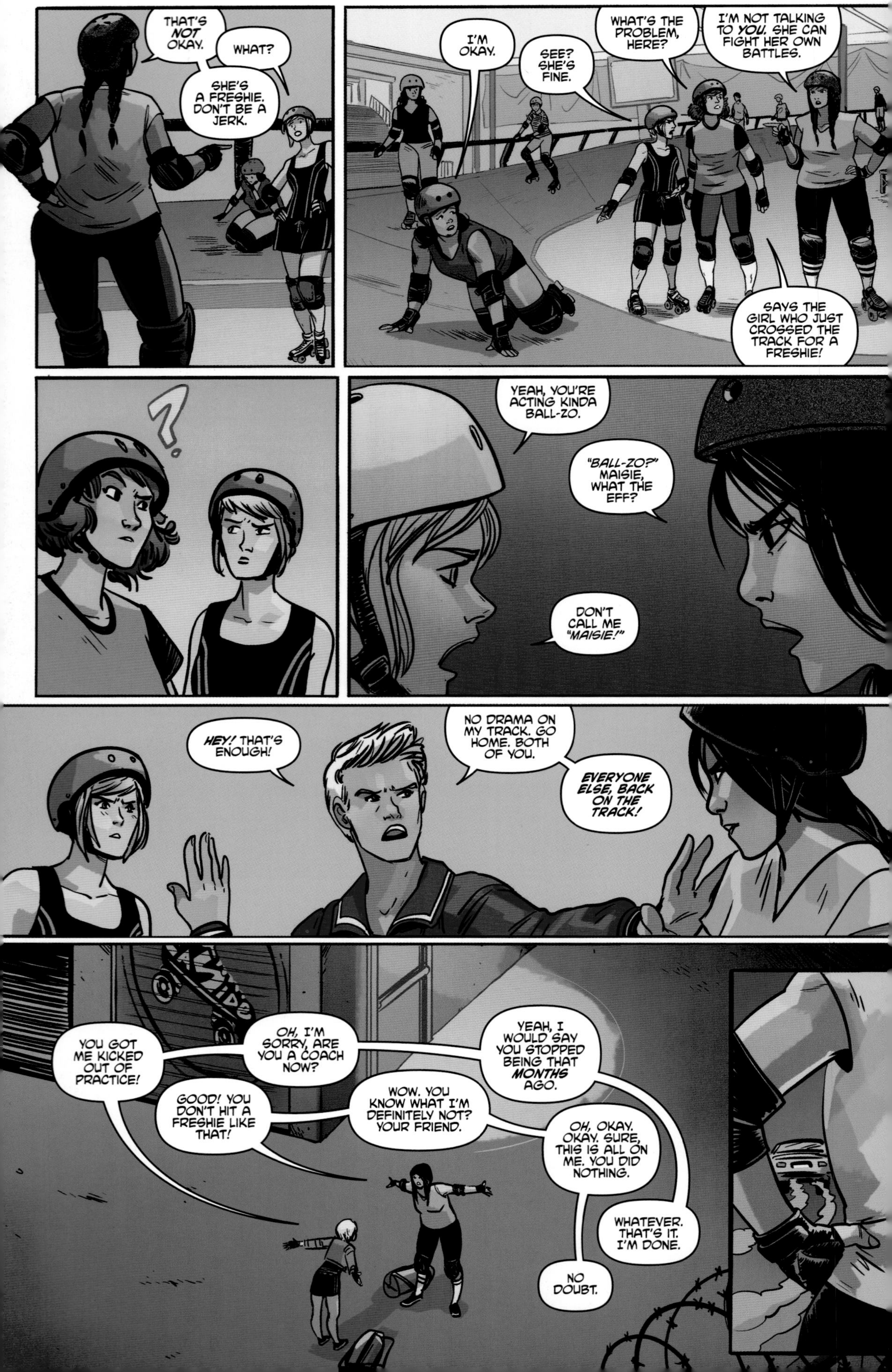
THAT'S *NOT* OKAY.
WHAT?
SHE'S A FRESHIE. DON'T BE A JERK.
I'M OKAY.
SEE? SHE'S FINE.
WHAT'S THE PROBLEM, HERE?
I'M NOT TALKING TO *YOU*. SHE CAN FIGHT HER OWN BATTLES.
SAYS THE GIRL WHO JUST CROSSED THE TRACK FOR A FRESHIE!
?
YEAH, YOU'RE ACTING KINDA BALL-ZO.
"BALL-ZO?" MAISIE, WHAT THE EFF?
DON'T CALL ME *"MAISIE!"*
HEY! THAT'S ENOUGH!
NO DRAMA ON MY TRACK. GO HOME. BOTH OF YOU.
EVERYONE ELSE, BACK ON THE TRACK!
YOU GOT ME KICKED OUT OF PRACTICE!
OH, I'M SORRY, ARE YOU A COACH NOW?
YEAH, I WOULD SAY YOU STOPPED BEING THAT ***MONTHS*** AGO.
GOOD! YOU DON'T HIT A FRESHIE LIKE THAT!
WOW. YOU KNOW WHAT I'M DEFINITELY NOT? YOUR FRIEND.
OH, OKAY. OKAY. SURE, THIS IS ALL ON ME. YOU DID NOTHING.
WHATEVER. THAT'S IT. I'M DONE.
NO DOUBT.

CHAPTER
FOUR

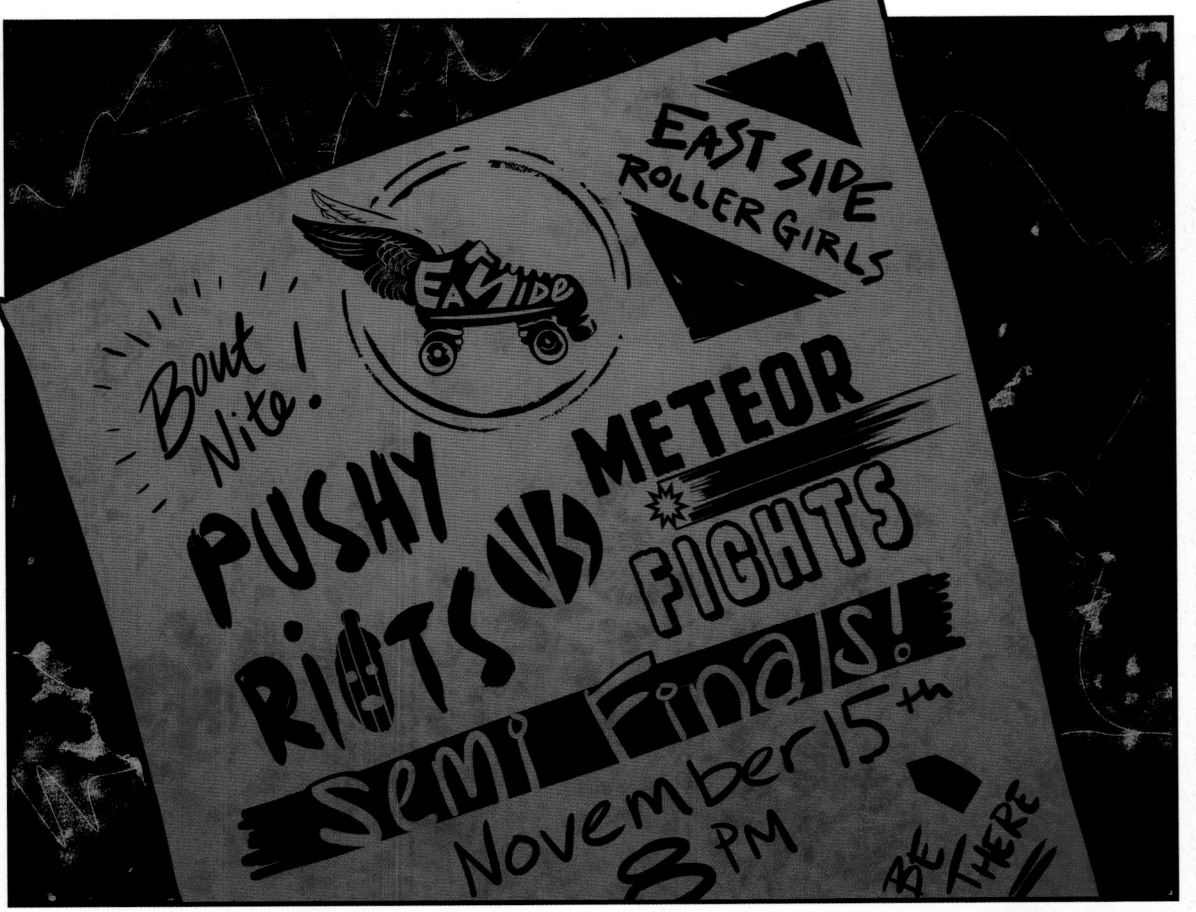
EAST SIDE ROLLER GIRLS
EASTSIDE
Bout Nite!
PUSHY RIOTS VS METEOR FIGHTS
Semi Finals!
November 15th
8 PM
BE THERE

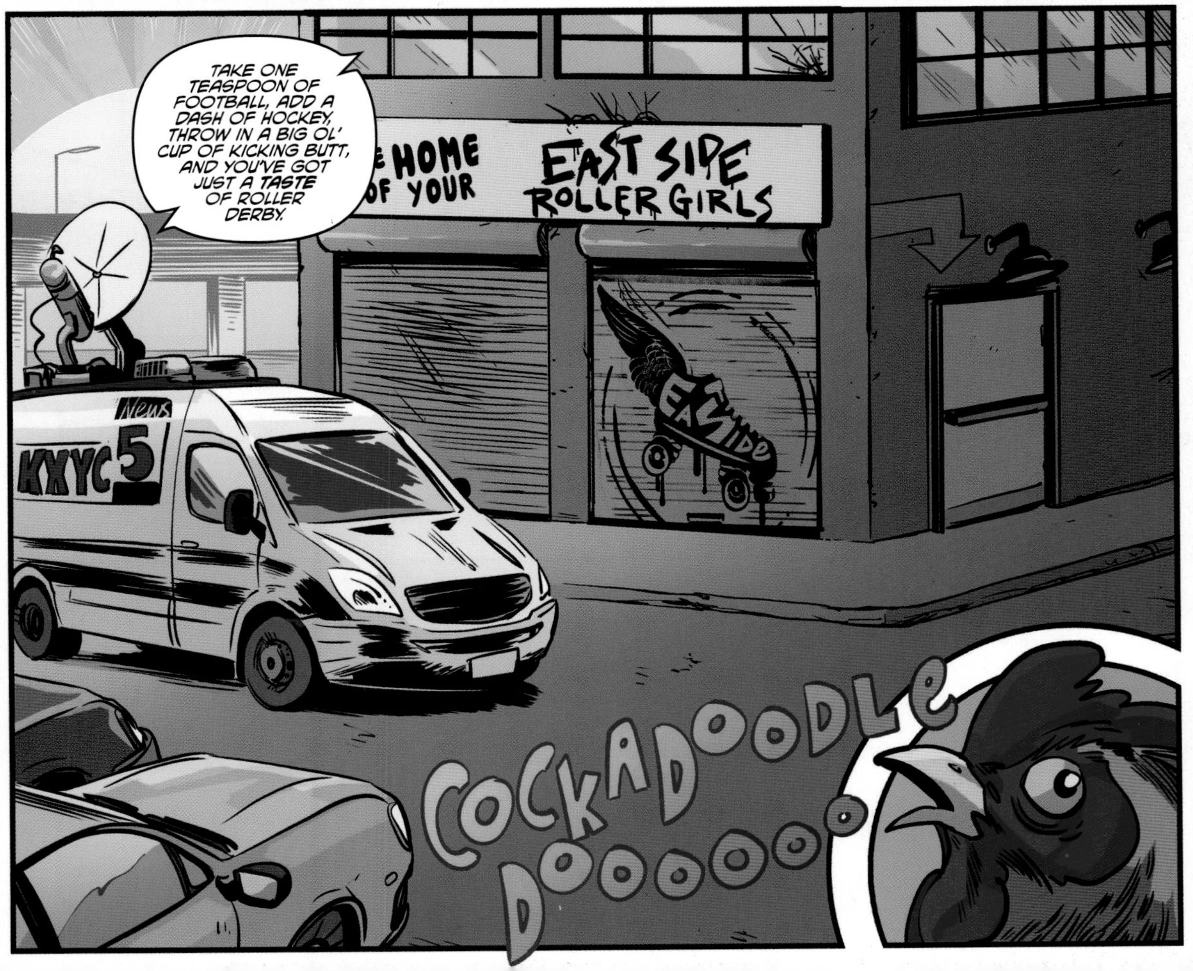
TAKE ONE TEASPOON OF FOOTBALL, ADD A DASH OF HOCKEY, THROW IN A BIG OL' CUP OF KICKING BUTT, AND YOU'VE GOT JUST A *TASTE* OF ROLLER DERBY.
HOME OF YOUR
EAST SIDE ROLLER GIRLS
News
KXYC 5
EASTSIDE
COCKADOODLE DOOOOOO

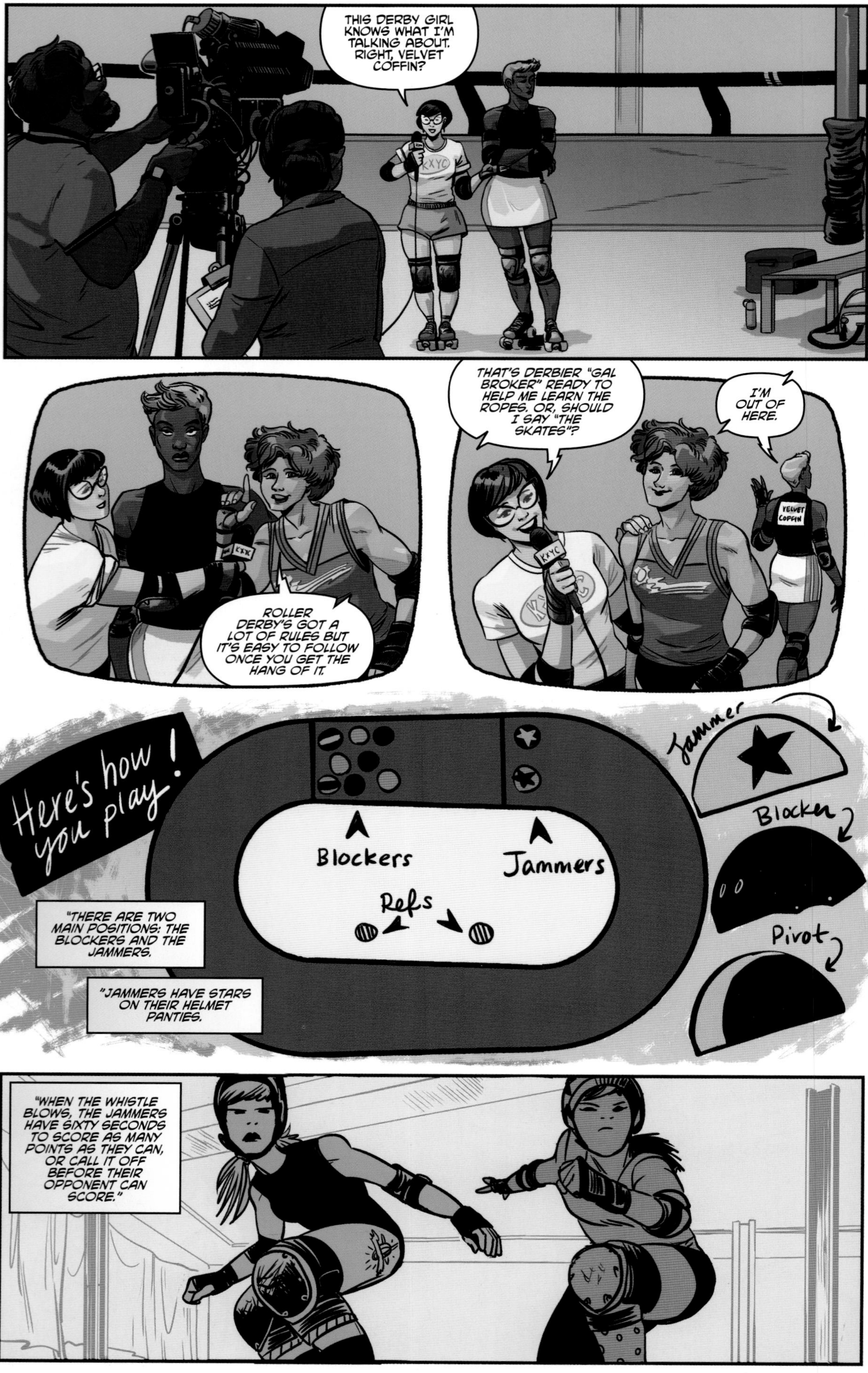

THIS DERBY GIRL KNOWS WHAT I'M TALKING ABOUT. RIGHT, VELVET COFFIN?
KXYC
ROLLER DERBY'S GOT A LOT OF RULES BUT IT'S EASY TO FOLLOW ONCE YOU GET THE HANG OF IT.
THAT'S DERBIER "GAL BROKER" READY TO HELP ME LEARN THE ROPES. OR, SHOULD I SAY "THE SKATES"?
I'M OUT OF HERE.
VELVET COFFIN
Here's how you play!
Blockers
Jammers
Refs
Jammer
Blocker
Pivot
"THERE ARE TWO MAIN POSITIONS: THE BLOCKERS AND THE JAMMERS.
"JAMMERS HAVE STARS ON THEIR HELMET PANTIES.
"WHEN THE WHISTLE BLOWS, THE JAMMERS HAVE SIXTY SECONDS TO SCORE AS MANY POINTS AS THEY CAN, OR CALL IT OFF BEFORE THEIR OPPONENT CAN SCORE."

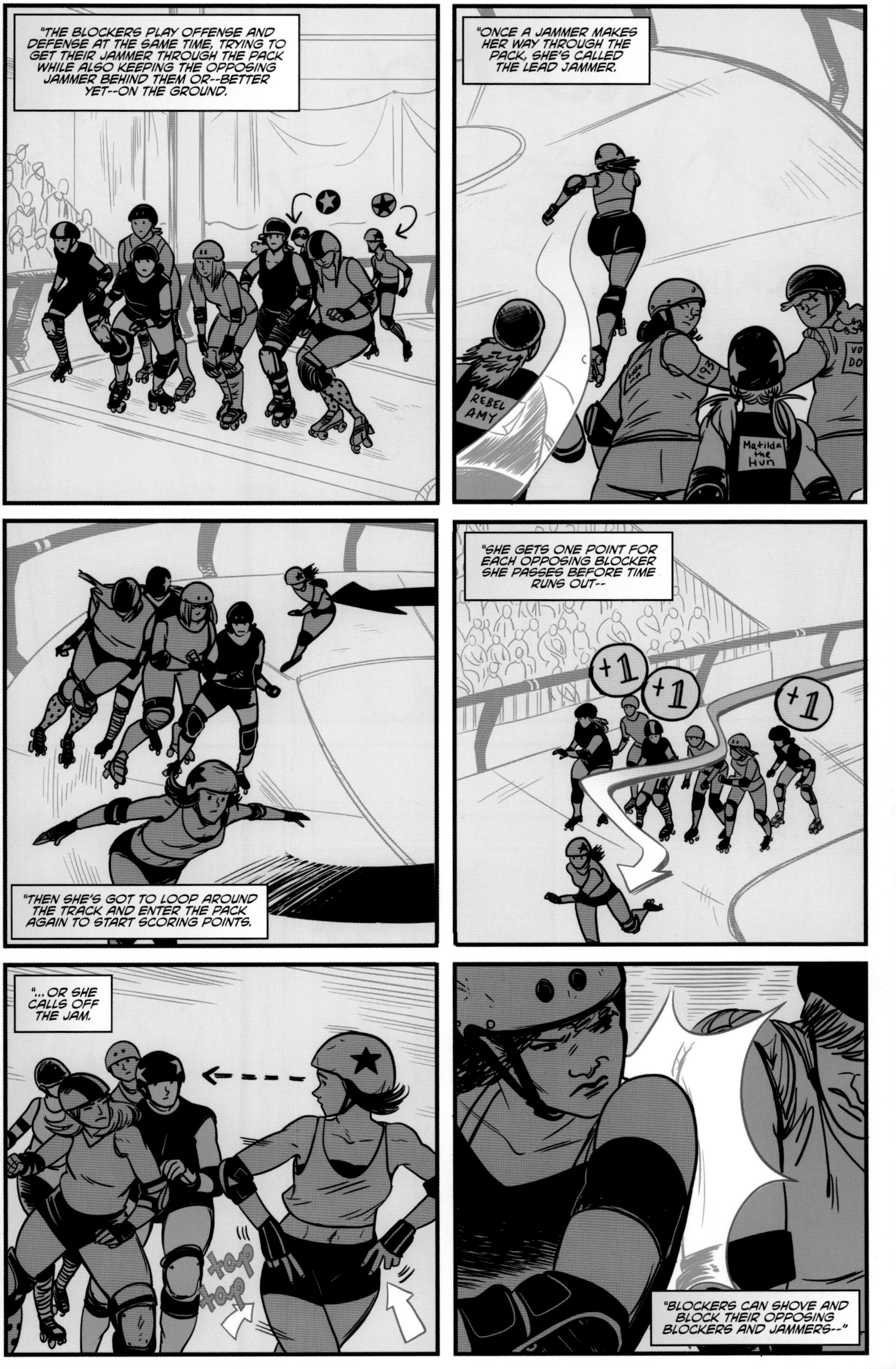
"THE BLOCKERS PLAY OFFENSE AND DEFENSE AT THE SAME TIME, TRYING TO GET THEIR JAMMER THROUGH THE PACK WHILE ALSO KEEPING THE OPPOSING JAMMER BEHIND THEM OR--BETTER YET--ON THE GROUND.
"ONCE A JAMMER MAKES HER WAY THROUGH THE PACK, SHE'S CALLED THE LEAD JAMMER.
REBEL AMY
Matilda the Hun
"THEN SHE'S GOT TO LOOP AROUND THE TRACK AND ENTER THE PACK AGAIN TO START SCORING POINTS.
"SHE GETS ONE POINT FOR EACH OPPOSING BLOCKER SHE PASSES BEFORE TIME RUNS OUT--
+1
+1
+1
"...OR SHE CALLS OFF THE JAM.
"BLOCKERS CAN SHOVE AND BLOCK THEIR OPPOSING BLOCKERS AND JAMMERS--"

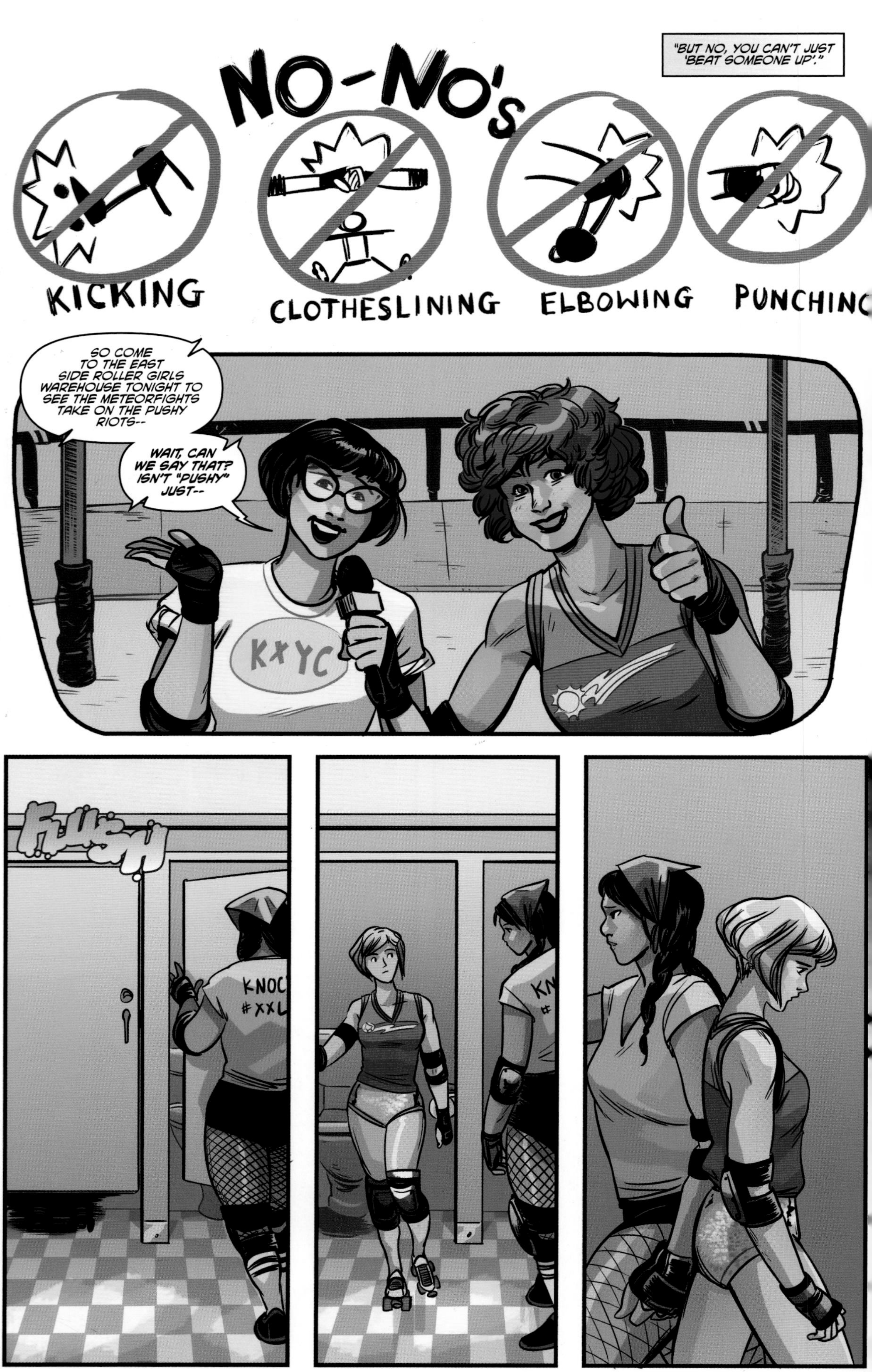
"BUT NO, YOU CAN'T JUST 'BEAT SOMEONE UP'."
NO-NO'S
KICKING
CLOTHESLINING
ELBOWING
PUNCHING
SO COME TO THE EAST SIDE ROLLER GIRLS WAREHOUSE TONIGHT TO SEE THE METEORFIGHTS TAKE ON THE PUSHY RIOTS--
WAIT, CAN WE SAY THAT? ISN'T "PUSHY" JUST--
KXYC
FLUSH

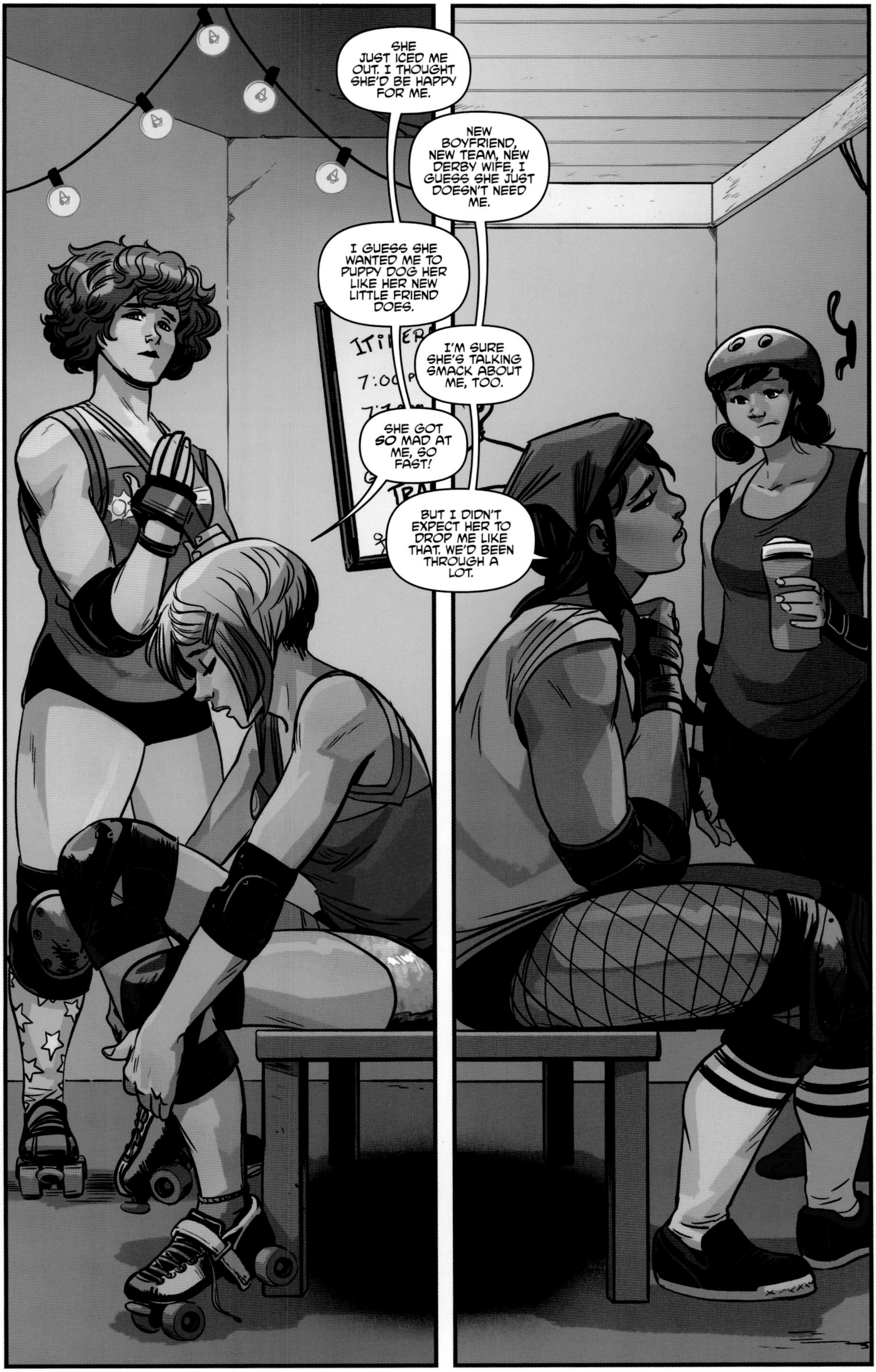
SHE JUST ICED ME OUT. I THOUGHT SHE'D BE HAPPY FOR ME.
NEW BOYFRIEND, NEW TEAM, NEW DERBY WIFE, I GUESS SHE JUST DOESN'T NEED ME.
I GUESS SHE WANTED ME TO PUPPY DOG HER LIKE HER NEW LITTLE FRIEND DOES.
I'M SURE SHE'S TALKING SMACK ABOUT ME, TOO.
SHE GOT SO MAD AT ME, SO FAST!
BUT I DIDN'T EXPECT HER TO DROP ME LIKE THAT. WE'D BEEN THROUGH A LOT.

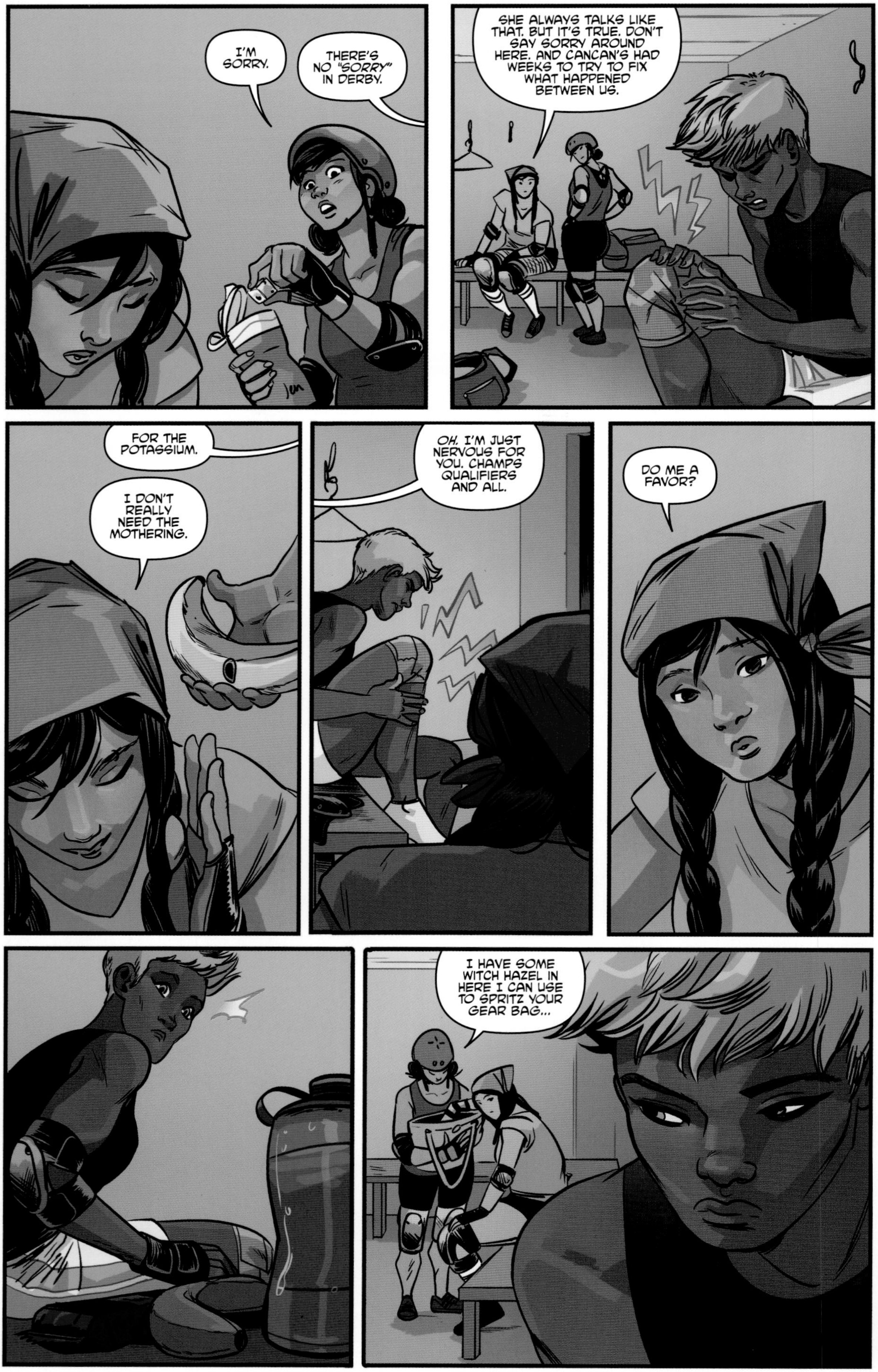
I'M SORRY.
THERE'S NO "SORRY" IN DERBY.
SHE ALWAYS TALKS LIKE THAT. BUT IT'S TRUE. DON'T SAY SORRY AROUND HERE. AND CANCAN'S HAD WEEKS TO TRY TO FIX WHAT HAPPENED BETWEEN US.
FOR THE POTASSIUM.
I DON'T REALLY NEED THE MOTHERING.
OH. I'M JUST NERVOUS FOR YOU. CHAMPS QUALIFIERS AND ALL.
DO ME A FAVOR?
I HAVE SOME WITCH HAZEL IN HERE I CAN USE TO SPRITZ YOUR GEAR BAG...

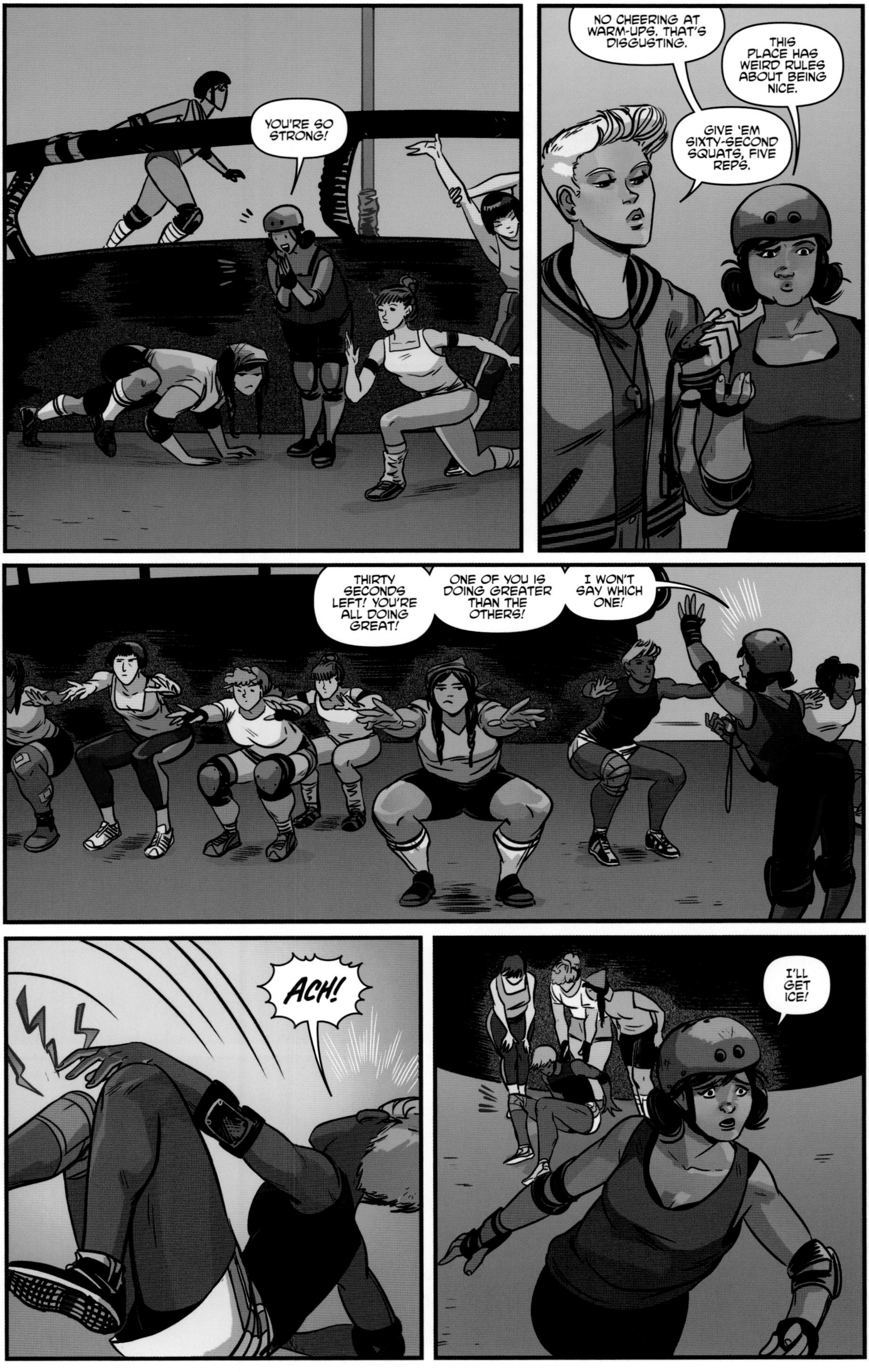
YOU'RE SO STRONG!
NO CHEERING AT WARM-UPS. THAT'S DISGUSTING.
THIS PLACE HAS WEIRD RULES ABOUT BEING NICE.
GIVE 'EM SIXTY-SECOND SQUATS, FIVE REPS.
THIRTY SECONDS LEFT! YOU'RE ALL DOING GREAT!
ONE OF YOU IS DOING GREATER THAN THE OTHERS!
I WON'T SAY WHICH ONE!
ACH!
I'LL GET ICE!

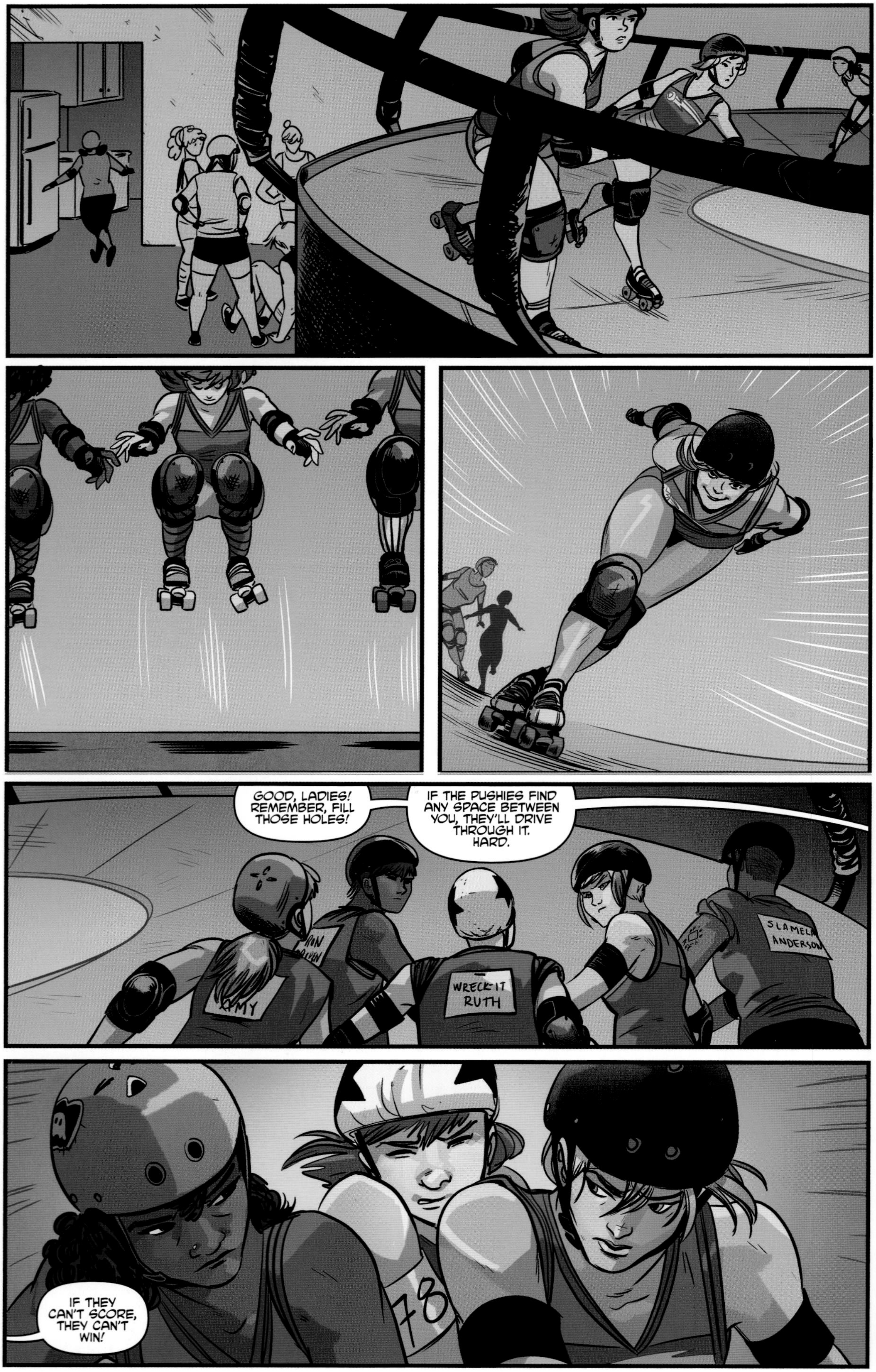
GOOD, LADIES! REMEMBER, FILL THOSE HOLES!
IF THE PUSHIES FIND ANY SPACE BETWEEN YOU, THEY'LL DRIVE THROUGH IT. HARD.
WRECK IT RUTH
78
IF THEY CAN'T SCORE, THEY CAN'T WIN!

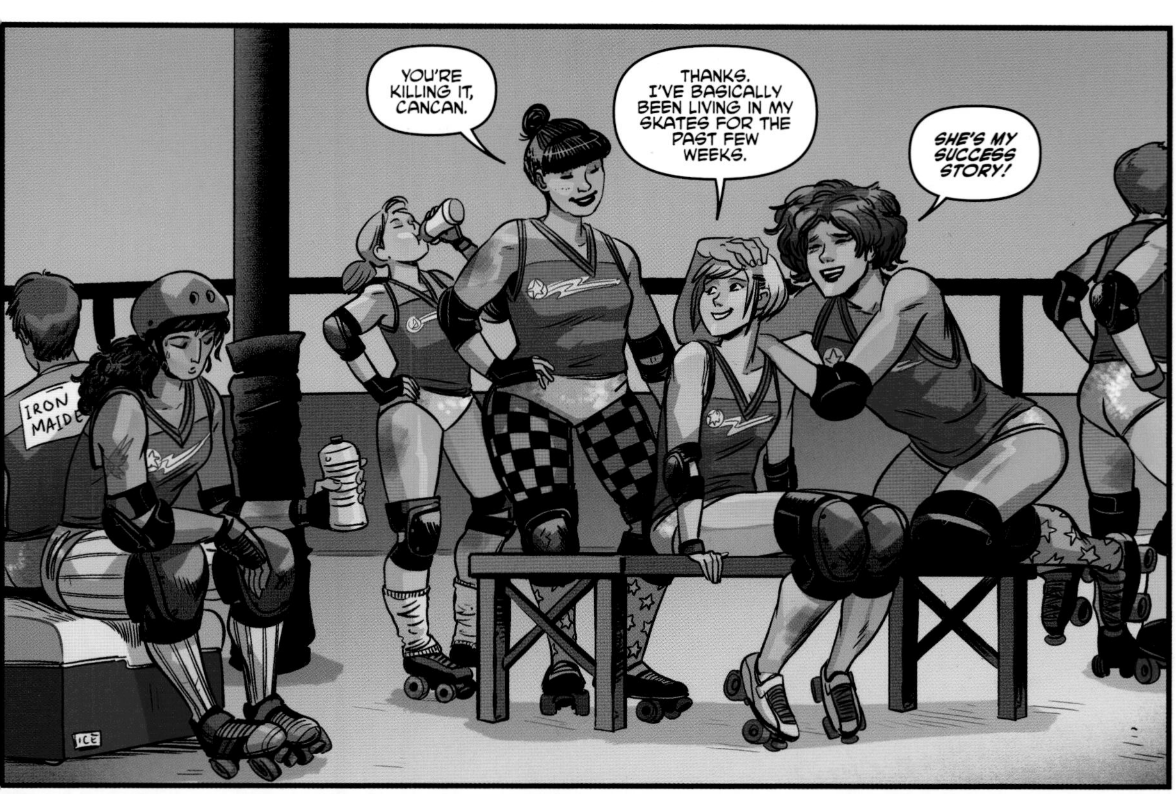
YOU'RE KILLING IT, CANCAN.
THANKS. I'VE BASICALLY BEEN LIVING IN MY SKATES FOR THE PAST FEW WEEKS.
SHE'S MY SUCCESS STORY!
IRON MAIDE
ICE

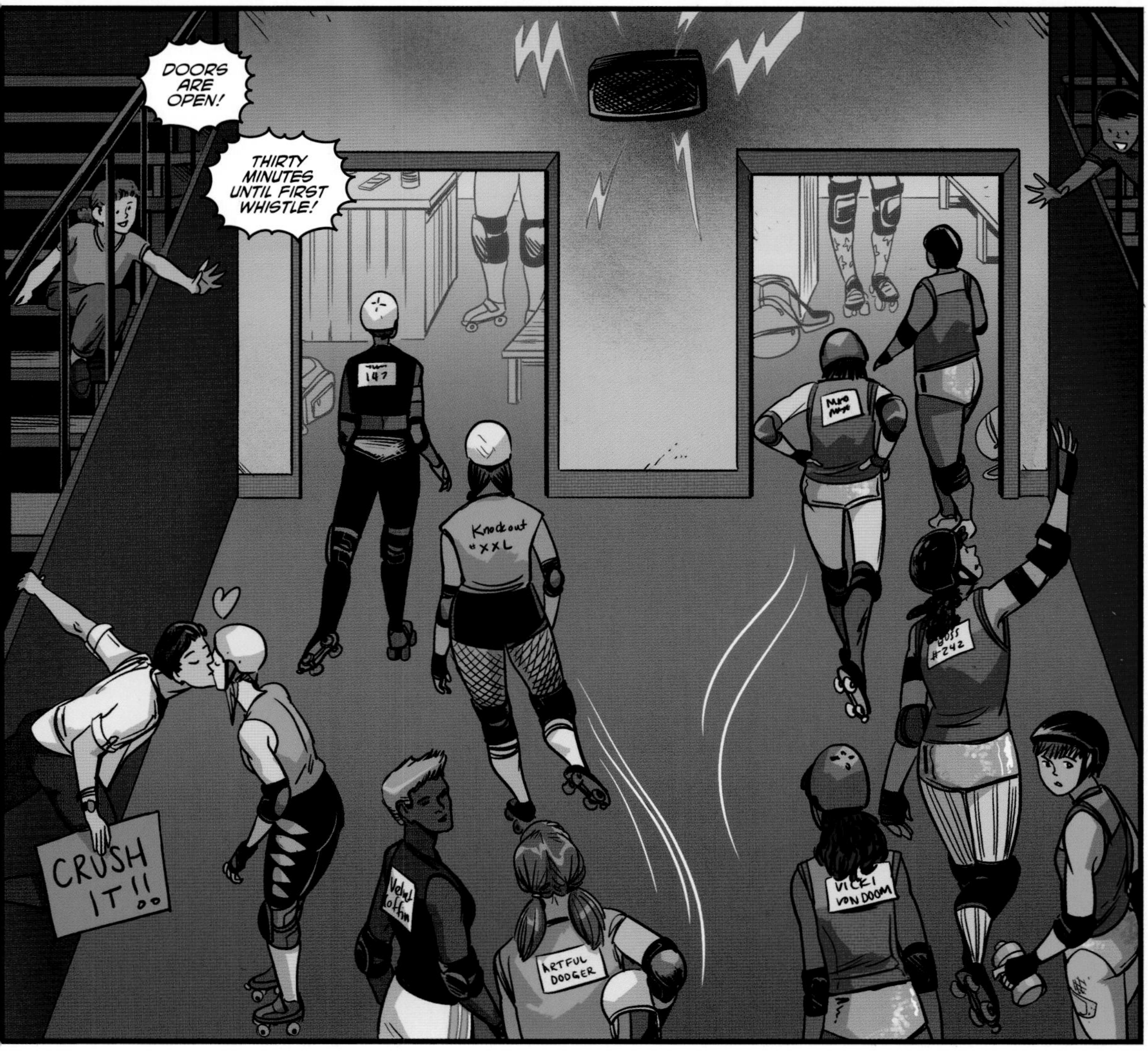
DOORS ARE OPEN!
THIRTY MINUTES UNTIL FIRST WHISTLE!
Knockout #XXL
CRUSH IT!!
ARTFUL DODGER
VICKI VON DOOM

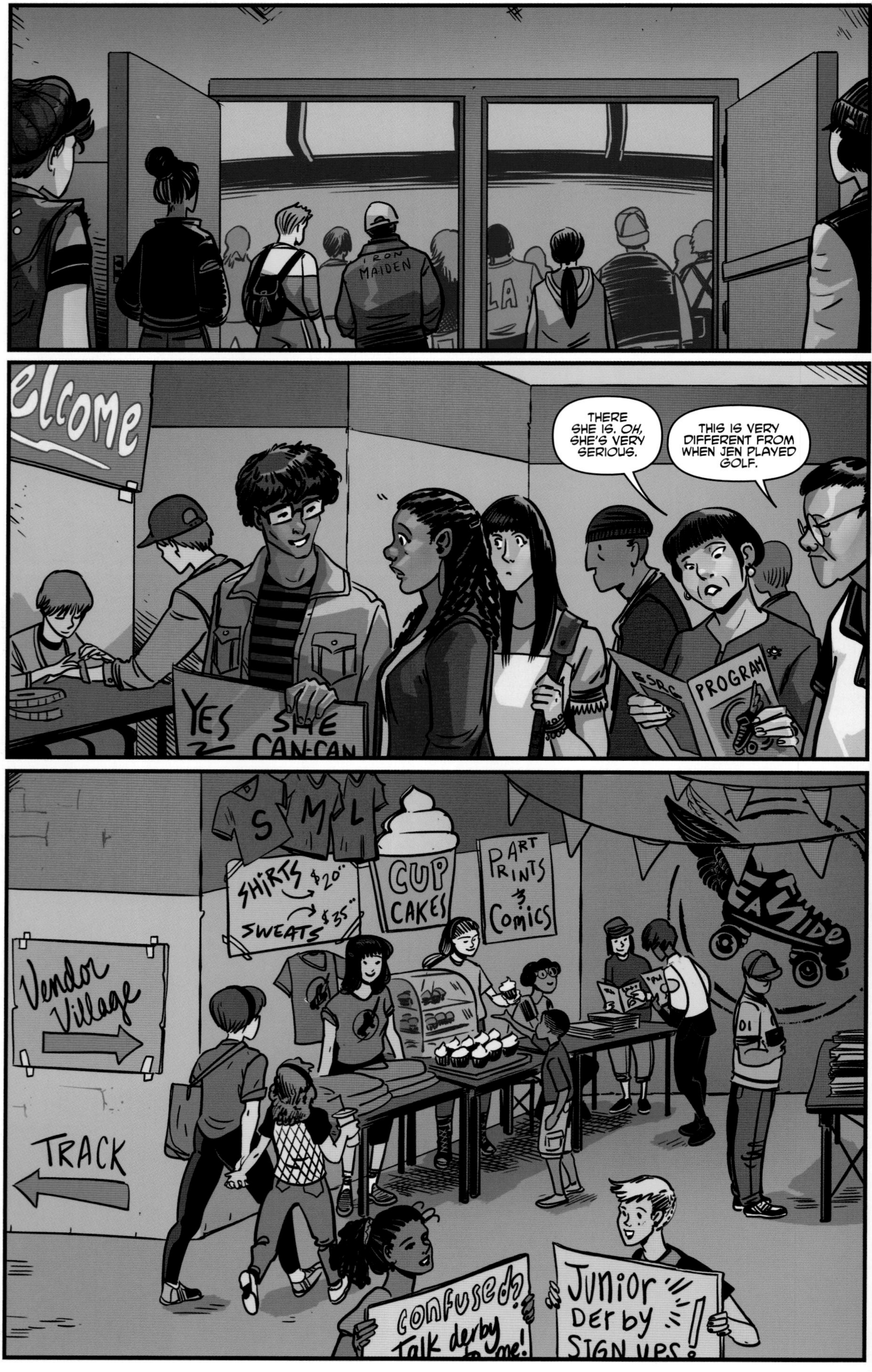
IRON MAIDEN
LA
elcome
THERE SHE IS. OH, SHE'S VERY SERIOUS.
THIS IS VERY DIFFERENT FROM WHEN JEN PLAYED GOLF.
YES SHE CAN-CAN
ESRC
PROGRAM
S M L
SHIRTS $20
SWEATS $35
CUP CAKES
ART PRINTS & COMICS
Vendor Village
TRACK
confused? Talk derby to me!
Junior Derby SIGN UPS!

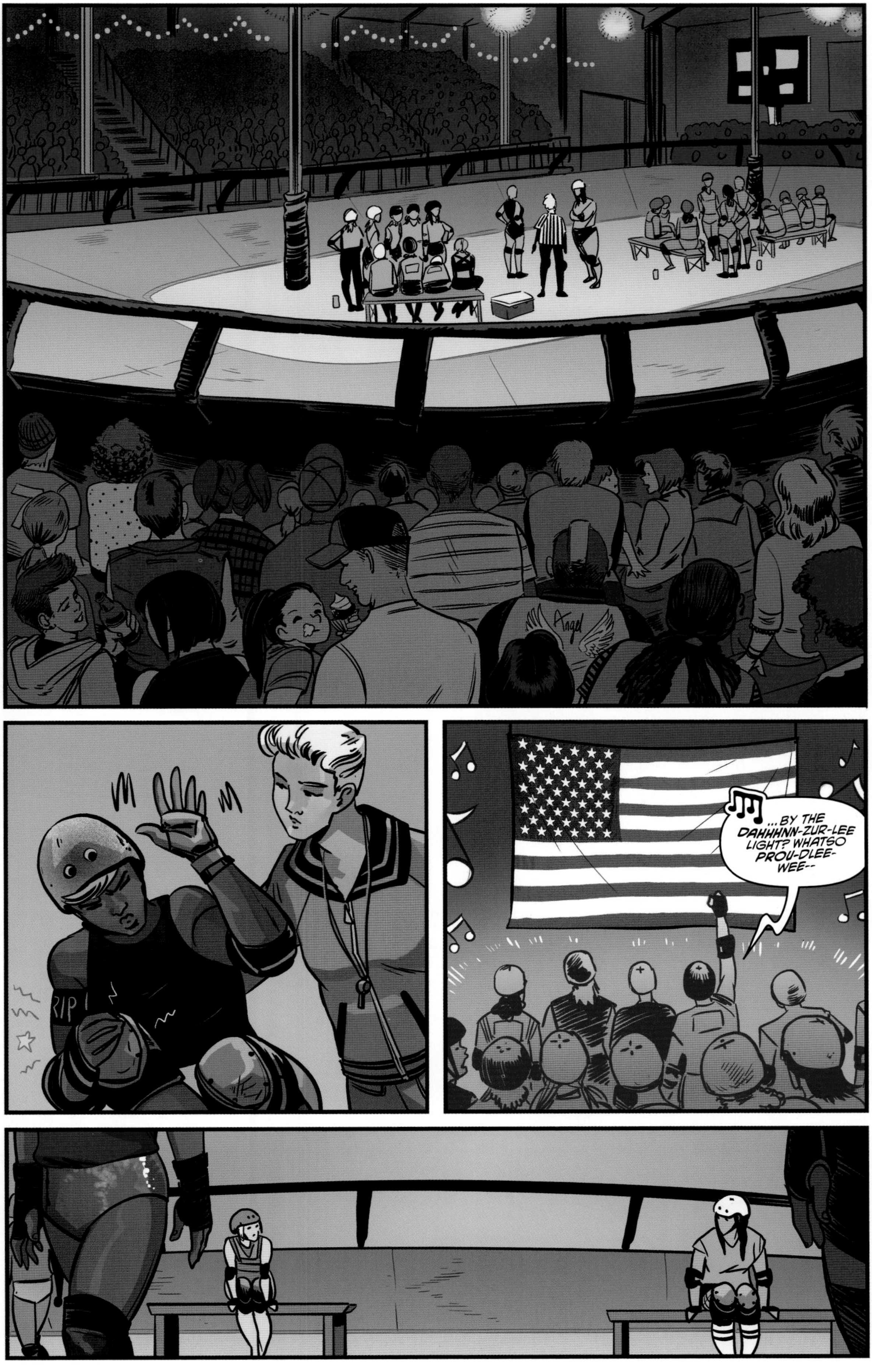
Angel
RIP
...BY THE DAHHHNN-ZUR-LEE LIGHT? WHATSO PROU-DLEE-WEE--

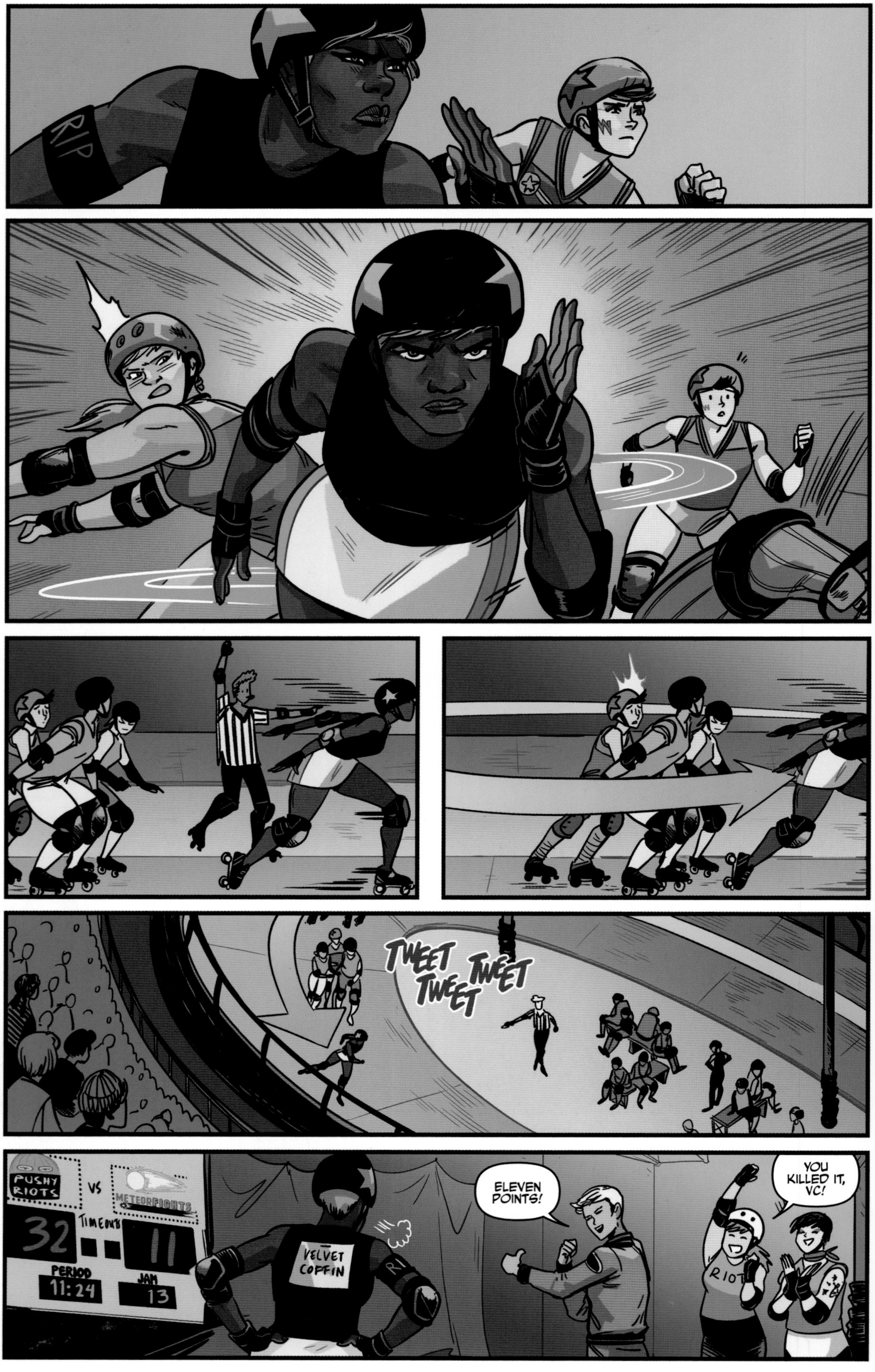
TWEET TWEET TWEET
PUSHY RIOTS
VS
METEORFIGHTS
32
TIMEOUTS
11
PERIOD
11:24
JAM
13
VELVET COFFIN
ELEVEN POINTS!
YOU KILLED IT, VC!

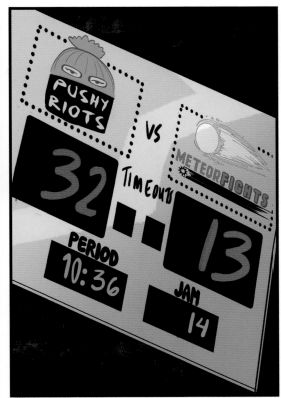

PUSHY RIOTS VS METEOR FIGHTS

32 TIMEOUT 13

PERIOD 10:36   JAM 14

SHE'S REALLY GOTTEN BETTER.

YEAH.

SHE WORKED REALLY HARD.

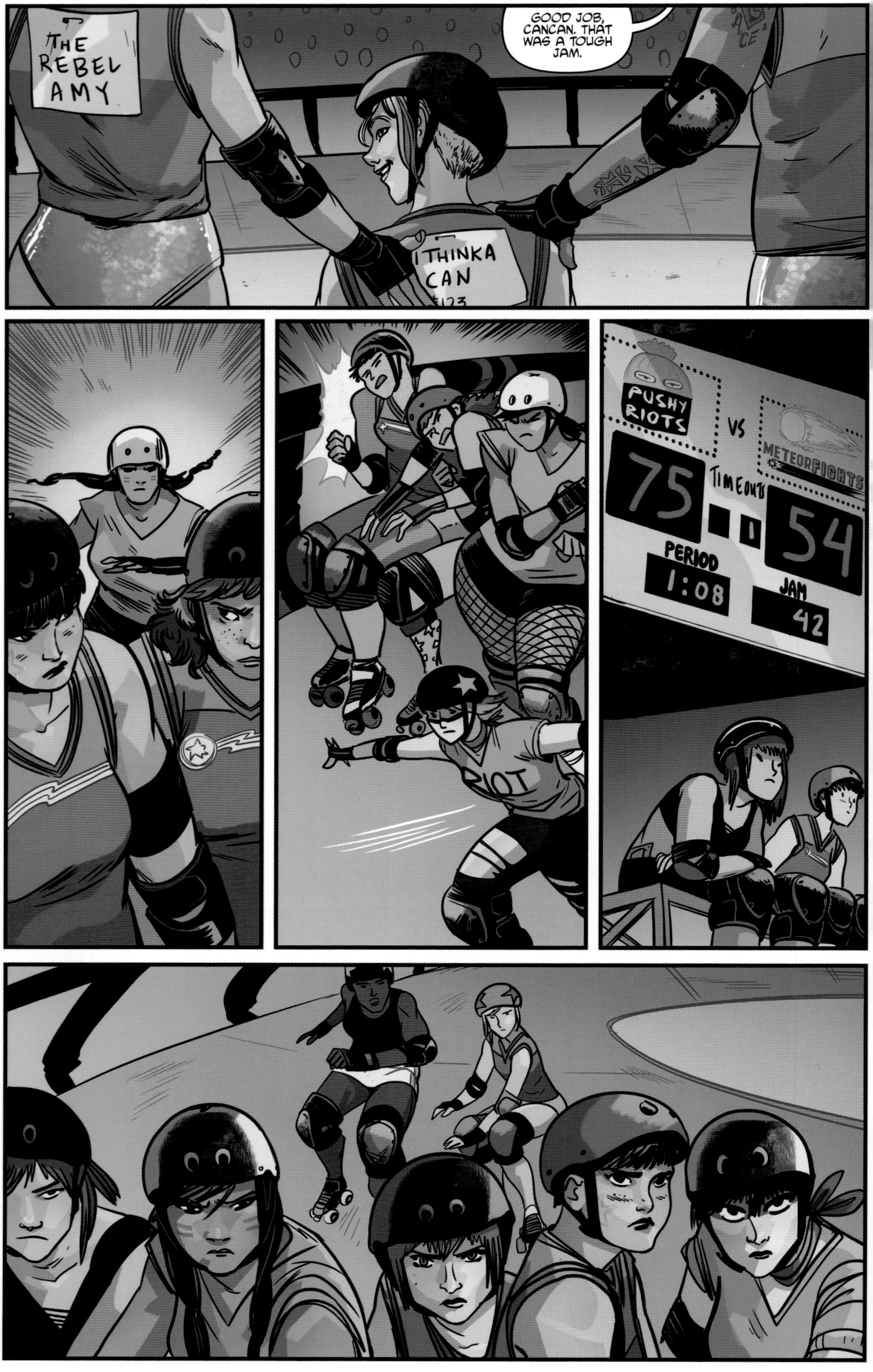

THE REBEL AMY
GOOD JOB, CANCAN. THAT WAS A TOUGH JAM.
ITHINKA CAN
PUSHY RIOTS
VS
METEORFIGHTS
75
TIMEOUTS
54
PERIOD
1:08
JAM
42
RIOT

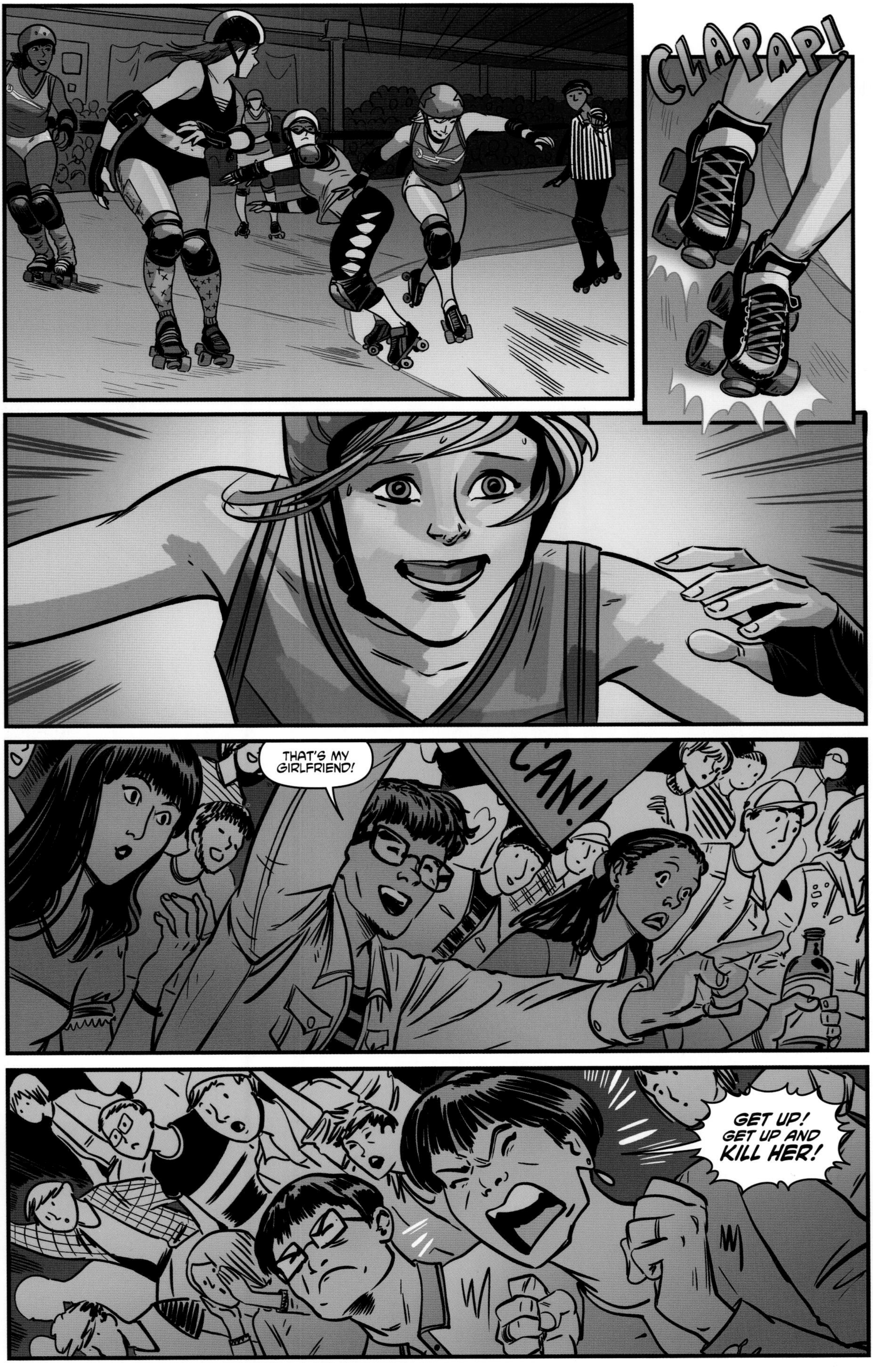
CLAPAP!
THAT'S MY GIRLFRIEND!
CAN!
GET UP! GET UP AND KILL HER!

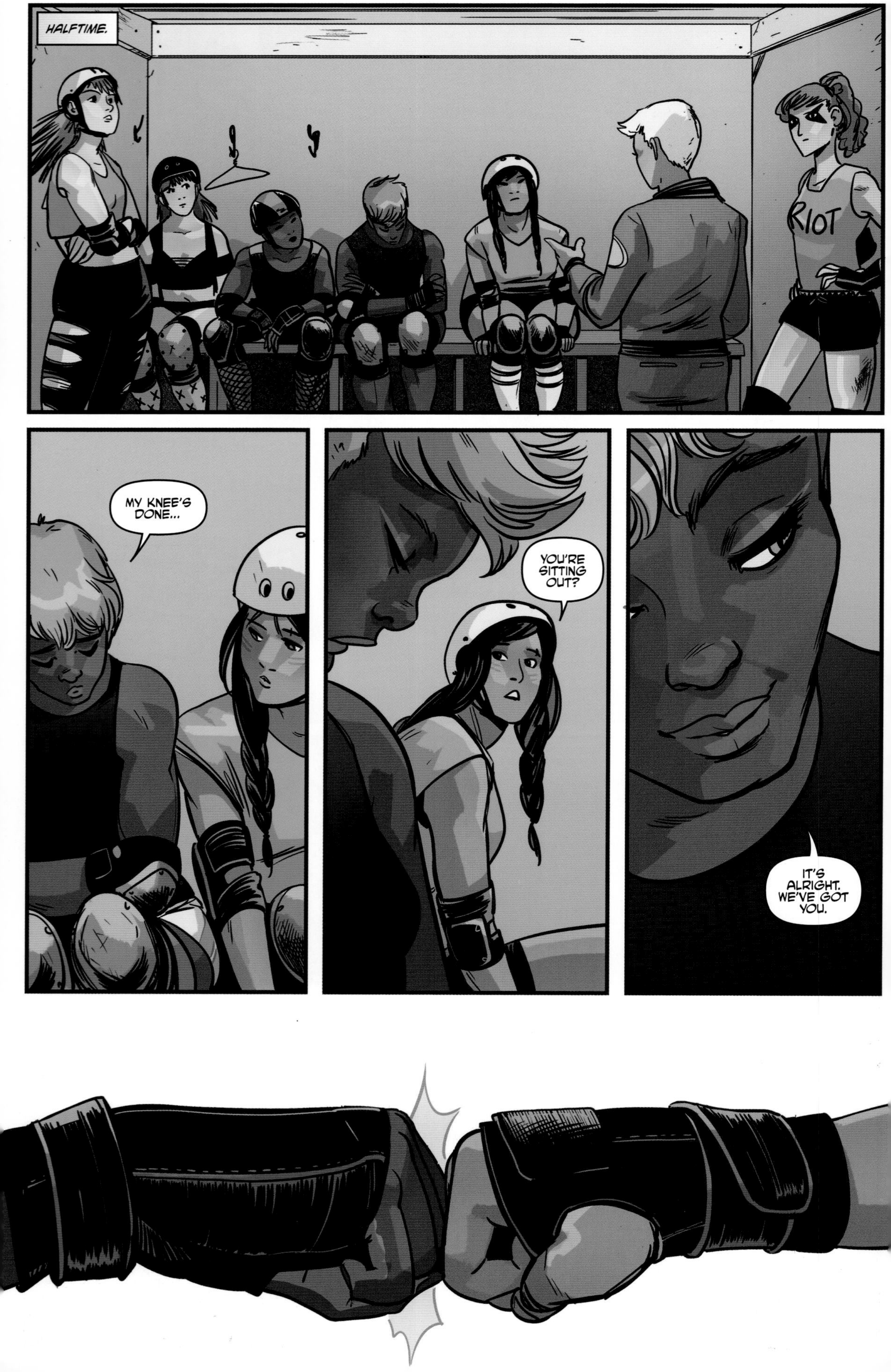
HALFTIME.
RIOT
MY KNEE'S DONE...
YOU'RE SITTING OUT?
IT'S ALRIGHT. WE'VE GOT YOU.

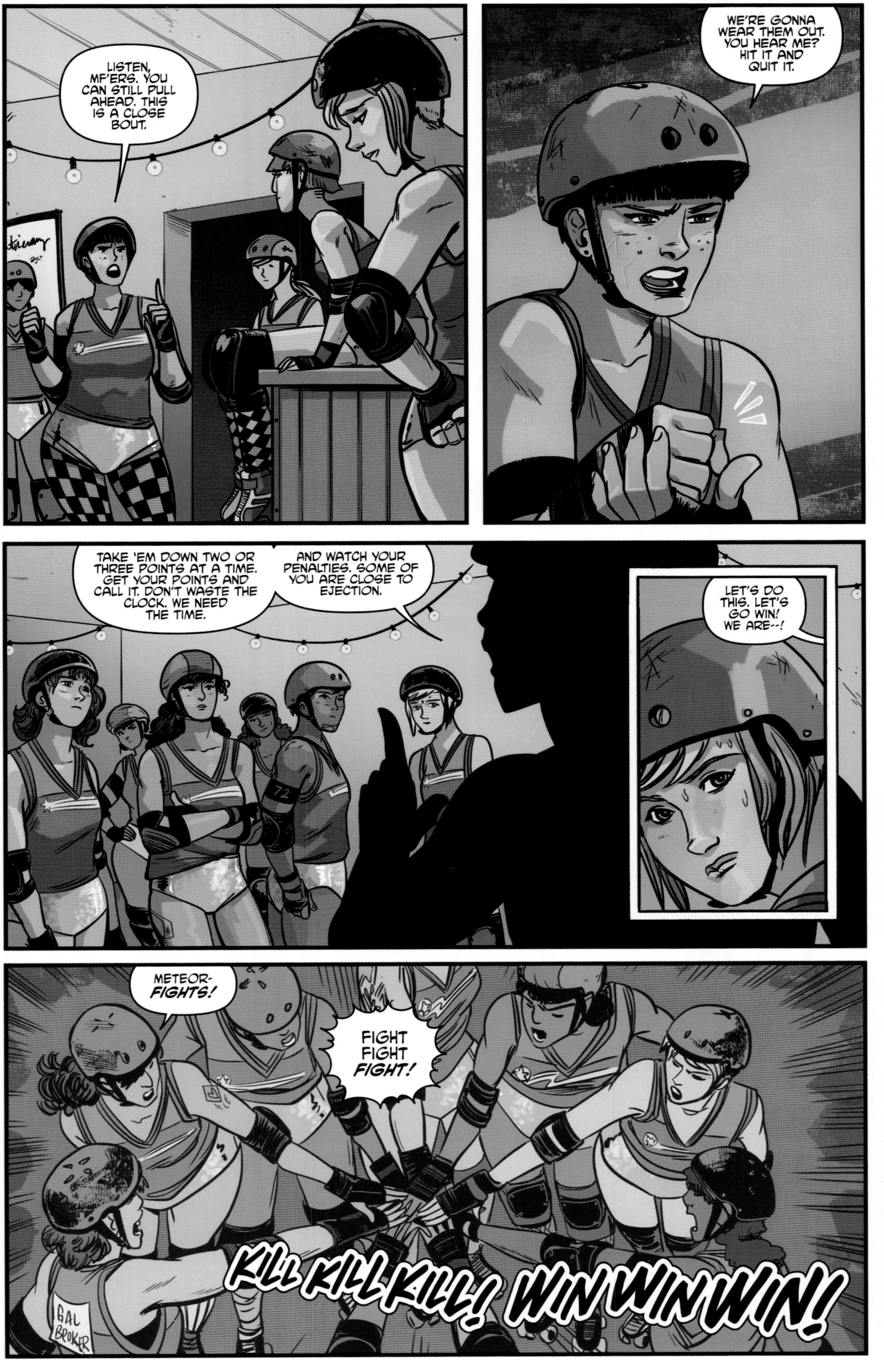

LISTEN, MF'ERS. YOU CAN STILL PULL AHEAD. THIS IS A CLOSE BOUT.
WE'RE GONNA WEAR THEM OUT. YOU HEAR ME? HIT IT AND QUIT IT.
TAKE 'EM DOWN TWO OR THREE POINTS AT A TIME. GET YOUR POINTS AND CALL IT. DON'T WASTE THE CLOCK. WE NEED THE TIME.
AND WATCH YOUR PENALTIES. SOME OF YOU ARE CLOSE TO EJECTION.
LET'S DO THIS. LET'S GO WIN! WE ARE--!
METEOR-FIGHTS!
FIGHT FIGHT FIGHT!
KILL KILL KILL! WIN WIN WIN!
GAL BROKER

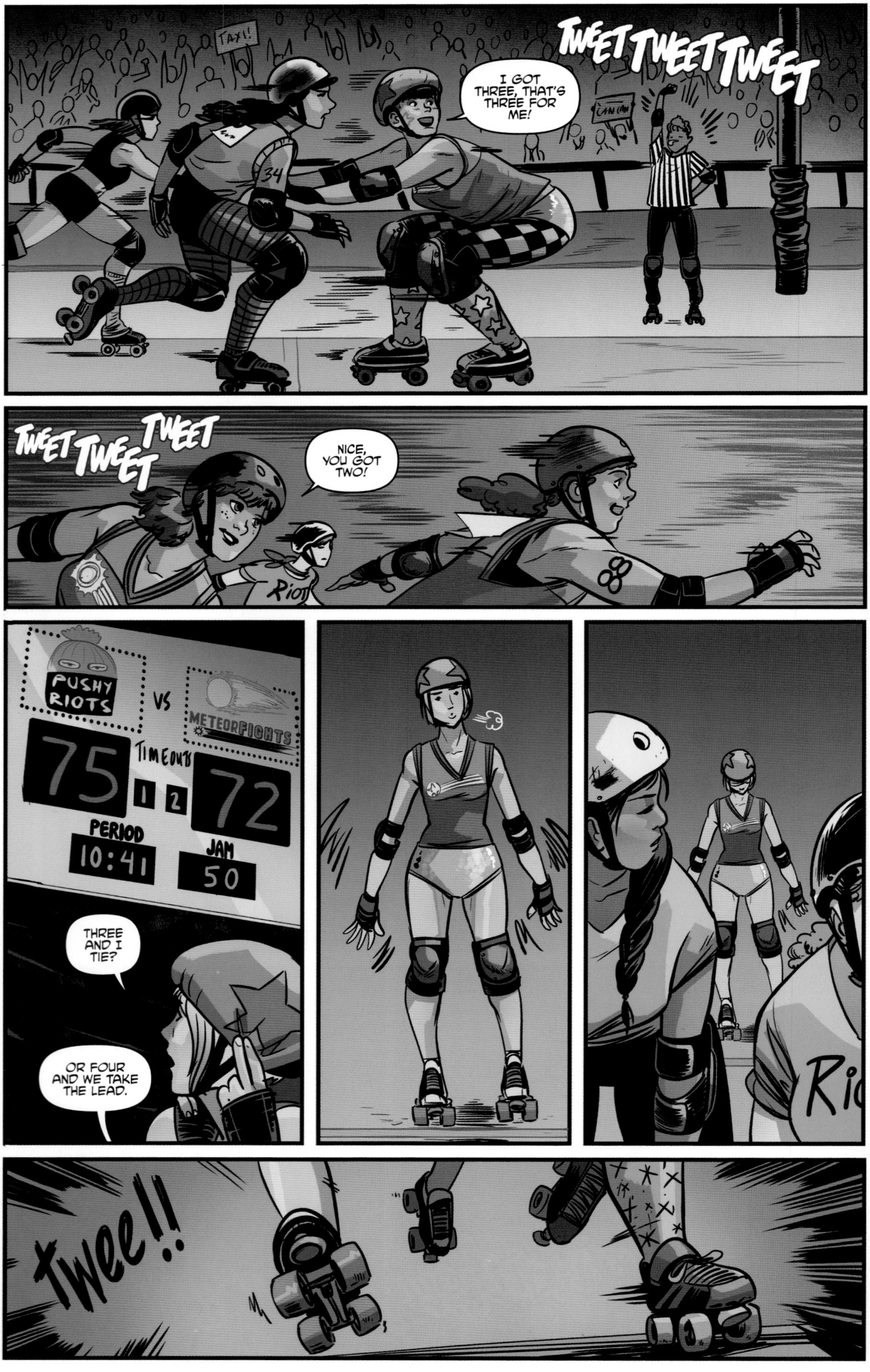
TAXI!
CAN CAN
I GOT THREE, THAT'S THREE FOR ME!
TWEET TWEET TWEET
34
TWEET TWEET TWEET
NICE, YOU GOT TWO!
RIOTS
88
PUSHY RIOTS
VS
METEORFIGHTS
75
TIMEOUTS
1 2
72
PERIOD
10:41
JAM
50
THREE AND I TIE?
OR FOUR AND WE TAKE THE LEAD.
Rio
TWEE!!

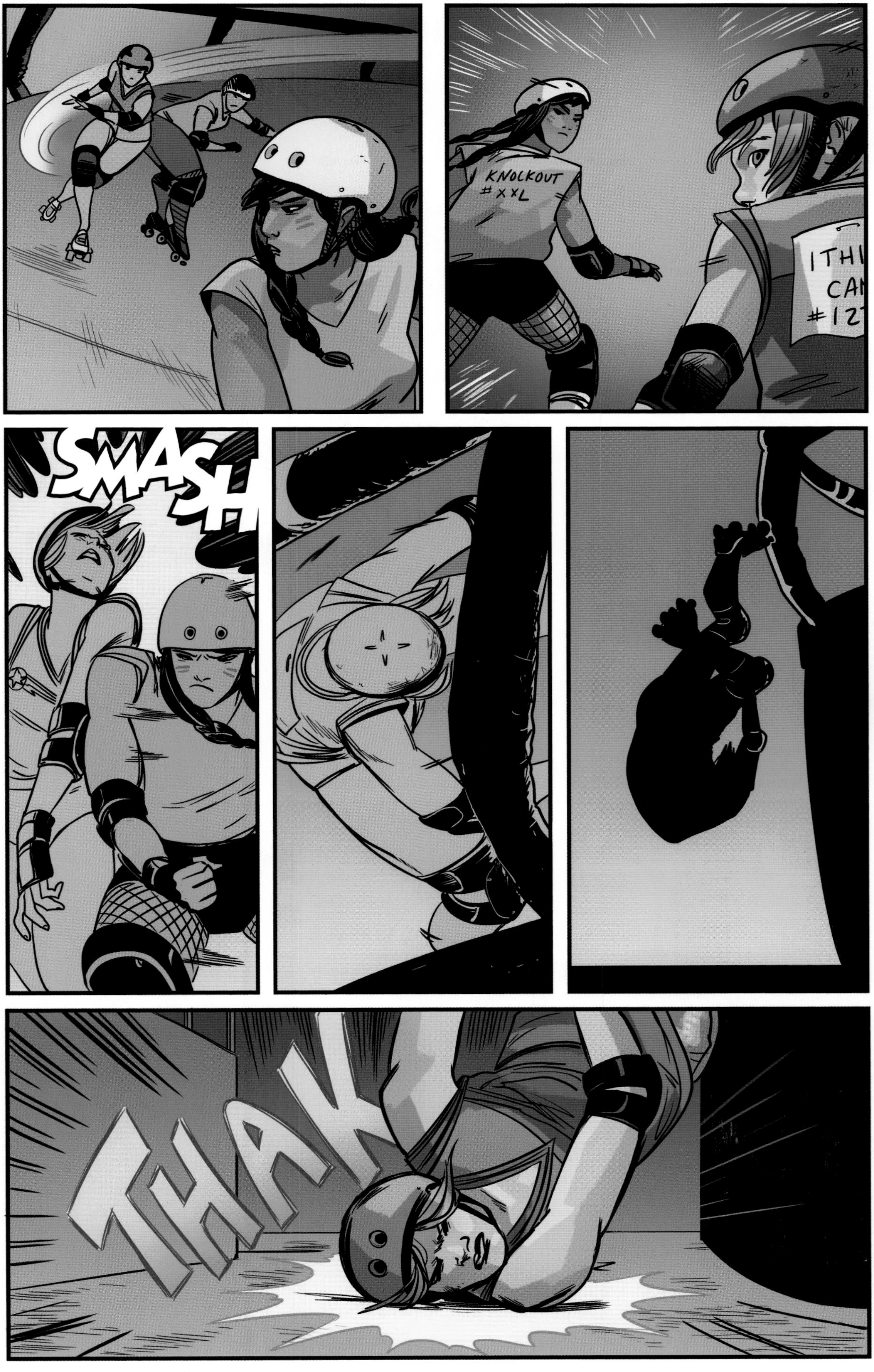
KNOCKOUT
#XXL
SMASH
THAK

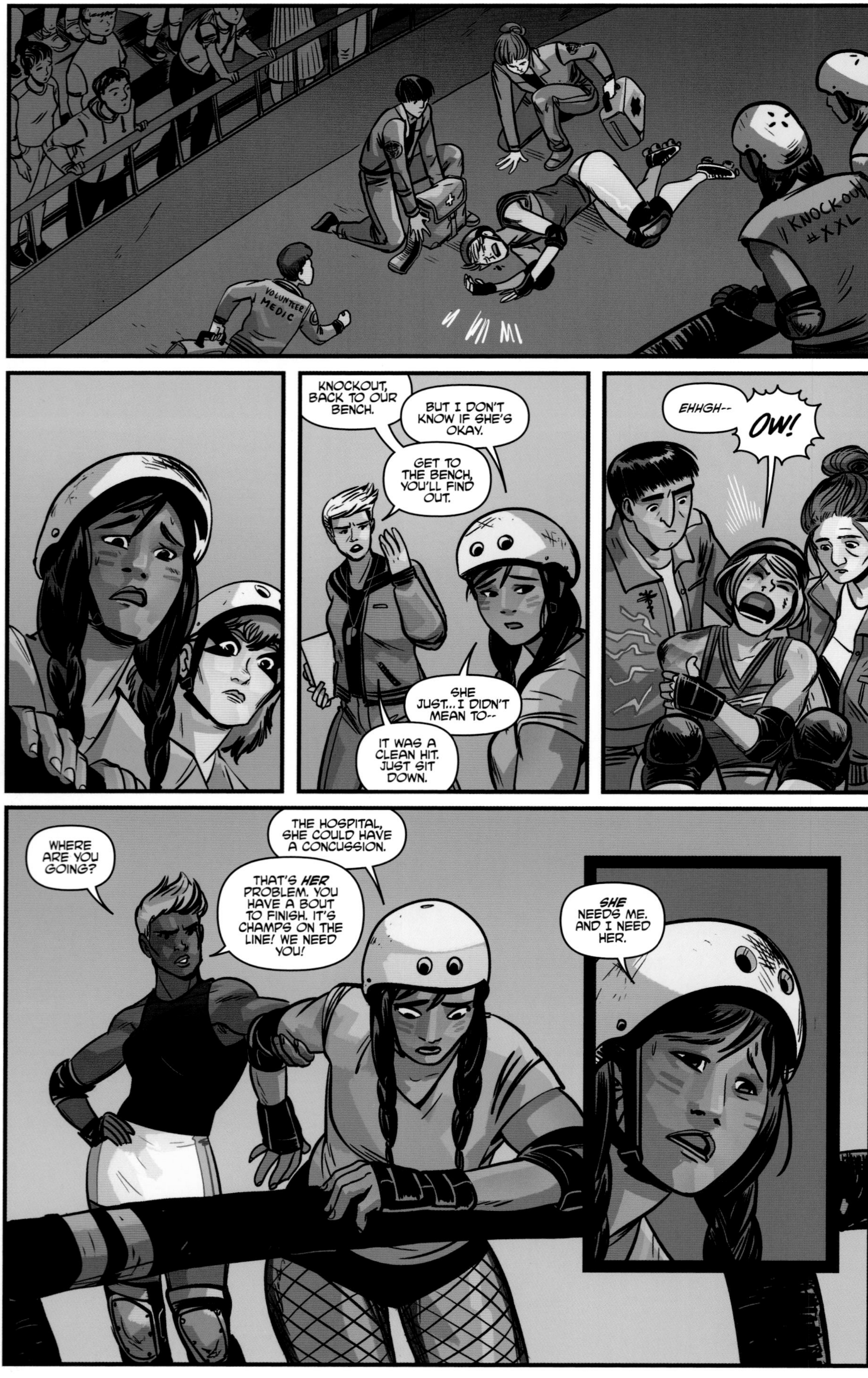
VOLUNTEER MEDIC
KNOCKOUT #XXL
KNOCKOUT, BACK TO OUR BENCH.
BUT I DON'T KNOW IF SHE'S OKAY.
GET TO THE BENCH, YOU'LL FIND OUT.
SHE JUST... I DIDN'T MEAN TO--
IT WAS A CLEAN HIT. JUST SIT DOWN.
EHHGH--
OW!
WHERE ARE YOU GOING?
THE HOSPITAL, SHE COULD HAVE A CONCUSSION.
THAT'S HER PROBLEM. YOU HAVE A BOUT TO FINISH. IT'S CHAMPS ON THE LINE! WE NEED YOU!
SHE NEEDS ME. AND I NEED HER.

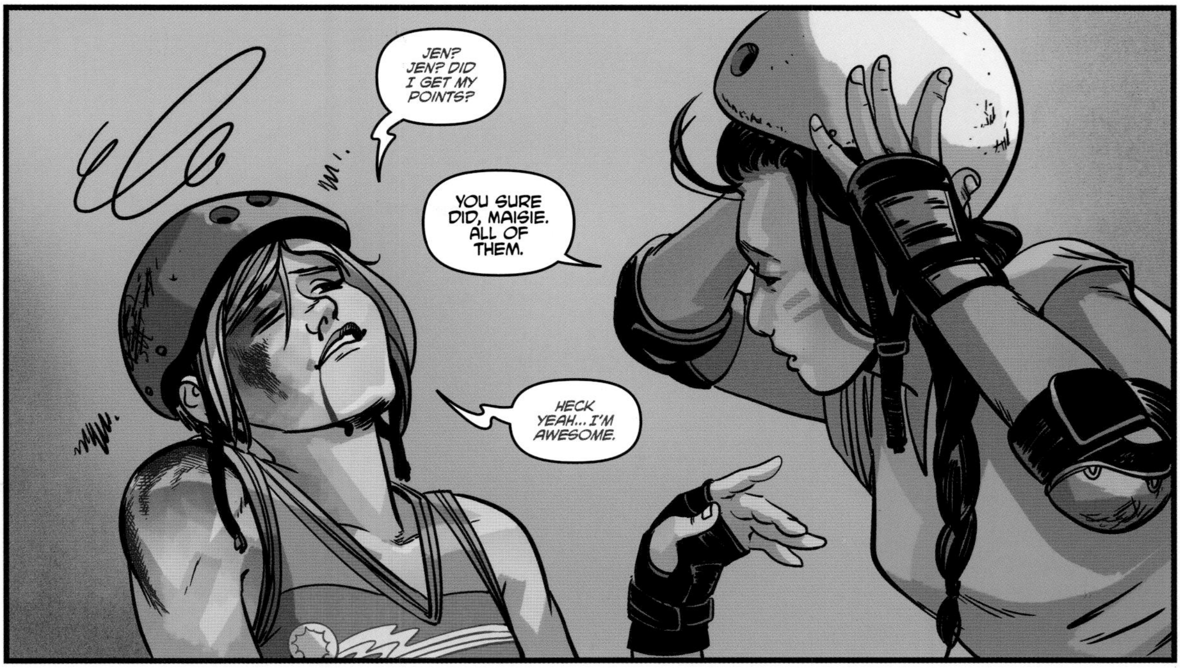
JEN? JEN? DID I GET MY POINTS?
YOU SURE DID, MAISIE. ALL OF THEM.
HECK YEAH... I'M AWESOME.

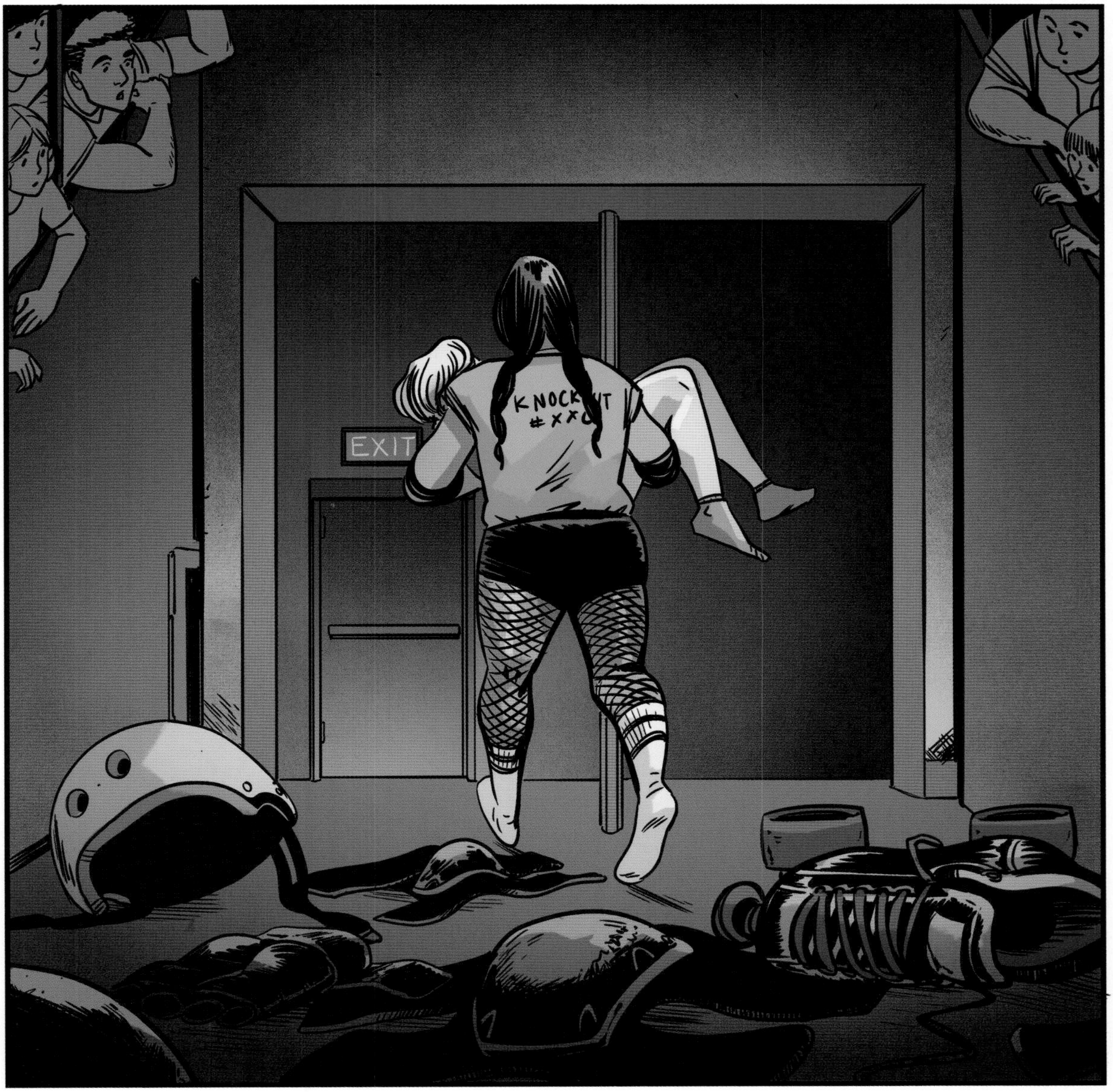
EXIT

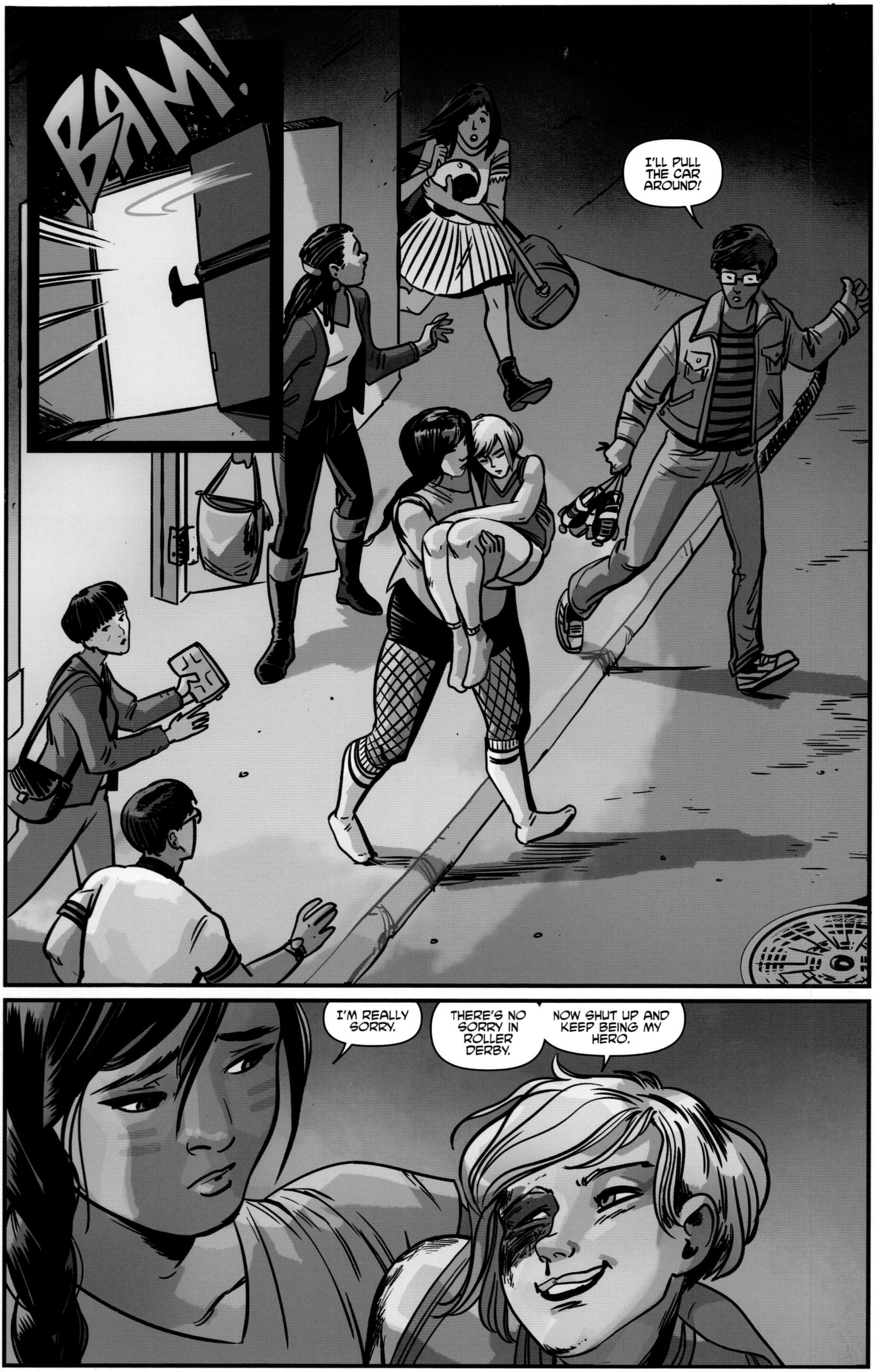
BAM!
I'LL PULL THE CAR AROUND!
I'M REALLY SORRY.
THERE'S NO SORRY IN ROLLER DERBY.
NOW SHUT UP AND KEEP BEING MY HERO.

ISSUE #1 MAIN COVER BY
VERONICA FISH

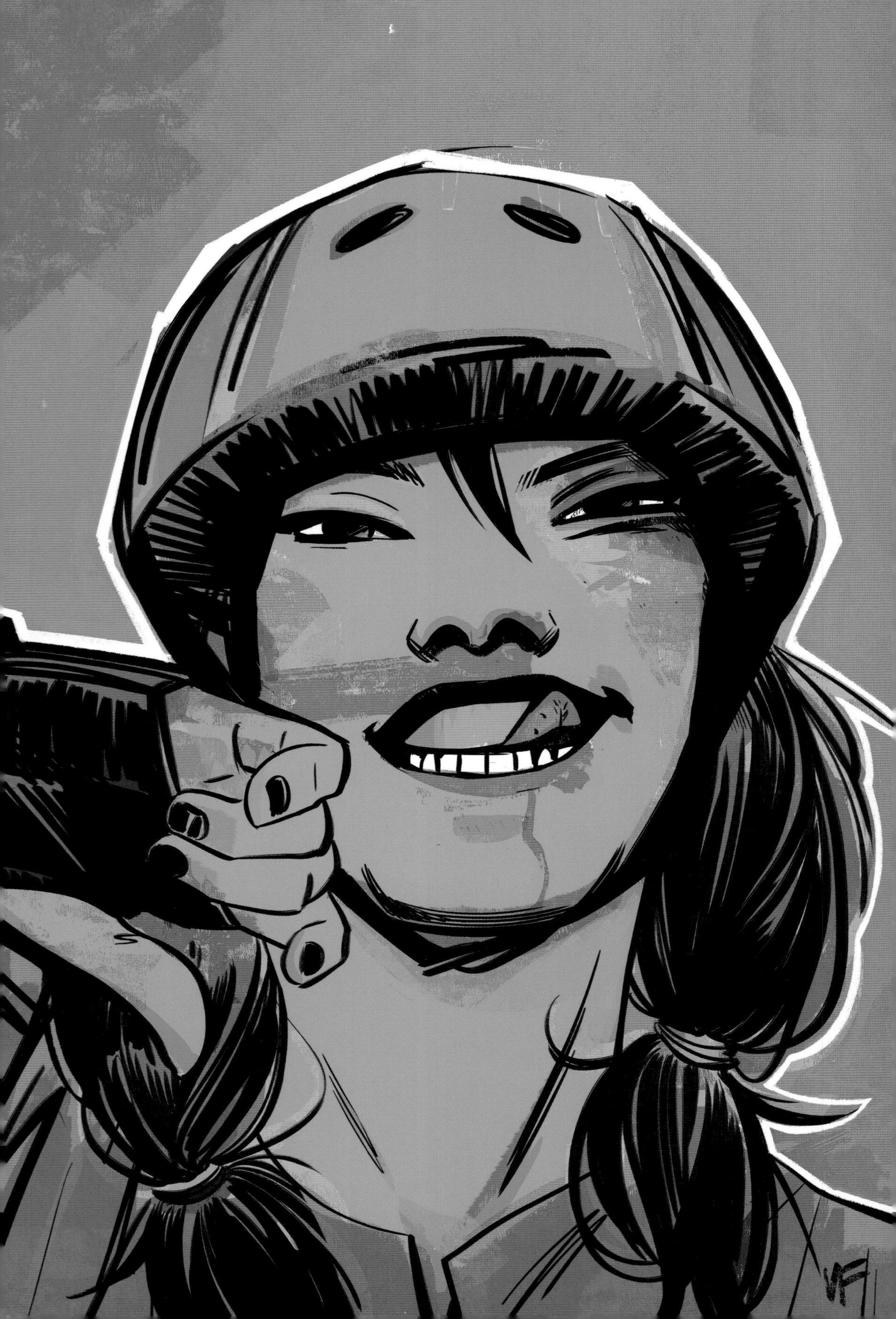
VF

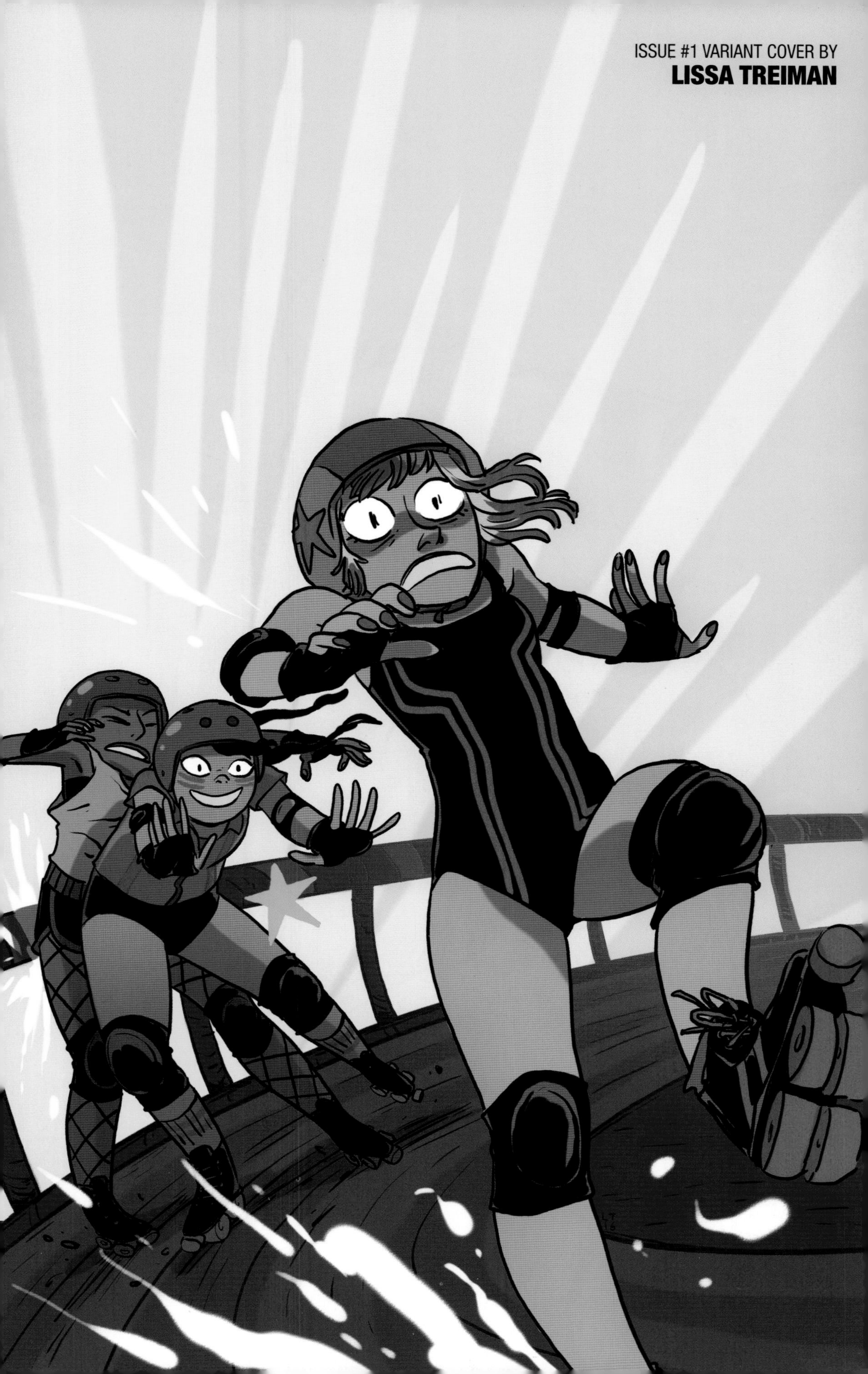

ISSUE #1 VARIANT COVER BY
LISSA TREIMAN

ISSUE #1 VARIANT COVER BY
JEN BARTEL

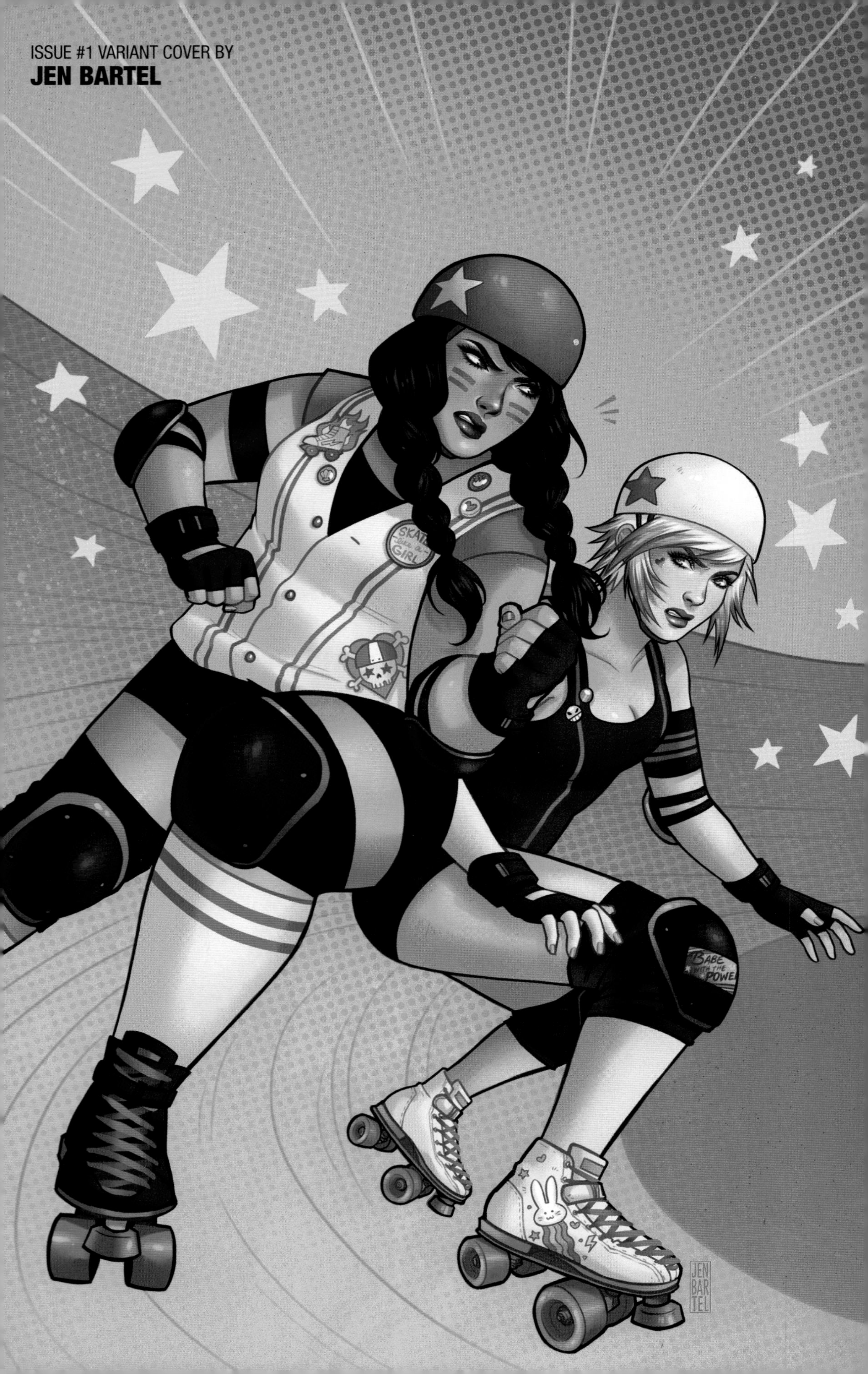
JEN BARTEL

ISSUE #1 SECOND PRINT COVER BY
VAUGHN PINPIN

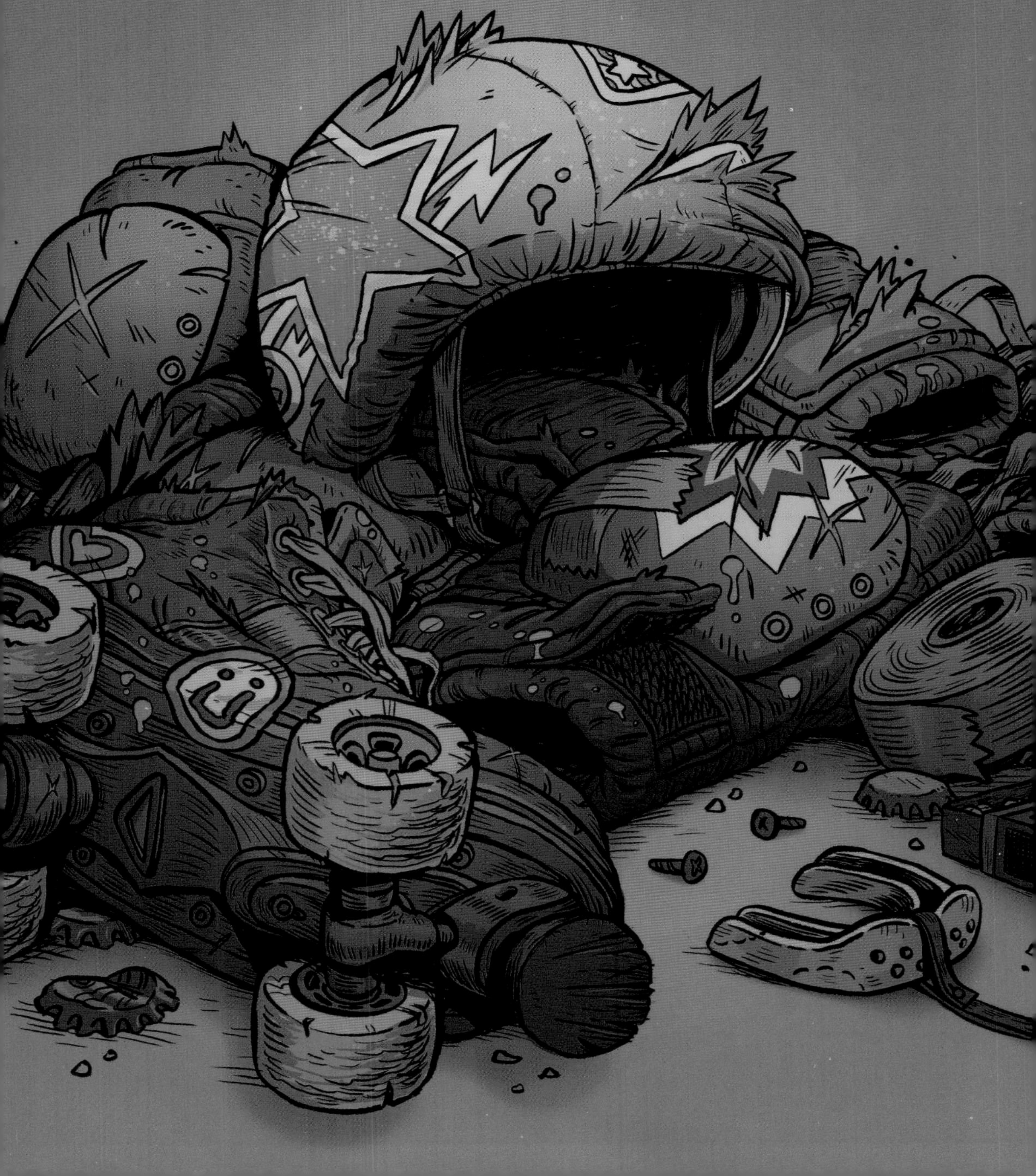

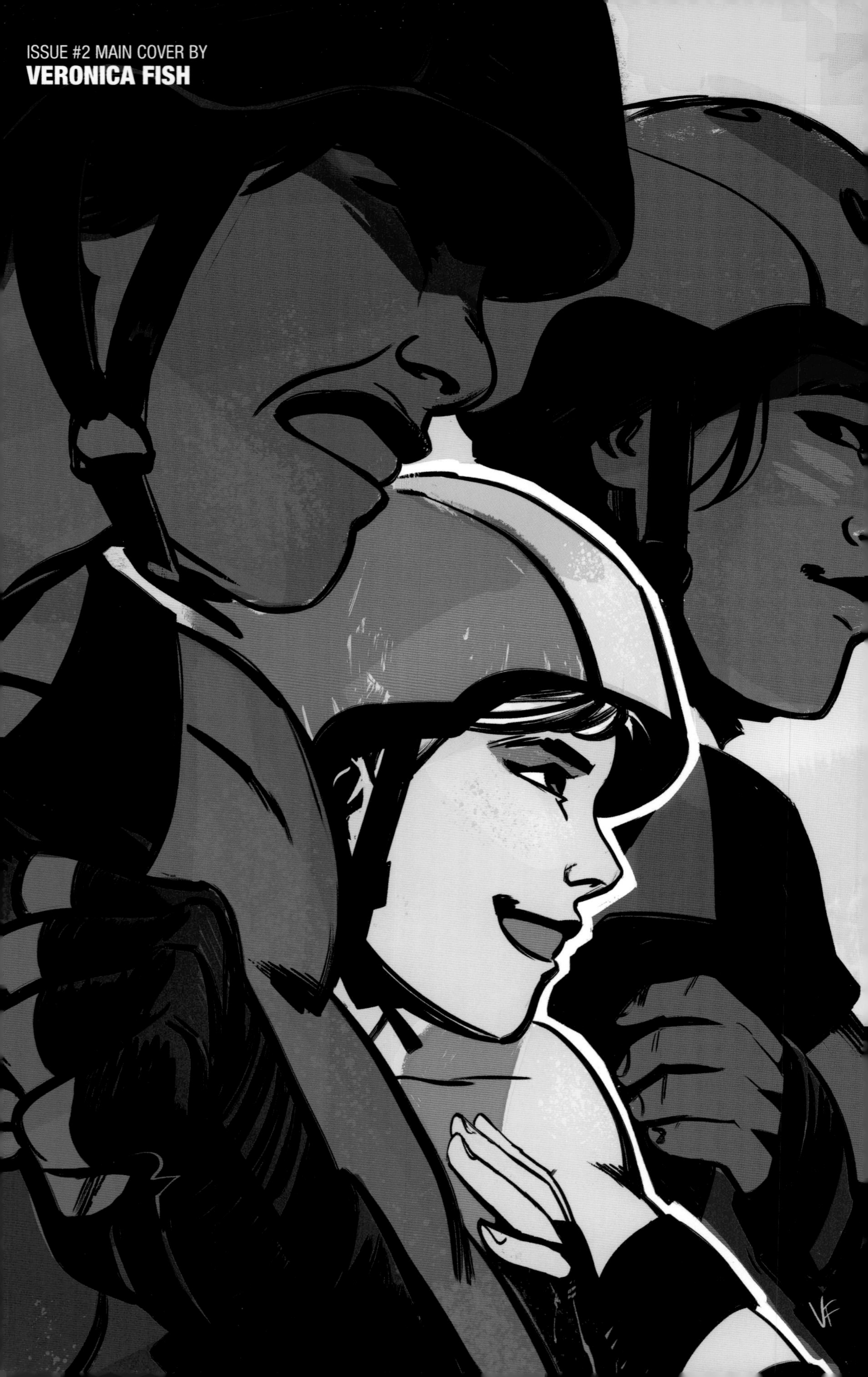

ISSUE #2 MAIN COVER BY
VERONICA FISH

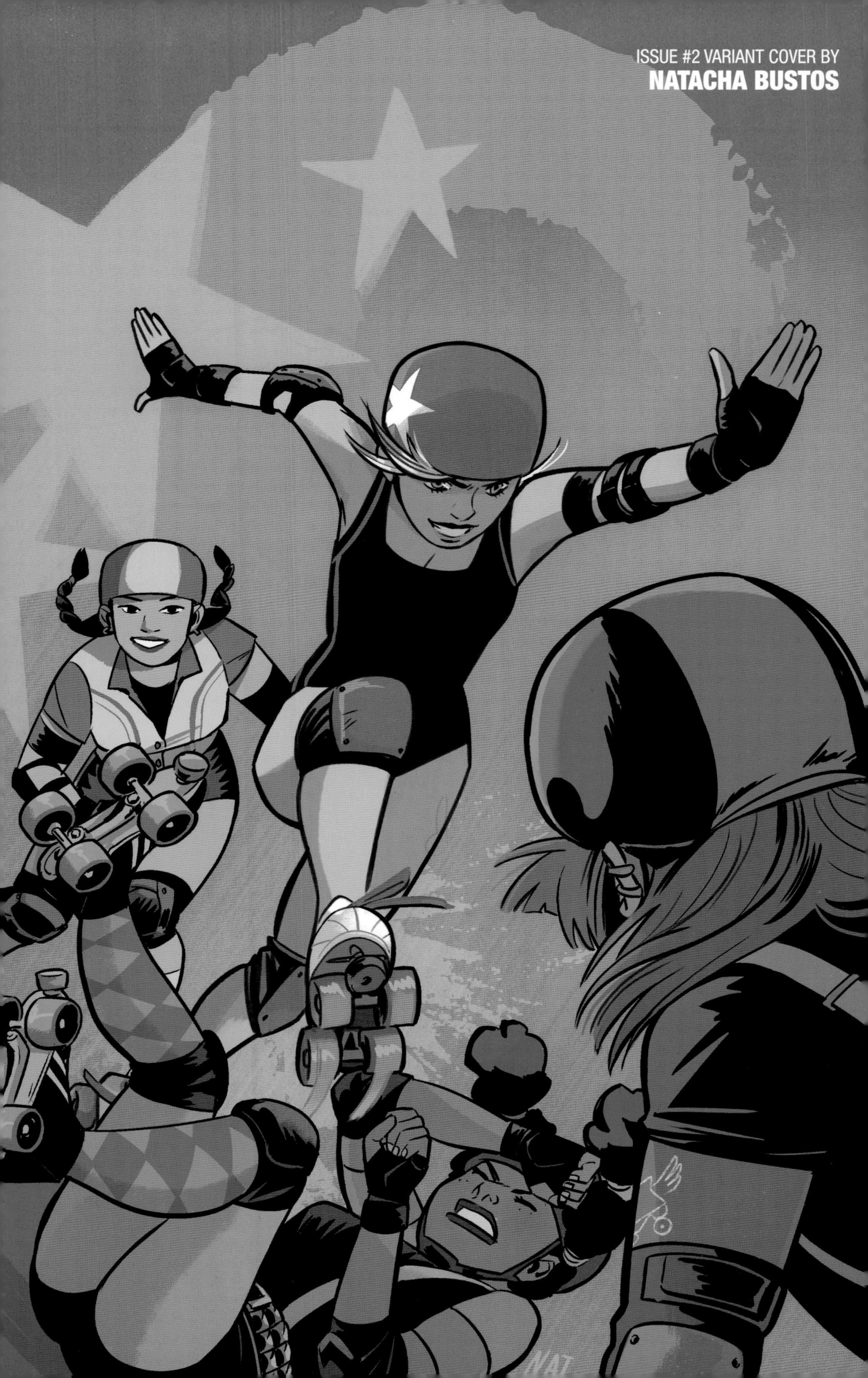

ISSUE #2 VARIANT COVER BY
NATACHA BUSTOS

ISSUE #3 MAIN COVER BY
VERONICA FISH

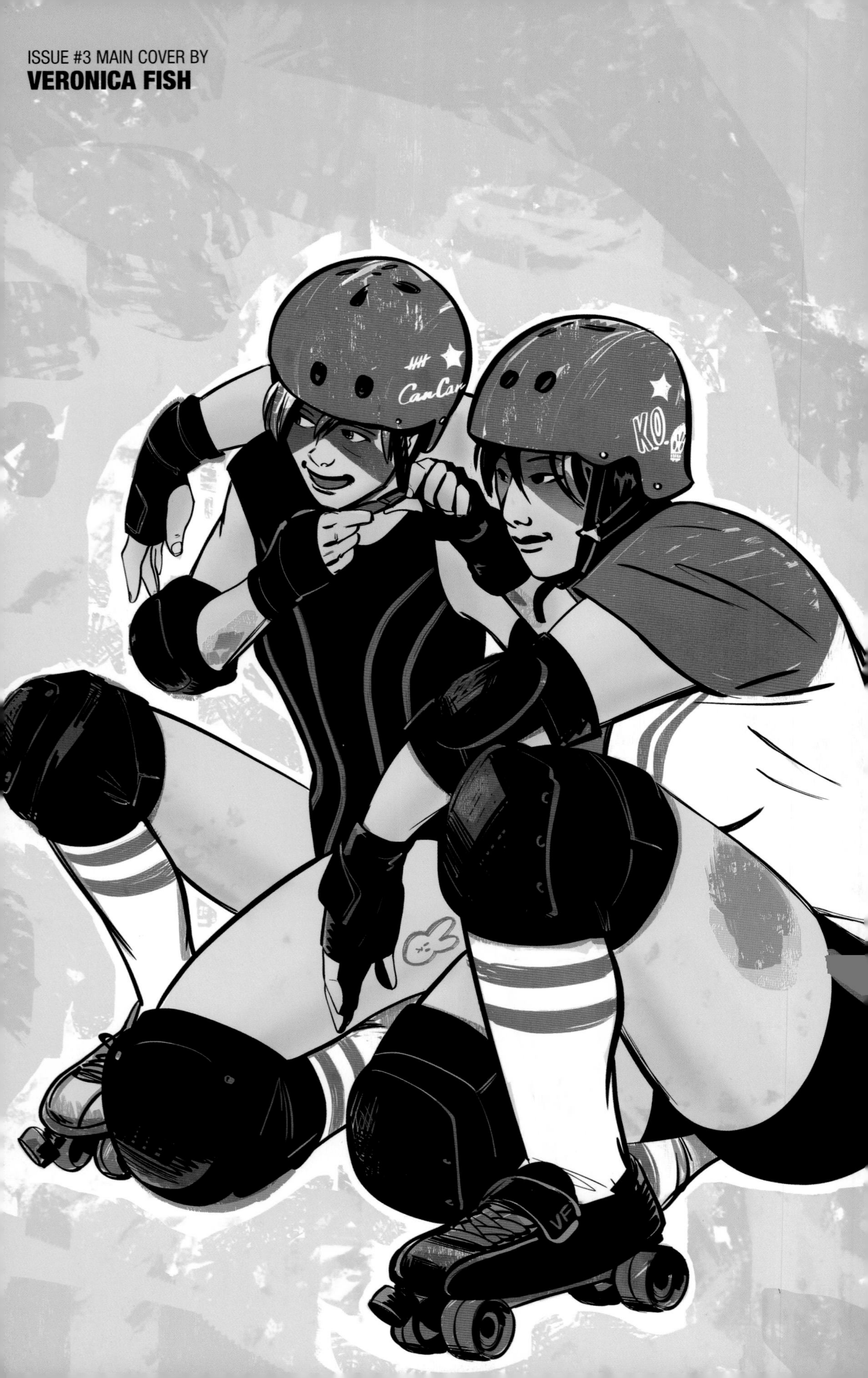

ISSUE #3 VARIANT COVER BY
JEN BARTEL

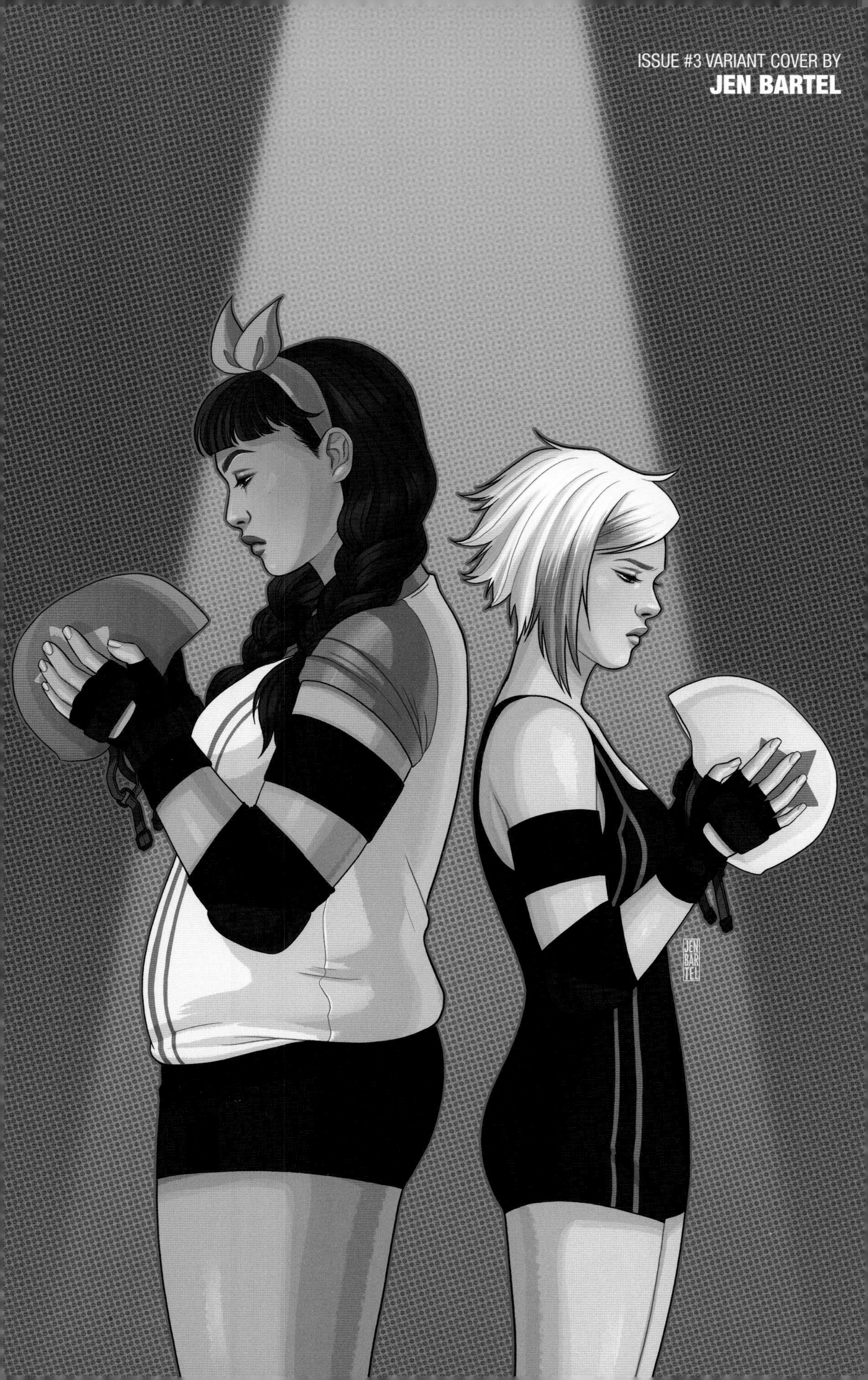
JEN BARTEL

ISSUE #4 MAIN COVER BY
VERONICA FISH

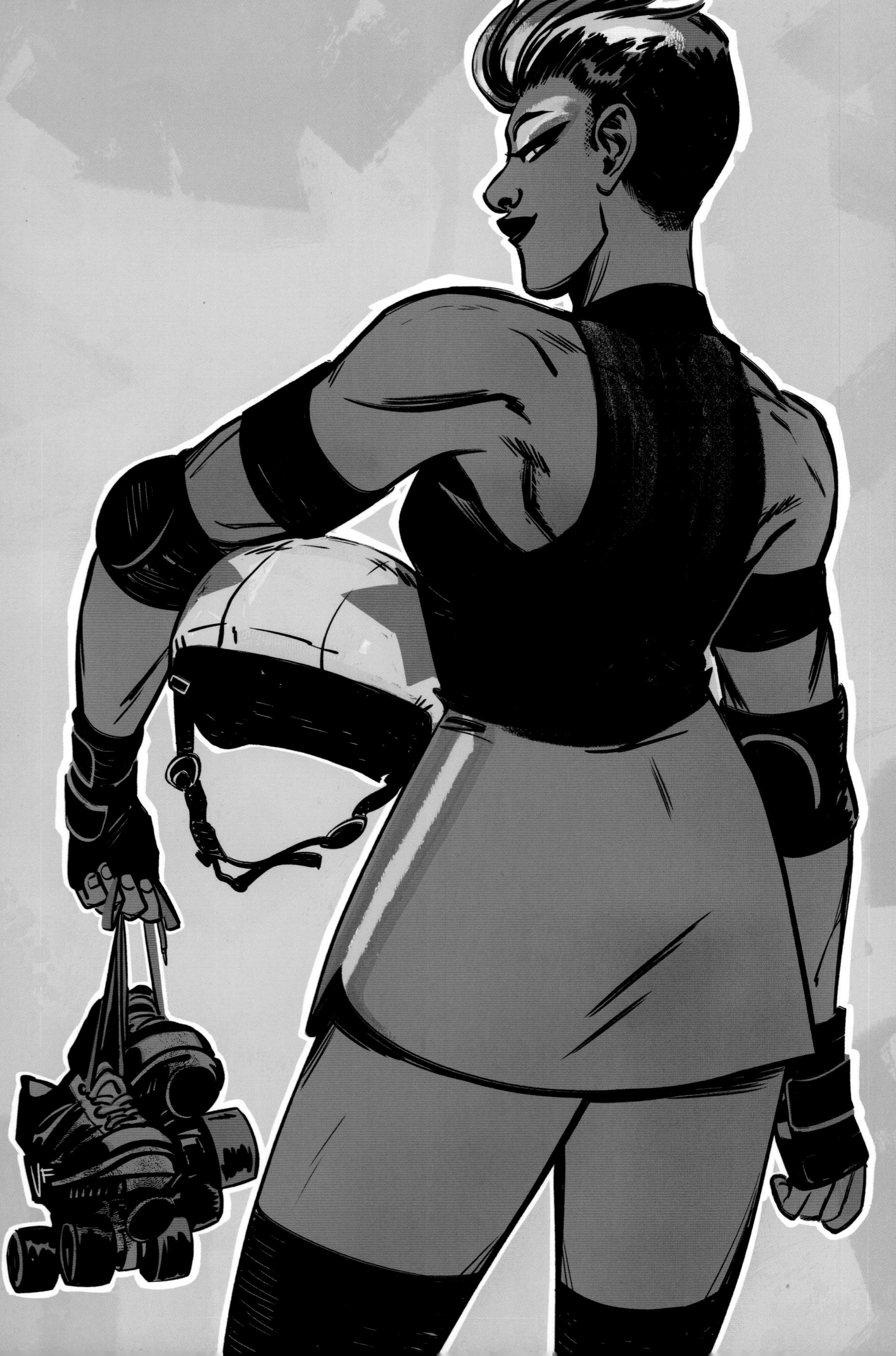

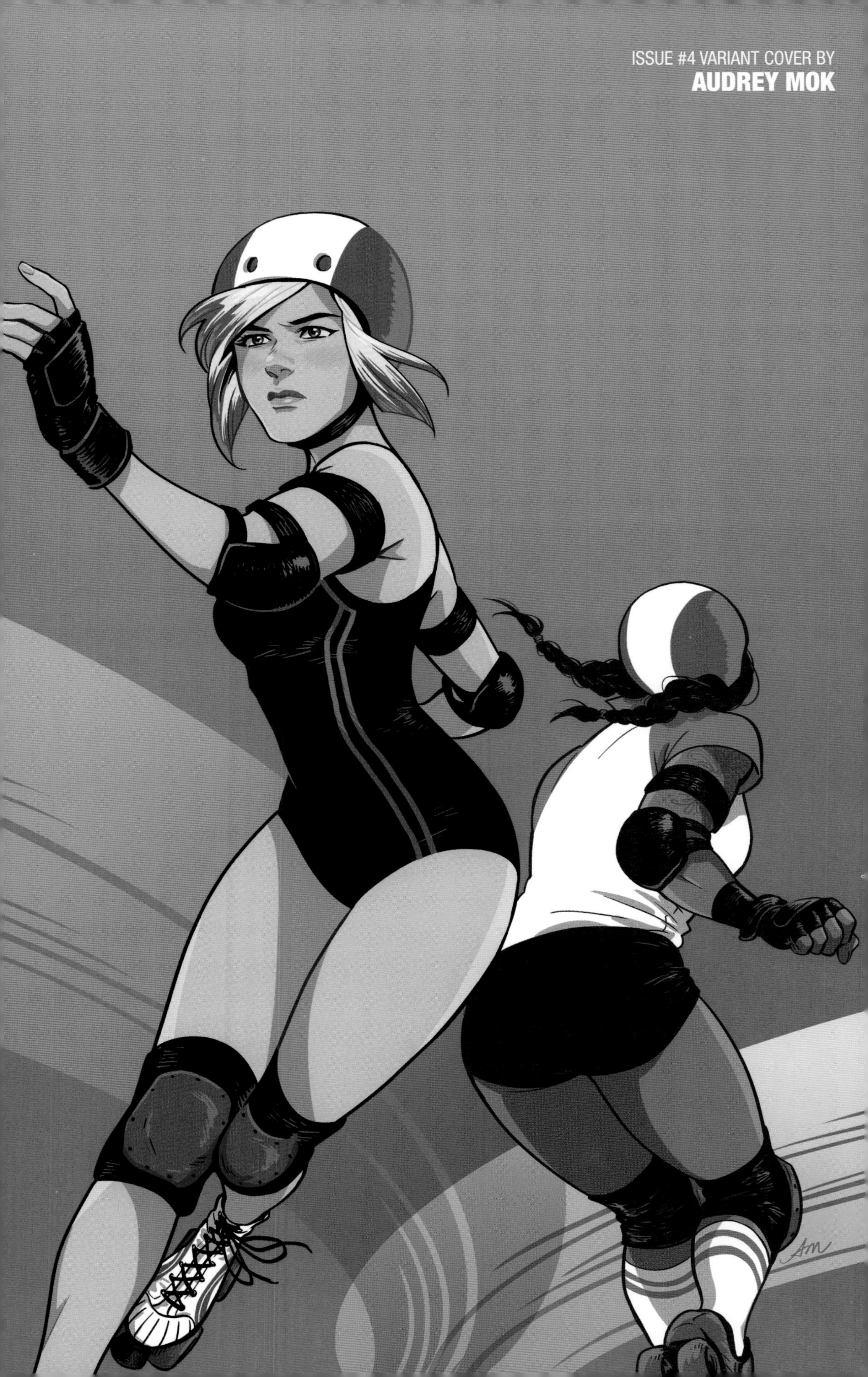

ISSUE #4 VARIANT COVER BY
AUDREY MOK

DISCOVER
ALL THE HITS

STEVENSON · ELLIS · WATTERS · ALLEN
LUMBERJANES
BEWARE THE KITTEN HOLY
NEW YORK TIMES BESTSELLING SERIES

Allison + Treiman + Cogar
GIANT DAYS
VOLUME ONE

JONESY
HUMPHRIES · BOYLE · QUINN
"A SPIRITUAL SUCCESSOR TO SCOTT PILGRIM"
"PURE CUTE"
VOLUME ONE

Hope Larson · Brittney Williams · Sarah Stern
GOLDIE VANCE
"Scoot over Nancy Drew..."
—Los Angeles Times
Volume One

THE BACKSTAGERS

TYSON HESSE'S
DIESEL
IGNITION

Lumberjanes
Noelle Stevenson, Shannon Watters, Grace Ellis, Brooke Allen, and Others
Volume 1: Beware the Kitten Holy
ISBN: 978-1-60886-687-8 | $14.99
Volume 2: Friendship to the Max
ISBN: 978-1-60886-737-0 | $14.99
Volume 3: A Terrible Plan
ISBN: 978-1-60886-803-2 | $14.99
Volume 4: Out of Time
ISBN: 978-1-60886-860-5 | $14.99
Volume 5: Band Together
ISBN: 978-1-60886-919-0 | $14.99

Giant Days
John Allison, Lissa Treiman, Max Sarin
Volume 1
ISBN: 978-1-60886-789-9 | $9.99
Volume 2
ISBN: 978-1-60886-804-9 | $14.99
Volume 3
ISBN: 978-1-60886-851-3 | $14.99

Jonesy
Sam Humphries, Caitlin Rose Boyle
Volume 1
ISBN: 978-1-60886-883-4 | $9.99
Volume 2
ISBN: 978-1-60886-999-2 | $14.99

Goldie Vance
Hope Larson, Brittney Williams
Volume 1
ISBN: 978-1-60886-898-8 | $9.99
Volume 2
ISBN: 978-1-60886-974-9 | $14.99

The Backstagers
James Tynion IV, Rian Sygh
ISBN: 978-1-60886-993-0 | $29.99

Tyson Hesse's Diesel: Ignition
Tyson Hesse
ISBN: 978-1-60886-907-7 | $14.99

Power Up
Kate Leth, Matt Cummings
ISBN: 978-1-60886-837-7 | $19.99

Teen Dog
Jake Lawrence
ISBN: 978-1-60886-729-5 | $19.99

Midas Flesh
Ryan North, Braden Lamb, Shelli Paroline
ISBN: 978-1-60886-455-3 | $14.99

Help Us! Great Warrior
Madeline Flores, Trillian Gunn
ISBN: 978-1-60886-802-5 | $19.99

BOOM! BOX™

AVAILABLE AT YOUR LOCAL COMICS SHOP AND BOOKSTORE
To find a comics shop in your area, call 1-888-266-4226
WWW.**BOOM-STUDIOS**.COM

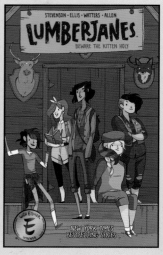

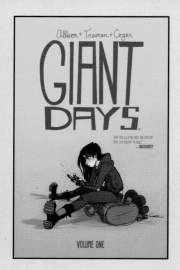

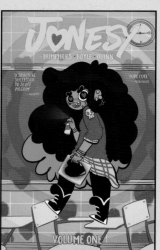

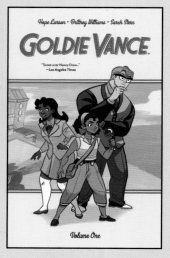

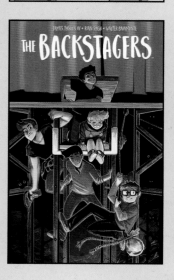

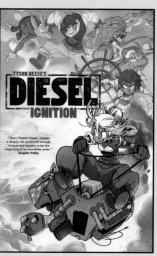